Bang to Rights

Jo Bavington-Jones

Bang to Rights

Published by The Conrad Press in the United Kingdom 2024

Tel: +44(0)1227 472 874
www.theconradpress.com
info@theconradpress.com

ISBN 978-1-916966-39-0

Copyright © Jo Bavington-Jones, 2024

The moral right of Jo Bavington-Jones to be identified as author of this work has been asserted in accordance with the Copyright, Designs and Patents Act 1988.

Typesetting and Cover Design by: Charlotte Mouncey, www.bookstyle.co.uk
The Conrad Press logo was designed by Maria Priestley.

Printed and bound in Great Britain by Clays Ltd, Elcograf S.p.A.

For Sam and Dirk

*'Perhaps it's good for one to suffer.
Can an artist do anything if he's happy?
Would he ever want to do anything?
What is art, after all, but a protest against
the horrible inclemency of life?'*

Aldous Huxley, *Antic Hay*

Prologue

Covid had killed the writing group. Well, that and the fact that one of its members turned out to be a serial killer, turning two others into murderers. Either way, 'Write Time, Write Place' was a thing of the past. Unlike Covid. That, apparently, was here to stay, and people were learning to live with it, much as Amy and Jenny were learning to live with killing Robert. They'd got away with it by making it look like suicide.

Their shared secret had bonded them for life, a pact made that they would never confess their crime to another soul. At first they'd sworn never to speak of it again, but sometimes, inevitably, the subject would come up; something would remind them of Robert – a song on the radio, or walking past one of the murder sites. It was impossible to escape the memories of his crimes when their hometown of Folkestone was awash with the art installations Robert, 'The Exhibitionist', had tainted forever with his victims' bodies. There had been talk in the town of removing the exhibits altogether, but that had never happened. Perhaps a committee somewhere had decided the notoriety would bring even more tourists to the town to satisfy their ghoulish curiosity.

Eventually, the shock died down and the killings became old news, replaced by the other madness going on in the world. For Amy and Jenny, however, it was always in the back of their minds, never forgotten for long.

CHAPTER 1

Willem

The sun had yet to peep over the horizon as Willem de Groot hefted his rucksack onto his shoulders and closed the front door, nudging his one-eyed ginger cat back inside with his foot as he did so. Cat, for that was the name Willem had given him when the cat had turned up at his door one day three years ago, mewled pathetically.

'Breakfast when I get back,' Willem muttered, to Cat. Or himself.

It was a twenty-or-so-minute walk to the harbour, where he hoped to capture the day's sunrise using the heavy Nikon camera he carried on his back. This was Willem's favourite time of day: before too many people were up and about to get on his nerves, which seemed to fray much more quickly nowadays. At fifty-seven, he could feel himself turning into the grumpy old man he had seen his father become. He saw his father looking back at him from the mirror now, the once dark-blonde curls steely grey and the lines around his blue eyes deepening year on year. He consoled himself with the fact that he was still in pretty good shape and his six-foot frame hadn't gone to fat.

Willem took the set of steps which ran down beside the row of terraced houses where he lived at number thirteen, grumbling about the broken glass and the hypodermic needles littered in his path.

'Fokken mense,' he said, reverting to the Afrikaans of his childhood. It was somehow more satisfying to curse in the tongue of the country he grew up in. He'd written to the council on a number of occasions, drawing their attention to the state of the steps, but nothing was ever done. He kicked some of the larger pieces of jagged green glass to the edge, making a mental note to come back and clear them away later. He couldn't abide littering of any sort, but this made his blood boil as he thought of the children and animals who might get hurt. As much as Willem didn't care for children personally, and had none of his own, he didn't want to see them injured.

Turning right at the bottom of the steps, Willem continued on his way, glancing to his left before crossing the road. He'd be surprised to see any traffic at this time of the morning, but better safe than sorry was his motto. Taking a shortcut through the car park of a block of flats, Willem nodded to another early riser, who was getting into his car. Since moving down from London just over three years ago, Willem found the people of the seaside town of Folkestone to be much friendlier in general than London folk.

As he walked he thought back to the first time he'd seen Folkestone. He'd driven down on a day off from his job at the publishing firm, fancying a day at the seaside would do him good. He missed the wild and rugged beauty of the South African coast and was sick of city life if he was completely honest. Who was it said, if you're tired of London, you're tired of life? Well, Willem *was* tired, of both. So, he'd jumped in his ancient Volvo estate, praised God when it started, and headed towards Dover with the notion of photographing the White

Cliffs. He'd found a narrow lane running parallel to the cliffs near Capel-le-Ferne and parked the car halfway up a bank so he could check out the view.

What Willem saw from the top of the cliffs at Capel – a white Martello tower and the Harbour Arm, with its lighthouse at the far end – piqued his interest and he got back in his car and found his way to the town of Folkestone. After that day, he'd found himself thinking of the place often, and just six months after that first visit he'd moved down.

Willem could smell the sea now, the salty tang in the air as he walked briskly to keep warm, swapping the heavy tripod from one arm to the other from time to time. He was thinking about the shot he was after on this particular April day, of the sun rising next to the lighthouse he'd come to know so well, and photographed so often. He was hoping to find the Harbour Arm deserted as, in his opinion, people rarely added anything to photographs. He didn't hate people, exactly, he just didn't want them in his shots.

Thankfully, there was no one in sight as he made his way to the upper walkway, shivering as the wind whipped around him, a flashback to the windy South African coast of his youth. He relished the big skies of the town he'd made his home and never tired of photographing them. This morning, like so many before, was looking promising as he set up his tripod and camera and waited for the sun to show itself. It wasn't many minutes until the sky lit up in a burst of orange, and Willem started shooting. This was why he'd left London and his soul-destroying job behind a desk.

Willem had been photographing as a hobby for about twenty years, but now he was attempting to make his living from it. It was scary but exhilarating; never knowing what money would be coming in month by month was not a comfortable feeling, but so far he was getting by.

It didn't take long for the sun to rise in the cloudless sky and Willem was soon packing his camera once more, satisfied with the photos he'd taken. People loved a sunrise, or a sunset, and he was pretty sure he'd have something saleable to go in the shop and on his market stall.

The walk home took a little longer, mostly uphill as it was. Willem took a different route, up the cobbled Old High Street in the Creative Quarter, with its independent shops and galleries. It was still too early for anything to be open and there was still no one else around. As Willem trudged up the hill, he glanced in the windows, stopping from time to time if something caught his eye. He was always on the lookout for work for sale by competing photographers. His own photos were available in a shop about halfway up the street, and he paused to check the window display, noting the framed lighthouse image, which was by far his bestseller, standing prominent. Nodding with satisfaction, Willem continued on his way.

It wasn't long before he was opening his front door once more. Cat greeted him, winding around his legs, and miaowing.

'Yes, yes, Cat, I'm hungry now too,' Willem said, stepping over the animal. He shucked off his rucksack and coat, unlaced the heavy work boots he favoured, replacing them with his well-worn slippers, and headed downstairs to the kitchen. He needed coffee and couldn't ignore the rumblings of his stomach.

Willem filled the kettle and got the coffee pot ready before turning his attention to Cat, who continued to try and trip him up.

'Ach, are you trying to kill me?' he exclaimed.

Soon Cat was happily eating his breakfast, crunching the small biscuits with his head turned to one side, using his few remaining teeth, and Willem turned his attention to making coffee, which he took into the lean-to on the back of the house. He always thought the lean-to had delusions of grandeur; it desperately wanted to be a conservatory but, sadly, whoever had erected it had done a pretty shoddy job, and it was a draughty, subsiding shed-cum-greenhouse clinging on to the back of the house like a needy girlfriend. The work needing to be done was on a very long list of jobs in Willem's head. In the meantime, he had squeezed a small table and chairs in amongst the work benches and tools and often took his morning coffee there.

Settling himself with a sigh, Willem gazed out at the rows of terraced houses standing in the shadow of the railway viaduct which spanned the horizon. He was content.

CHAPTER 2

Amy

Amy stretched and yawned, waking naturally to the sun shining through the bedroom window, an orange warmth creeping up the bed to her face. Since she moved into her little terraced house in Folkestone seven months ago, she hadn't bothered closing the bedroom curtains, not wanting to shut out the morning light which somehow had a magical quality to it. She was pretty sure no one could see in as her house was on the uppermost row of terraces and the houses opposite were some way away, connected by the viaduct, which she never tired of looking at, the trains seeming to fly through the sky. She'd always lived near the sea, but this particular seaside town just had something about it she couldn't put her finger on. Apart from the big skies and the creative vibe, this was also the hometown of her now best friend and literal partner in crime, Jenny.

Amy was feeling good on this particular morning. She'd slept deeply and hadn't been woken by the nightmares that sometimes had her waking shaking and scared. She hoped that time would shrink the memories, that they would fade like pictures bleached by the sun. Certainly the flashbacks to that horrific day at Robert's house when she'd seen photographs of one of his victims happened less frequently now. She still heard the gunshot, felt the recoil and saw the blood spatter some nights, and would wake with a pounding heart, sweat prickling her skin. She didn't feel guilt at what she'd done, not

12

exactly – Robert deserved to die – but she regretted the fact that she'd been the one to pull the trigger. She wasn't proud to have got away with murder, but she sure as hell was relieved. And hell was hopefully where Robert was now, eternally paying the price and being punished for his crimes.

Her friendship with Jenny had become the most important relationship she had, and they met two or three times a week. It was one such meeting today and they were meeting for coffee at Eleto at ten o'clock. Looking at the clock on the bedside table, Amy saw it was almost seven and she had time for a couple of hours of writing before she had to go out. *Shower and breakfast first*, she thought.

Standing in the shower, Amy let her thoughts drift to her current work in progress. She was writing her fourth novel and had reached a particularly sticky patch in the middle, one of the drawbacks of being a pantser rather than a planner. She knew it would sort itself out somehow and probably lead the story in an unexpected direction. Obstacles like sticky patches and timeline hiccups kept the writing interesting for her too, never knowing where, or when, she might come out the other side. So, she wasn't overly worried. She might just brainstorm with Jenny over coffee later. Something would come up, a light-bulb-over-the-head moment. Jenny despaired at Amy's lack of planning. All her own stories were meticulously planned. They really were such different people in so many ways, but they were united by an unbreakable, unshakeable bond, a viaduct between their houses of shared guilt.

After a quick breakfast of homemade granola and yoghurt (she was on a mission to cut back on her sugar intake), Amy sat down at her desk and switched on her laptop. Her office was underneath her bedroom and enjoyed the same view of the viaduct. She still looked up every time a train went over. Just last week she'd watched the Flying Scotsman steam across it on its tour of Kent. Most weekends, and more often in the summer, she also saw a Spitfire fly over, and had learned to recognise the sound of its Merlin engine. Just another thing that made Folkestone so very special.

Soon Amy was lost in her story, having circumvented the sticky patch, and was surprised when her phone trilled to tell her it was time to finish and head out to meet Jenny. She always set an alarm now, knowing that if the writing was flowing she would become so absorbed she was unaware of the passing of time.

Another advantage of living where she did was that Amy could walk into town in a matter of minutes and, even better, be at the beach in ten. Shrugging into her favourite khaki jacket, she grabbed her bag and headed out. Turning her face up to the sun, Amy was delighted to find the chill which had been lingering into April had been replaced by the first real warmth of the year. She smiled and set off walking.

Jenny had beaten her to the cafe and she waved from the table she'd bagsied in the window. Amy waved back, smiling at her pink-haired friend.

'Hello, you,' Amy said as she pushed open the door.

'Hello to you,' Jenny replied. 'I ordered your usual.' This meant a coconut milk cappuccino and a gluten-free brownie. (Well, she'd been good at breakfast.)

'Thank you,' Amy said, hanging her jacket on the back of the chair and sitting down opposite Jenny. 'How's you?'

'Mighty fine, thanks for asking,' Jenny said.

Amy smiled. 'I'm very glad to hear it. What you been up to?'

'Sewing.'

'Ooh, you're turning into quite the little seamstress, aren't you?'

Jenny's sewing habit had started during the pandemic, when she began making masks for herself and friends, usually out of fabric with cats on. Cats were Jenny's other big passion.

'I think I'm addicted to sewing. And buying fabric.'

'With cats on?' Amy queried.

'With cats on,' Jenny confirmed with a nod.

'You thought about starting a little business, selling your wares? You're very good.'

Jenny pulled a face. 'Not sure. It takes me bloody ages to make anything. I made a bag last week and it took ten hours. At that rate I'd have to charge about a million pounds for it.'

Amy laughed. 'Don't discount the idea. You might get quicker.'

'Half a million pounds,' Jenny said, deadpan.

Just then their drinks and cakes arrived, a hot chocolate and matching brownie for Jenny, and the conversation paused while they ate, words giving way to appreciative noises.

'So good,' Amy said once the brownie was devoured.

'Very yummy indeed,' Jenny agreed.

'Anyhoo, apart from sewing, what else have you been doing?' Amy asked.

'More sewing.'

'Okay, I get the picture. Well, I've been writing.'

'How's it coming along? Hit any bumps in the road yet? Any literary potholes, as it were?'

Amy looked sheepish. 'Er... maybe...'

'That's a yes then. Told you, you need to plan.'

'Yes, Miss,' Amy said, before muttering 'never gonna happen' under her breath and smiling sweetly at her friend.

'Well, don't come running to me when you get stuck,' Jenny said.

'Well, I won't be able to, will I?' Amy said, pulling a face.

Jenny looked blank.

'If I'm stuck. Dur.'

Jenny stuck her tongue out.

Amy returned the favour.

'How've you been otherwise?' Amy asked her friend, her expression serious. 'You know… at night and stuff.'

'Fine. If I ever have a bit of a wobble I give myself a good talking to,' Jenny said. 'He got what he deserved, Amy,' she added, lowering her voice. 'I refuse to let guilt ruin my life.'

Amy was silent, her gaze cast downwards as she absent-mindedly ran her finger across the chocolate sauce used to decorate the brownie plate and sucked the chocolate off. 'I s'pose,' she said eventually, nodding slowly, but thinking maybe it was easier for Jenny – she hadn't been the one to pull the trigger and put a bullet in Robert's brain.

Amy could feel Jenny watching her, reading her mind.

'I know it's not the same for me, Amy, I do know that, but I'm here *for* you and *with* you, you know that,' Jenny said, reaching over and squeezing Amy's hand.

Amy smiled and nodded, not trusting herself to speak just yet.

'Anyway, changing the subject to something a bit cheerier,' Jenny said, 'my gas and electricity bill came this morning.'

Amy pulled a face. Energy prices had rocketed in recent months. 'How bad?'

'A hundred and fifty-one thousand and eight pounds. And sixty-seven pence,' Jenny informed her, deadly serious.

Amy, who was taking a sip of her coffee at the time, managed to control herself and not spray Jenny with a mouthful. 'What?! You're joking?'

Jenny shook her head. 'Look, I took a photo of the bill,' she said, getting her mobile out and showing Amy the offending item.

'Bloody hell! Have you turned the entire house over to growing cannabis or something?'

'No, my law-breaking days are over. I think I might've read the meter wrong,' Jenny said sheepishly. 'I'll give them a call when I get home.'

'You seem remarkably calm about it,' Amy said, thinking her friend would normally be pretty anxious about something like this.

Jenny just shrugged. 'Yeah, I don't sweat the small stuff anymore.'

'Well done, you. I'm currently sweating the small, medium and large stuff. Not sure what size this one is, but I've applied for a place to sell my books in a shop on the Old High Street. Got my fingers crossed. Just not sure if they're crossed in the hope of getting it, or not getting it.'

'Ooh, that's exciting. I'm sure you'll get it,' Jenny said.

CHAPTER 3

The shop

After breakfast, Willem settled himself in front of the two large screens in his office and downloaded the photographs he'd taken of the lighthouse that morning. Then he selected the one he thought was the strongest image and opened it in Photoshop. He didn't do much in the way of post-production, apart from increase the contrast a little to really make the colours sing, and to sometimes add a vignette. He had a strong dislike of the over-processed, over-saturated images he saw elsewhere. He'd made the switch to digital happily enough, but he was still a traditionalist where his photographs were concerned. He wanted honesty in his work. In all aspects of his life in fact.

When he was happy with the image, he printed it out on one of his two huge printers. When it had dried out he would mount and frame it ready for sale. He sighed as he thought of the shop. He knew it was a necessary part of making a living from his photography, but he dreaded the one day a week he had to spend working in the space he shared with six other artists. He'd picked Monday as his day because that was when the Old High Street, where the shop was located, was the quietest. Admittedly, he had to suffer the occasional bank holiday, but he figured it was an acceptable trade-off.

Willem was the only photographer in the shop. It was agreed they would not have other artists who were in direct competition. They were an eclectic bunch, as mixed as the arts and crafts they produced. They called themselves 'Coastal Creatives', which Willem thought lacked imagination, but he could live with it, and he could just about live with the other artists. Well, most of them anyway. He thought back to the day he'd met with the group, a sort of interview process to see if he was the right 'type' to join them.

The woman who seemed to be in charge was called Gloria. She recreated the paintings of the Old Masters using collage techniques and paper from old magazines and books. Willem didn't hate her work, but his dislike of the woman herself, definitely soured his opinion.

'So, Willem, what makes you think you're a good fit for our happy little band?' Gloria asked, peering at him earnestly over her round, metal-framed glasses. She was sitting opposite him wearing dungarees, which Willem would come to realise were her go-to item of clothing most days, and with a vivid scarf wrapped around her wild grey curls. Willem just knew she was vegan and didn't shave her armpits.

While Willem thought he most certainly *wasn't* a good fit, he realised he had to play nicely and say all the right things to convince Gloria and the others that he absolutely *was*.

'Well,' he began, 'looking around your wonderful shop, at all these stunning pieces…' he said, gesturing around the shop (he was actually making himself feel sick), 'I think my photography would add a completely new dimension, adding to rather than detracting from the rest of all your amazing work.'

It was working. Gloria was practically simpering, doing her best 'oh-you're-too-kind' act, and batting away the compliments like flies buzzing around her head.

Nobody else was saying anything. Willem got the distinct impression that what Gloria wanted, Gloria got, and that it wasn't worth wasting their collective breath trying to interject and offer an opinion. In the main they were slouched in their chairs with their arms crossed, and resigned looks on their faces. He managed to catch the eye of a younger artist, who rolled his eyes, and Willem knew he'd found an ally. He managed to keep a straight face as he turned his attention back to Gloria, who was droning on about all the rules and regulations he would have to adhere to should they accept him.

'Yes, yes, of course, no problem,' Willem said, nodding, when Gloria finally stopped to draw breath.

'Well, we will make a decision in the next couple of days and let you know,' Gloria said, making it clear the interview was over and that Willem could take his leave.

'I'll see you out,' the young man whose eye Willem had caught said to him as Willem rose to go.

'Thank you. Sorry, I don't know your name,' Willem said. Gloria hadn't thought it necessary to do introductions, apart from her own: 'Gloria de Dieu, lovely to meet you,' which she managed to make sound like 'lovely to meet me'.

'It's Finn,' he said, offering his hand to Willem.

'Nice to meet you, Finn,' Willem said, shaking the proffered hand.

'You too,' Finn said, leading Willem to the door.

'I don't suppose you've got time for a coffee, have you?' Willem asked.

Finn looked at his black smartwatch. 'Um… I have a meeting in about forty minutes, but I could do a quick one,' he said.

'Great, thank you. It would be good to find out a little bit more about the shop,' Willem said.

'Sure, no problem. Folklore okay with you?' Finn said, pointing across the street to the bar.

Willem offered no objection, and soon they were ordering Americanos, no milk, no sugar, a similarity which was to prove the first of many Willem and Finn would share.

Finn gestured for Willem to choose a table and followed him to a two-seater in the window with no other tables nearby. It was the one he would have chosen.

'So, is that a South African accent I detect?' Finn asked.

'It is. Dutch parents but I grew up in South Africa. Twenty years in London have softened the accent, but I don't think it'll ever go completely,' Willem shrugged.

'Beautiful country,' Finn said. 'Don't you miss it? The weather especially.'

'When I get off the plane there and for a couple of days, I ask myself why I ever left, but then I remember all the problems and...' Willem shrugs the end of the sentence.

'Fair enough,' Finn nods. 'Well, shall I try and fill in the gaps left by Gloria at the meeting?'

'Yes, please. I can't believe she only introduced herself. Glory of God, for goodness' sake. I tried to interrupt her – it felt very rude not to learn who the rest of you were, but I soon realised I wouldn't get a word in edgeways,' Willem said.

Finn smiled. 'That's our Gloria. We've all come to accept that's the way she is and it's easier to just go along with it than make waves. You'll get used to her,' Finn said, pulling a face that suggested otherwise.

As Finn spoke, Willem took in his appearance. The quietly spoken young man in front of him looked to be in his early thirties, with a neat, dark beard and almost shaved head. He had deep brown, intelligent eyes and a shy manner. Willem liked him, and thought he might just have made a new friend. His circle of friends was small; most people got on his nerves these days.

'I think I can cope with Gloria. I've met her type before. Besides, I assume working different days in the shop, I won't have too much contact with her. Although I suspect any amount of contact with her is too much,' Willem added, raising his eyebrows.

Finn grimaced again. 'You should probably brace yourself for regular interference, at least in the early weeks. She does like to throw her weight around and micromanage everyone.'

'Oh great. I look forward to that. I will just keep my mouth shut I think,' Willem said.

'Very wise,' Finn nodded. 'She should leave you in peace eventually. Once she's convinced you're competent enough to run the shop. Although she didn't leave poor Harry alone for months.'

'Harry? Please tell me he's the potter?' Willem said, having admired some stunning raku pots in his whistle-stop tour of the shop.

Finn laughed. 'He prefers ceramicist but, yes, Harry is our potter. Harry's pretty much straight out of art school. He works Monday to Friday on the IT helpdesk at the university in Canterbury, so he does Saturday or Sunday in the shop, alternating weeks with Gloria. He's a nice guy. All the ladies love him, but he's oblivious to it.'

'And the others... they seem pretty nice,' Willem said, hopefully.

'Yeah, they are. I'll introduce you to everyone when the opportunity arises, although they'll probably all pop in to the shop at some point while you're there, to replace stock and stuff.'

'Thank you, Finn, I'd appreciate that. I noticed some pretty flamboyant jewellery too. I was trying to work out which one of them was responsible when Gloria was in full flow.'

'Who did you decide on?' Finn asked.

'Maybe the young woman with the dreadlocks?'

'Ah! Lunette. No, the jeweller is actually Geraldine, the larger lady who was sitting on my left. She used to teach religious studies but took early retirement due to ill health. She's also a celebrant – you know, does weddings and funerals. She's lovely.'

'You sound very fond of her,' Willem remarked, taking a sip of coffee.

Finn smiled. 'I suppose I am. She doesn't have any family and has kind of adopted me. Or maybe I adopted her. I try and help her out when she gets in one of her muddles.'

'Is that often?'

'Well, yes, fairly often. Gerry can be a bit clumsy. I try and cover up for her before Gloria finds out, which means being available with my toolkit on Gerry's days. I don't mind though. Happy to do it.'

'That's good of you. I promise to try not to break anything.'

'Thanks! I get the impression you can probably fix most things yourself though?'

'I do have a pretty comprehensive toolkit of my own,' Willem confirmed.

'Good to know! So, Geraldine, Gerry, is our jeweller, then there's Lisa, who makes pieces of art from beach finds

– driftwood, sea glass, pebbles and stuff. Lisa's lovely too, just very nice and normal. Married with a couple of kids at secondary school. I sometimes make miniature houses and things to go on her driftwood scenes.'

'So… presumably the woodwork I saw is yours then?' Willem said.

'Yep, that's me. I do pyrography and wood carving.'

'Very nice. I like to work with wood when I have the chance too.'

'So, who does that leave…?' Finn mentally looked around the shop. 'Oh, how could I forget our resident candle- and soap makers, Lunette and Benoit? French, obviously, not sure what their history is, but they're actually leaving for Glastonbury in about a week to sell their aura-cleansing soap there.' Finn said this with a totally straight face.

'Their what?' Willem exclaimed.

'Aura-cleansing soap.'

'That's what I thought you said. You're going to have to explain that one.'

'That'll have to be a story for next time, I'm afraid. I have to get to my meeting – someone who wants to commission a chess set.'

'Of course, don't let me hold you up. Thank you so much for your time. Perhaps we can arrange to meet again soon to continue our chat, whether I'm accepted in the shop or not?'

'Yeah, sure, that would be good. I'm sure it's just a formality with the shop. Gloria needs you more than you need her. She just likes to make people sweat before she tells them magnanimously that they're worthy of joining the cast of Coastal Creatives.'

Finn had been right and Willem had actually got the call from Gloria the very next day telling him he was in. Glory be to God.

CHAPTER 4

Antisocial media

Willem was well established in the shop now. He'd survived induction-by-Gloria by the skin of his teeth. She'd plagued him for weeks with her micromanagement and fussiness, rearranging things constantly and generally carrying on as if she was the only one really capable of running the place. He'd had to bite his tongue on many an occasion, and swallow a cutting remark or six. He'd been on the verge of quitting more than once too, telling Gloria where she could shove her shop. He also wondered if she was flirting with him from time to time. Willem wasn't the best at picking up signals from the opposite sex, so he might have been reading her wrong, but he got a definite sense that she wasn't happy he appeared to be immune to her charms. Now, thankfully, she mainly left him in peace, keeping her meddling to about once a month. He thought she probably got the DTs if she left it any longer. He remembered one conversation in particular on his second Monday in the shop.

'So, Willem, can I call you Will?' Gloria said as her opening gambit.

'No,' Willem replied.

Gloria seemed off-kilter at this. She wasn't used to men saying no to her. (Even if they were saying yes just to keep the peace.) 'Oh,' she said. 'Oh, well, anyway, what brings you to this wonderful little town of mine?'

Willem raised his eyebrows at her taking ownership of the town, and was about to speak when Gloria continued.

'Of course, I've lived here all my life. Oh, the changes I've seen! You wouldn't believe how different the place is now, much more gentrified,' she said, clearly implying how much better this suited her.

Willem didn't attempt to join the conversation, sitting back in his chair behind the counter and resigning himself to one of Gloria's monologues. He only half listened, hoping his grunts and nods were appropriately interjected. The other half of his brain was busy planning a night shoot to Dungeness.

'Gone are all the tacky amusements from the seafront – you might have heard of the Rotunda – and the nightclubs, of course. Most unsavoury,' Gloria wrinkled her nose in disgust.

Willem nodded obediently, thinking all the while of the Milky Way.

'Of course, not everyone is happy about the new apartment blocks being built on the beach now, but they're terribly short-sighted about the prosperity this will bring to the town.'

Gloria proceeded to name-drop some local VIPs, some of whom Willem had heard of. He was deeply unimpressed, however, and stifled a yawn. Thankfully, after about ten minutes, he was saved by that rarest of creatures: a Monday shopper.

He rarely saw more than a handful of customers on his Monday shifts. There had been the odd occasion when he didn't have a single customer, not even a browser. He didn't mind though, apart from the obvious fact that he made no sales of his or anyone else's goods, and therefore no money. He kept himself busy working on his images and preparing social media posts for the week. The discovery of the scheduling tool on Facebook had been a revelation and enabled him to create a week's worth of posts in advance.

Willem hated social media. In an ideal world he wouldn't have any accounts, not Facebook or Instagram, Twitter or the rest, but social media was a necessary evil if you had something to sell. So, Willem did them all, as well as having an online shop linked to his website, an Etsy shop, and photographs in all the image libraries.

He had managed to build an audience of over two thousand on Instagram and this had become his number one platform. He was now considering using his TikTok account for something other than watching funny pet videos too.

The posts were scheduled to appear at six p.m. on Facebook and nine p.m. on Instagram as, according to some algorithm, they were peak times for his audience. If only that was the end of it, but no, then he had to reply to all the comments his posts received. Most evenings were spent checking intermittently and thanking people for commenting. Usually with a bottle of Windhoek lager or a tot of Kraken Black Spiced Rum to dull the pain.

He didn't take much notice of who was commenting on the whole. He did appreciate all the 'wows' his images got, but the whole business was really a huge pain in the arse. He just reminded himself that every like was a potential sale and got on with it. He didn't think much of it when he started seeing the same comment pop up several days in a row: *Awesome image, stunning location!* It was always the first comment the posts received, and was accompanied by a 'Love' heart rather than a 'Like' thumbs up. One evening, Willem noted the heart appeared split seconds after the post went up. Almost as if the person posting was waiting for it. He shrugged it off and took a long swig of his beer. Someone else obviously had as sad an existence as he did, and nothing better to do with their time than trawl social media.

Willem's friendship with Finn had strengthened over the months, and Willem had a great deal of respect for the younger man he'd grown to like very much. Each would often pop into the shop when the other was on shift, and they met for coffee or lunch every couple of weeks. It was a week or so after Willem joined the shop before Finn had the chance to tell him the story of Lunette and Benoit, the French couple who'd now moved to Glastonbury to peddle their amazing soap.

'So, you probably already know that the aura-cleansing soap started life as candles? They were hand-poured soy-wax candles in recycled glass jars. They didn't just pour the wax in though, the jars were filled with the "outpourings of their loving union", whatever the fuck that meant, and also contained a little parchment scroll and a crystal in the bottom of the jar,' Finn began.

Willem just stared at him, mystified.

'The idea was,' Finn continued, 'that you burn the candle down and when it's all used up you remove the crystal, wash it and put it in your drinking water.'

Willem started to speak, but Finn raised his hand to stop him.

'Wait, it gets better. The little parchment scroll has a link on it to a personalised piece of music they recorded. I kid you not.'

'The mind boggles,' Willem said, wide-eyed.

'Indeed. But, apart from how completely bonkers the idea

was, it had one fatal flaw, as they discovered when customers started reporting that the scroll caught fire when the wick burned all the way down.'

'No! Oh my God, that's hilarious. So, that's when they made the switch to soap?'

'Yep,' Finn nodded. 'Cleanse your body and your aura at the same time, with the crystal and scroll safely encased in plastic in the middle of the bar of soap.'

'Did the good people of Folkestone actually buy this soap?' Willem asked, incredulously.

'Not in any great quantities, hence the move to Glastonbury.'

'I think they'll do very well there,' Willem nodded. 'I visited with my camera last year and Glastonbury High Street is awash with bizarre hippy shops.'

'I think you're probably right. Thankfully I think we've found someone to take their place in the shop – a local author who, I'm happy to report, seems very sane and normal.'

'Oof!' Willem exclaimed. 'Don't speak too soon. I worked in publishing for many years. I forget who said all writers are shy megalomaniacs, but in my experience they weren't far off the mark.'

'Well, time will tell. Anyway, Amy's books should be going in any day and she'll be taking over Lunette and Benoit's Thursday shift.'

'Okay. I daresay our paths will cross at some point and I will reserve judgment until then,' Willem said, bowing his head.

'Let's hope she's the exception that proves the rule,' Finn said, holding up crossed fingers.

'Indeed. What sort of books does she write?'

'Novels. Women's fiction, whatever that means,' Finn

shrugged. 'We've never had books in the shop before, so it'll be interesting to see how they go.'

Willem hadn't given Amy or her books a second thought after that. The books had appeared on the shelves that used to hold the candles and soaps, and he still chuckled to himself when he remembered Finn's story of the burning parchment.

CHAPTER 5

Dutch courage

It was about a month since Amy had joined Coastal Creatives and she'd come to the attention of a local radio presenter, Fay McFarlane, who had the ten 'til one show on Radio Folkestone. Amy had always shied away from public speaking and interviews as she was naturally a shy person and definitely didn't enjoy blowing her own trumpet. Or any other instrument. A megalomaniac she most certainly wasn't.

Between Jenny nagging her, and her own fervent desire to make something of her writing career, Amy had reluctantly agreed to go on Fay's show. She met up with Jenny for a drink the night before.

'Why did I agree to this?' she groaned, putting her face in her hands and pressing the tips of her fingers into her eyes.

She and Jenny were sitting at a small table in The Pullman. It was a Monday evening and the place was pretty quiet.

'Here, drink this,' Jenny said, holding out a shot glass.

Amy took her hands away from her face. 'Ew. What is it? I don't really do shots.'

'Shut up and drink it,' Jenny instructed. 'It'll make you feel better.'

Amy did as she was told and downed the dark treacle-coloured liquid. It burned as it went down, but did feel oddly soothing, like cough medicine.

'What was that?' she asked Jenny.

'Jägermeister,' her friend informed her.

Amy raised her eyebrows. 'Who knew?' she said. 'It's surprisingly pleasant.'

Jenny nodded. 'It is. It gets a bad rap because of Jägerbombs, but it's actually a digestif made with... hang on...' Jenny said, typing something into her phone, 'fifty-six herbs and spices.'

Amy raised her eyebrows. 'Sounds positively healthy.'

'Practically salad,' Jenny nodded her bright pink head.

'I think I'll have another one,' Amy said.

'Steady on,' Jenny cautioned. 'One is medicinal, more is anaesthetic.'

Amy pulled a face. 'Anaesthetic sounds quite appealing right about now. I feel sick thinking about tomorrow.'

'You'll be fine. I know Fay and she's brilliant: really funny and down to earth. She'll help you out if you're floundering.'

'Urgh, don't say floundering. I don't want to flounder. I want to sound professional and confident,' Amy groaned.

'And you will. Even if you don't feel it on the inside, you'll come across as confident – you always do.'

'Do I? I always imagine the audience can hear my heart beating nineteen to the dozen. And smell the fear.'

'Well, you don't have to worry about that at least, not on the radio,' Jenny grinned.

'Thanks, but that's not much consolation.'

'What can I do to help?' Jenny asked.

'I don't know. Come with me? Hold my hand. And my hair when I throw up?'

'You're not going to throw up.'

'I might,' Amy pouted.

'Well, as long as you don't do it in the paper bag you're

hyperventilating into,' Jenny giggled.

Amy regretted telling Jenny that particular story.

'It only happened the once,' she said mournfully. 'Oh God, what if I throw up live on air?'

'Well, it'll be a great dinner party story for years to come.'

Amy groaned again. 'Seriously though, will you come with me?'

'Yes, of course I will, dopey. I can pretend to be your PA and demand a bowl of blue M&Ms and a pure white Persian cat with one green eye and one blue be available to you for the duration of the interview.'

Amy laughed, in spite of herself. 'And don't forget the bottle of Jägermeister,' she added.

'Your wish is my command, Your Majesty,' Jenny mock-tugged her forelock. 'Seriously, though, if you ever do turn into a diva, I will unfriend you immediately, remember that.'

'Never gonna happen.'

'Yeah, yeah, I can see you on the red carpet now… Jenny who?'

'I promise never to forget you… er… what was your name again?'

'See? One local radio appearance and you've already forgotten us little people,' Jenny said, shaking her head sadly.

'Perhaps if you could all wear name badges?'

The friends lapsed into silence for a few moments, Amy lost in thoughts of dread and embarrassment and Jenny of white Persian cats. Eventually it was Amy who spoke.

'Drink? What are you having?'

'Um… tonic with a squeeze of lime please,' Jenny said.

'I might join you,' Amy said, getting up to go to the bar.

'What a pair of party animals we are,' she added as she turned away.

'You know it,' Jenny said to her departing back.

Amy didn't notice the bearded man sitting at the other end of the bar. Willem was nursing a glass of rum after a particularly testing day in the shop. It involved Gloria. He didn't look up.

Amy took the drinks back to Jenny and sat down again.

'Cheers,' she said, holding up her glass to clink against Jenny's.

'Cheers, ears. Right, do you want to run through some of the stuff Fay might ask you?' Jenny said.

'Ugh, no, thanks. I think that would just make me more nervous. Can we talk about something completely different?'

'Yep, sure. Cats or sewing?' Jenny said.

'How about both? What are you making at the moment?'

'Well, I may have popped into the fabric shop today – damn you and your irresistible fabrics and patterns, Miss Gingers – and bought a pattern for dungarees and some bright pink, leopard print fabric.'

'Hm... I suppose big cats count. Dungarees, eh? That reminds me, I keep forgetting to tell you about Gloria in the shop.'

'Is she the bossy one who thinks she's in charge?' Jenny asked.

'Yes, do you know her?'

'Only by reputation.'

'Well, it's quite funny really. I was expecting her to be a right bossy cow when I joined, but she's actually been super helpful – can't do enough for me. She seems to be quite impressed by the fact that I'm an author and treats me like a local celebrity. She even put a poster up in the window telling people as much.'

Jenny pulled a face.

'Exactly! What must the others have thought? It made me cringe. Anyway, I took it down on my shift. Denied everything when she asked me if I knew what had happened to it.'

'Wise move. Wait 'til she hears you on the radio! Blue M&Ms and everything next time you're in the shop.'

'I haven't told them I'm on the radio,' Amy admitted. 'Does anybody actually listen to Radio Folkestone anyway?'

Jenny raised her eyebrows. 'You'd be surprised, especially Fay's show. She's won awards I'll have you know.'

Amy groaned. 'Oh God, I was happier when I thought no one would be listening.'

On the other side of the pub, Willem was thanking the barman and making his way to the door. He barely noticed the two women as he passed them. He was preoccupied with thoughts of the radio appearance he'd agreed to the next morning. He'd already had three rums. Any more and he'd have a thick head when he woke up. He was dreading being on the radio enough already without turning up hungover.

Amy and Jenny's conversation, meanwhile, moved on to the shop.

'So, how's it going in the shop?' Jenny asked. 'Apart from bossy old Gloria throwing her weight around.'

'Okay, thanks. They seem like a nice bunch on the whole. I haven't met Harry yet – he makes the raku pots – or the new photographer, Willem. The others seem nice though. Geraldine – she makes the oversize jewellery – reminds me of the Vicar of Dibley. She's really lovely. Always breaking things, I gather. Regularly knocks things over with her bum or boobs. Not someone you could ever be cross with though.'

'She sounds like my nan. At least your books aren't fragile,' Jenny said.

'Unlike my ego,' Amy sighed.

'Maybe you do need another shot?' Jenny said.

'Yeah, in the head.'

Jenny raised her eyebrows as Amy realised what she'd said.

'Jägermeister?'

'Definitely,' Jenny nodded.

CHAPTER 6
Faces for radio

The next morning Amy and Willem woke in their respective terraced houses at opposite ends of the viaduct, each unaware of the other, but both groggy and lacklustre from too much grog in The Pullman, and a restless night worrying about being on the radio.

'Urgh, Jägermeister,' Amy groaned. 'Never again.'

'You're getting old, man, can't hold your liquor any more,' Willem said aloud to no one, pressing his fingers to his temples.

Amy dragged herself out of bed and pulled on her robe from where it hung on the back of the door, running her fingers through her hair as she made her way downstairs, yawning all the way. 'Coffee,' she said. 'Need coffee.' In the kitchen, she filled the reservoir of her Tassimo machine, inserted an Americano Grande pod and pressed start. 'Shush,' she said to the machine as it did its job. She didn't ask Alexa to play music as she would normally have done in the morning. She did wonder about how many inanimate objects she spoke to in the house though. While she waited for the coffee she took a couple of paracetamol with a glass of much-needed water.

Willem made it to a sitting position on the side of his bed, groaning at the aches and pains that were a sign of his advancing years, as well as a result of too much rum. 'Why did you carry on drinking when you got home?' he asked himself. 'Silly old fool. Should know better.' He took an ancient grey dressing gown off the foot of the bed and shrugged into it, shoved his feet into a pair of battered old sheepskin slippers and plodded down the stairs to make coffee. He didn't take anything for his headache. Willem didn't like taking painkillers. Unless the pain was killing him. He made a pot of strong coffee which he took upstairs to his office with his favourite mug, which read: *I have the patience of a Saint. Saint Cunty McFuckoff.* It had been a leaving present from one of his colleagues at the publishing firm. Willem liked to start the day by catching up on the news, which he watched on his PC.

Amy took her coffee back to bed and waited for it, and the painkillers, to do their work. She hoped a long hot shower would complete the rejuvenation, or at least make her feel human enough to get through the radio interview. She wasn't on until quarter past eleven and had arranged to pick Jenny up at ten-thirty, as Jenny didn't drive. All she wanted now was for the whole thing to be over. After her shower, Amy took her time getting ready, blow-drying her hair and applying a little makeup. She might only be going on the radio, but she needed the added confidence looking good gave her. It took a little more concealer than usual to achieve a look she was happy with.

After two mugs of coffee, Willem showered quickly, washing face, hair and body with two-in-one shampoo and conditioner – whatever had been on offer at the supermarket when he did his shopping. Another time it could be shower gel. Or dog shampoo. Willem didn't give a monkey's about that sort of thing. He figured they probably all had the same ingredients in anyway. He dried himself off roughly and dressed in grey jeans and his favourite T-shirt, which just happened to be at

39

the top of the pile. It had a picture of a camera on it and said: *I shoot people. And sometimes I cut their heads off.*

While she ate breakfast – a bacon sandwich made with two slices of bread with butter and ketchup, for her hangover – Amy listened to Radio Folkestone. They actually played some pretty good music, she concluded. Thinking about her appearance on air made her feel sick though, so she turned off the radio and busied herself with doing the breakfast dishes and a few little bits around the house (that didn't require bending or loud noise). At ten-twenty she picked up her bag and jacket and set off to collect Jenny. She experienced a moment of panic when she remembered the paper bag she'd left ready by the door and wondered if she should go back and get it. *Get a grip, woman,* she told herself, *you'll be fine.* The truth was she couldn't be bothered to turn around and go back to the house, park the car and go back indoors. Amy avoided parallel parking unless it was absolutely unavoidable.

Willem also had bacon sandwiches for breakfast. Unlike Amy, though, he had four slices of toast, a whole pack of bacon and a good dash of hot sauce. He applied hot sauce to pretty much all his meals, that or mustard anyway. *That's cleared the sinuses,* he thought as he rinsed the dishes. Checking his watch, he saw it was time to set off for the radio station, which was based in a local school not too far from his house. After a quick scrub of his teeth, he grabbed his favourite black jacket from the bannisters, shrugging into it as he left the house. It would only take ten or fifteen minutes to walk to the school and he figured the walk would help clear his still-muzzy head.

Amy pulled up outside Jenny's house a couple of minutes early, but Jenny was ready and waiting and waved to her friend from the lounge. Amy smiled. Jenny had obviously just had her hair done and it was the brightest shade of pink imaginable. Amy unlocked the car doors – locking them while driving alone had become a habit – and Jenny climbed in next to her.

'Morning,' Jenny said brightly. 'How're you feeling?'

'Morning. Pretty grim, thanks. Hair looks fab by the way. Glad I've got my sunglasses on though.'

'Thanks. Nerves or hangover? You'll be fine. Got your paper bag just in case?'

'Both and no, I forgot it. I just keep telling myself I'll be fine. And squirting Rescue Remedy in my mouth.'

'Not listening to Fay's show?' Jenny asked. 'Shall I put it on?' She didn't wait for an answer but simply turned the car stereo on and selected Radio Folkestone. The song playing was just coming to an end and soon they heard Fay introducing her first guest.

'So, joining me in the studio today is local photographer, Willem de Groot. Thanks for being here, Willem,' Fay began. She didn't ask if she could call him Will.

'Thanks for having me, Fay, it's great to be here,' Willem said, hoping he was the right distance from the microphone and that he wasn't speaking too loudly.

'I introduced you as a local photographer but, of course, as people might be able to hear from your accent, you're not originally from this part of the world, are you?'

'No, that's right. I grew up in South Africa – that's the accent you can hear. I moved to the UK when I was twenty-seven, spent twenty-plus years in London before making Folkestone my home.'

By this time, Amy and Jenny had reached the radio station

41

and were sitting in the car park listening to Willem's interview.

'Oh, that's Willem from the shop,' Amy said. 'You know, the photographer who joined just before me. Still haven't actually met him.'

'Oh yeah, I know who you mean,' Jenny said. 'I think I've seen him when I've been out walking early. Get the impression he's a bit surly. Sounds alright though.'

They listened for a few more minutes before deciding they really ought to go and check in at reception. Once they'd signed in Amy and Jenny sat down to wait.

'We're way too early,' Jenny remarked.

'Yeah, I know, sorry.'

Jenny shrugged. 'Doesn't matter. Nothing better to do.'

They sat in silence, with Amy fidgeting from time to time and dosing herself up with Rescue Remedy.

In the studio, Willem was telling Fay about his lifelong love of photography and how he was now trying to make a living from his hobby.

'So, where can people find your work then, Willem?' Fay asked.

'On my website,' Willem said, 'and also in the Coastal Creatives shop on the Old High Street. You can see all my latest work on Instagram too if you follow me.'

Fay then dutifully gave out Willem's web address and Instagram account details before rounding off the interview by thanking Willem once again.

'It's been my pleasure, Fay, thanks for having me on,' Willem said. He waited while Fay told her audience about her next guest.

'So, don't go anywhere because at eleven-fifteen I'll be talking to local author, Amy Archer, about her latest novel, set right here in Folkestone. Before that, here's a bit of Duran Duran for you.' The introduction of 'Girls on Film' started up and Fay rose from her chair to show Willem out.

'Thanks again, Willem,' Fay said as she ushered him out. As Willem passed the outer office he heard phones ringing and saw anxious faces, but didn't think too much of it, heading back down the corridor and through the double doors into reception. He was just glad that was over. In reception he passed two women, one with bright pink hair, who he vaguely thought he recognised, and another one he felt he should know. He screwed up his face as he tried to place her. Then, remembering Fay's words, he wondered if that was the local author she had as her next guest, Amy Archer whose books were in the shop. He nodded at them as he passed, noticing that the one with brown hair looked very nervous, her leg jiggling up and down and fingers fidgeting. They both smiled at him and he went on his way, pausing only to check out at the desk.

'So, that was Willem, eh?' Amy said to his departing back.

'That was Willem. Can't believe your paths haven't crossed yet, both of you being in the shop.'

Amy shrugged. She had other things on her mind.

It was a few more minutes before the double doors opened again and Fay approached them. She smiled at them. Jenny got up and hugged her.

'Hi, Jenny,' she said, returning the hug before turning her attention to Amy. 'Amy, hi,' she began, 'great to finally meet you. I'm really sorry to do this to you, but we're going to have to postpone your interview. I really am so sorry to mess you around.'

'Oh,' Amy said, surprised to feel a little disappointed. 'Oh, no problem.' She didn't ask why.

'Yeah, can't be helped, gonna be doing an extended news piece I'm afraid.'

Amy and Jenny realised how grim Fay's expression was as she spoke.

'What's happened? Has something happened?' Jenny asked.

Fay nodded. 'I'm afraid it has. A body's been found.'

CHAPTER 7

The beach huts

Amy and Jenny hurried back to the car and turned on the radio. Fay was just apologising to listeners about the change to the programme. Straight afterwards, the newsreader came on air.

'Police have reported a body has been found in suspicious circumstances at one of the Folkestone beach huts. The body of a woman, believed to be in her late forties, was found sitting in a deckchair in front of one of Rana Begum's one hundred and twenty colourful beach huts situated on the seafront between Folkestone and Sandgate along Lower Saxon Way. We have our reporter Bella Harp at the scene and she's joining us on air now. Bella, hi, what can you tell us?'

'Hi, Fern, well, you join me on the beach just below the Lower Leas Coastal Park, where police have cordoned off a stretch of promenade and about a dozen of the brightly coloured beach huts, which locals will know are part of this year's Creative Folkestone Triennial. At approximately seven-twenty this morning the body of a woman was found by a man walking his dog. He's here with me now.'

'It's always a dog walker who finds the body, isn't it?' Jenny interrupted.

'Shh!' Amy said, reaching over and turning up the volume.

'So, can you tell me what happened this morning?' the reporter continued.

'Yes, well, I came out to walk Juno at seven a.m. as usual,' he said, stroking the head of the black Labrador panting at his side. 'We always take the same route in the mornings. We walked past the beach huts and I noticed a woman sitting in front of one of them – the yellow and green one,' he said, pointing to the hut at the centre of the police cordon.

'Did anything seem unusual about the woman?' Bella asked.

'No, not at first, not really. I did think it was unusual to see someone sitting there at this time of day, but there wasn't anything obvious that made me suspicious. She had a hat on, and sunglasses, so I couldn't see her face – I just thought she was enjoying some peace and quiet at the start of the day. Her dog was lying with its head on her feet and didn't move when we went past. I just said "morning" and carried on walking.'

'You didn't think it was strange when she didn't answer you?'

The man paused. 'Well, no, not really. Not everybody wants to be sociable, do they?'

'So, what *did* make you think that perhaps all was not well when you came back past on your way home?'

'Um… they were just too still, I think. The dog hadn't budged at all.'

'So that was when you stopped? To check if she was okay?'

'Yes, that's right. I called Juno back and put her on the lead first. The other dog whined and lifted its head when I went over. I spoke to the woman, but got no response. Even when I shook her shoulder – nothing. That's when I called the police.'

'Did you check for a pulse at all?'

'No. I didn't really want to touch her again. I've watched enough police dramas to know you don't move a body in case you contaminate the scene or something.'

'So, did you realise she was dead at this point?'

'Yeah, I was pretty sure she was dead.'

'Was there any sign of injury or anything that might explain what had happened to her?'

'No, although there was what looked like mud or something around her mouth when I looked closer. Apart from that she just looked like she was sleeping.'

'Thank you for speaking to me,' Bella ended the interview and handed back to the studio.

Amy turned off the radio and turned to Jenny. 'I wonder why they're treating it as suspicious?' she said.

'Dunno,' Jenny shrugged. 'Maybe they know something we don't? You know, how they don't always release all the details – stop the nutters and the copycats.'

'Yeah, s'pose so. Given me the willies though,' Amy shuddered.

'Hardly surprising, is it? We haven't had any murderers on the loose since we did you-know-what to you-know-who.'

'Robert. The Exhibitionist,' Amy whispered.

'Forget about him, Amy, he's ancient history. Anyway, I'm more concerned with what will happen to the woman's dog,' Jenny said.

'Poor thing. Presumably it had a name tag on, so the police will be able to trace the owner's identity that way?'

'Yeah, probably. Hopefully.'

'I wonder what happened to her? What the cause of death was?' Amy continued, looking pensive.

'Whatever it was, don't get involved, Amy. Let it go.'

'Yeah, I know, it's just…' Amy began.

'I know,' Jenny said, smiling sadly at her friend.

Amy drove Jenny back to her house, promising to see her soon, and went home to try and write. Try as she might though, she couldn't shake the dead woman from her thoughts, and abandoned her work in progress. At lunchtime she turned on the television to watch the local news. There was a reporter at the same spot the radio reporter must have stood at earlier.

'You join me here at Mermaid Beach in Folkestone, where police are investigating the death of a local woman who has now been identified as Angela Falconer, a forty-eight-year-old married mother of two who worked in a jeweller's in the town. The cause of death is as yet unknown, but police are treating it as suspicious. Neighbours and colleagues describe Mrs Falconer as a kind and friendly woman who was well liked in the community, and are shocked by her death.'

Apart from a name, Amy learned little about the woman's death, turning the television off and wondering what to do with herself. She couldn't shake the feeling of foreboding which had overcome her.

Willem didn't hear about the body until the following morning when he did his usual coffee and news catch up. After he'd left the radio station he'd gone straight home to work on some images and he hadn't had the radio or television on, listening instead to a Foo Fighters CD in his work room. He'd photographed the beach huts only a week or so earlier – his customers loved beach hut images almost as much as they loved ones of the lighthouse.

He was sad for the town he'd grown to love; it was still recovering from the shocking Exhibitionist murders the previous spring. Like everyone, he still thought about the victims when he passed one of the art installations Robert Seymour had defaced with their bodies. 2020 should have been a Triennial year, but Covid had meant it was postponed until 2021. Willem couldn't help thinking a new batch of beautiful artworks would bring up the ugly business all over again. Personally he thought the installations should have been removed out of respect for the victims and their families. He found the idea of the town cashing in on their serial killer abhorrent. People were awful creatures, Willem thought, as Cat jumped up on the desk in front of him, mewling for his breakfast.

CHAPTER 8

The Plot

In a run-down bungalow on the outskirts of the town, some-one else was watching the news, gleefully sucking up all the attention the body at the beach huts was getting, like Slush Puppie up a straw. It was like oxygen to him. It had been too long, and he felt alive for the first time in months.

He knew he'd got ahead of himself – the Triennial didn't start for another few weeks – but he couldn't resist giving them a little appetiser, a taster of what was to come.

He'd waited impatiently for the announcement with the new dates for the fifth Folkestone Triennial. It was due to start on the 22nd July and they were running it longer than usual, right up until November 2nd. They were calling it 'The Plot' and there would be more than twenty outdoor, newly commissioned public artworks set around the town, available to everyone free of charge. It thrilled him to think of himself in the news. He'd have more than fifteen minutes of fame, and his art would be remembered long after the other artists' had been forgotten.

He admitted to feeling a little frustrated; there was so little he could do to prepare until he knew the details. He wasn't worried though. He knew the ideas and inspiration would come. *Just when you thought it was safe to go back in the water, Folkestone*, he chuckled to himself. He'd lived in the seaside town his whole life and seen the dramatic changes wrought, especially in recent years with the arrival of Creative Folkestone, the arts charity responsible for putting on the Triennial. Gone was the Rotunda Amusement Park on the seafront, along with the old nightclub La Parisienne. He had so many memories of mini-golf and fairground rides, of nights out involving way too many shots with half-naked girls, and eating hot ring dough-nuts at the Sunday market. The town had been gentrified and transformed into a creative hub. True, they'd brought back a Sunday market, but it was nothing like the one of his youth. Instead it was all arts and crafts stuff. He didn't hate it. He actually quite liked some of the art installations dotted around the town and had a lot of respect for the ingenuity of some of the artists. He wasn't going to lie though, some of it was just pretentious shit. Well, whatever this year's exhibits were like, he was confident he could improve them and take that ingenuity to a whole other level.

Jenny was excited about the Triennial too. For slightly differ-ent reasons. She'd taken a job as one of the hosts responsible for manning the exhibits and telling visitors about them. She'd tried to persuade Amy to apply too.

'Pleeeeease,' Jenny said, putting her palms together in prayer and pouting at her friend.

Amy couldn't help laughing. 'I can't, I'm sorry, I've just got too much on.'

'No, you haven't,' Jenny interrupted.

'Yes, I have. Apart from finishing this damn book, I have the shop, and I've been asked to write some short stories for a couple of anthologies.'

Jenny was momentarily sidetracked. 'Ooh, short stories! Love a short story. However, there's a clue in the name – they're *short* so they don't take long to write, so that excuse doesn't work.'

'Pah! You know how I feel about short stories. It's a very different skill to writing a novel. And one I don't have.'

'Rubbish! I would remind you of a certain short story you wrote for the group last year, of the lovely Laura and the elephant tranquiliser,' Jenny said, raising her eyebrows and cocking her head.

Amy pulled a face. 'Fluke. Beginner's luck. It's going to take me ages to write them. If I can even come up with ideas to begin with.'

'I'll help you. What are the themes?'

'One's "The British Seaside Resort: the dark side", the other's "Tipping Point",' Amy told her.

'Easy!' Jenny insisted.

Amy just sort of growled at her.

'Anyway, back to the host job. Pleeeeease!'

'No, Jenny, I really can't. How about this though – I'll come and keep you company sometimes. When it's quiet we can brainstorm short story ideas.'

Jenny thought for a few moments. 'Deal,' she said finally. 'That's actually even better really as if we'd both been hosts, we'd probably have been in different places anyway.'

'Good, that's sorted,' Amy said. 'So, when do you start?'

'July. We have some training for a couple of days before it all kicks off.'

Amy was quiet.

'I know what you're thinking, Amy,' Jenny said. 'You're worried it's going to bring up the Robert thing all over again.'

Amy nodded. 'I can't help it.'

'I know. It's bound to remind people, but with everything

the town's been through with Covid and stuff, I think it's ready to get back to some sort of normal and to celebrate a bit. The last thing anyone wants is to think about a dead serial killer.'

'I know you're just trying to make me feel better, and I appreciate it.'

'Is it working?' Jenny asked.

'No, not really,' but Amy couldn't help smiling at her friend.

'Would cake help?'

'Always,' Amy laughed.

It was to be Willem's first Triennial. Of course he was familiar with them; you couldn't see a small pink house floating in the harbour and not ask questions. He'd actually been asked by Creative Folkestone to do some photography for them, as well as some drone work. His reputation as a photographer was growing and, only last week, he'd seen one of his images reproduced on one of the recycling bins in the town centre. They'd obviously got it from one of the images libraries Willem supplied. It had made him chuckle, especially as it was a drone shot and he could see himself standing with the controller next to a Martello tower.

He'd been asked to attend a preview on July 21st to photograph the artists with their work, along with local dignitaries. It wasn't the sort of work Willem enjoyed, but he needed the money. He would just have to grin and bear it. And hope there was free booze.

CHAPTER 9

Amy and Willem

The weeks were flying by and Amy was in the Coastal Creatives shop one Thursday at the end of June, desperately trying to come up with ideas for her tipping-point story. Thankfully the shop had been pretty quiet, giving her time and space to think. Unfortunately, neither the time nor the space had helped and she was starting to feel the pressure of a July deadline as a tight band around her head, which she now had in her hands, not hearing Willem as he entered the shop.

'Er... hello,' Willem said to the brown head of hair behind the desk.

Amy looked up in surprise. 'Oh! Sorry, I didn't hear you come in,' she said, feeling flustered.

'No, you look like you have the weight of the world on your shoulders there, Amy... it is Amy, isn't it?'

Amy nodded, 'Yes, I'm Amy. And you're Willem? I saw you at the radio station that day.'

It was Willem's turn to nod. 'Yes, you were with the lady with the pink hair, I think.'

'Yes, that's my friend, Jenny. She was there for moral support. I was a bit nervous,' Amy confessed.

'I understand. Me too. So, how did it go?' Willem asked.

'It didn't,' Amy said. 'I was cancelled!'

'No! Why?'

'Because of the body. You must know – the one they found at the beach huts.'

'Ah, yes. I'm sorry you were cancelled though,' Willem said.

'I was quite relieved, to be honest,' Amy admitted, looking sheepish. 'I was absolutely dreading it. Honestly thought I might throw up on air.'

Willem laughed.

Amy smiled at him. He had a nice laugh.

'Will you go back another time?' he asked.

'Hm… maybe. If they ask me. I won't be volunteering.'

'You should. Fay is very down to earth and easy to talk to.'

'We'll see. In the meantime, I'm tearing my hair out over this bloody short story I have to write,' Amy groaned.

'I'm afraid I'm not familiar with your writing,' Willem apologised.

'No reason why you should be,' Amy said.

'What's the short story about?' Willem asked.

'I have no idea, that's the problem.'

'Do you have a theme?'

'Yes, it's tipping point, and I'm rapidly reaching mine. Into insanity.'

'So, something that tips a person over the edge, perhaps?' Willem said.

'Yep, something like that,' Amy confirmed.

'The straw that broke the camel's back, in other words? Hm. Well, I know what will be mine one day…' Willem began.

'Oh?'

'Yes, it will be someone who gets in my shot just as I'm about to push the button on something I spent ages planning. That will be my straw.'

As Willem spoke a small lightbulb had gone on in Amy's writer's brain. 'By George, I think you've got it!' she said. 'Thank you!'

'I have? And who's George?' Willem said, smiling at Amy's sudden animation and thinking how it transformed her face quite beautifully. He was embarrassed and looked away to regain his composure.

'The idea,' Amy enthused. 'Can I nick it, please? No idea who George is, it's just something we say.'

'Oh, okay. Well, you are welcome to use the idea, for what it's worth. Perhaps I could read the story when it's finished?'

'Yes, of course, if I ever do finish it,' Amy said. 'Although now I have an idea, there is more chance of that happening. Thank you!'

'You're welcome,' Willem said, grinning. Amy's enthusiasm was contagious.

'Sorry, I've totally forgotten to ask why you're here. Can I help with anything? I'm such a bad shopkeeper,' Amy said, pulling a face.

Willem laughed. 'You're fine. I just brought some more stock in, that's all.'

'Ah, okay. Let me guess, lighthouses?'

'Yes, lighthouses, what else?'

'I imagine sales of beach hut images haven't been helped by that woman's body being found?'

'Indeed. I pray they never find a body at the lighthouse,' Willem said. 'Or I will go broke.'

'Now there's another story idea, right there,' Amy said. 'Might nick that too.'

At that moment the sound of the door opening and a

customer coming in put an end to their conversation. The customer was wearing a mask, so Amy and Willem quickly put theirs on too.

'Good morning,' Amy said. 'Welcome to Coastal Creatives. Just let me know if you need any help.'

Willem held up the bag he was holding, and pointed to his section of the shop, moving quietly away from the desk.

The customer approached the desk as he went. 'Do you have any images of the lighthouse?' she asked.

Amy grinned behind her mask. 'Funny you should ask,' she said. 'Let me introduce you to our resident photographer, Willem de Groot.'

'I finally met Willem,' Amy said.

She and Jenny were having one of their regular coffee and cake catch-ups in Eleto. It had got to the point where they didn't even have to ask for gluten-free salted caramel chocolate brownies.

'And? What's he like?'

'Um… nice.'

'Nice? That's a bit beige,' Jenny said. 'Call yourself a writer? You must have a better word to describe him than nice. Consult your inner thesaurus at once.'

'Well, firstly, I don't call myself a writer, as well you know, and secondly, what's wrong with nice? Nice is… nice,' Amy shrugged.

'Still got imposter syndrome, eh?'

'Yeah, when people ask me what I do for a living, I still say, "well, I'm not really working at the moment, but I write a bit".'

'I wonder how many books it will take for you to think of writing as your job?' Jenny queried.

'Dunno. Maybe when I start making a proper living from it?' Amy replied.

'Yeah, s'pose. You'll have to practise saying in the mirror, "I'm an author", until you can say it without pulling a face or giggling.'

'And people will say "that's nice",' Amy laughed.

'Indeed. Anyway, back to Willem. Is he a bit surly?'

'No. At least I didn't find him surly. He actually gave me an idea for one of my stories.'

'Ooh, so he's your muse now is he?' Jenny joked.

'No! Well…' Amy began, looking down at her plate and fidgeting with the fork.

Jenny cocked her head and stared at her friend. 'Amy… spill… is something going on I should know about?'

'No! God, no, he's so not my type.'

'I sense a but,' Jenny said.

'Well, I do find myself thinking about him rather a lot since we met. It's rather surprised me.'

'You like him!'

'I don't like him,' Amy insisted. She paused. 'Well, maybe I do. I don't know. It's been a while since I liked anyone. Almost forgotten what it feels like.'

'Ah, dating in the age of Covid. Hasn't that been fun? Not.'

Amy groaned. 'Virtual dating, no thank you.'

'So, are you going to ask him out?' Jenny wasn't letting go.

Amy shook her head. 'No, absolutely not. I don't even know if he finds me attractive. He could be married for all I know.'

'I'm pretty sure he's single. You should find out.'

'Can we change the subject now please?' Amy said. 'When's your training?'

'Spoilsport. Um, next Monday and Tuesday. Then they've got some preview thingy on the Wednesday for all the local bigwigs.'

'Cool. I hope you enjoy it.'

'Thanks. I figure, even if I hate it, it's only 'til November,' Jenny shrugged.

In his workroom Willem was thinking about Amy. She kept popping into his head and surprising him. He hadn't been in a relationship for a really long time and certainly wasn't expecting to meet someone. He wondered if their paths would cross again. He hoped so. Perhaps he could find an excuse to call in to the shop again when she was there. *Silly old sod*, he said to himself, *as if she'd be interested in a bad-tempered old dinosaur like you!* Nevertheless, he was whistling along with 'Here comes the sun' as he returned to framing yet another lighthouse image.

CHAPTER 10

Preview day

The day of the Triennial preview, July 21st, dawned bright and sunny and saw Willem down on Sunny Sands early to capture yet another glorious sunrise. He never tired of the big skies and the fantastic light in Folkestone. He could see France clearly on the horizon, some twenty-six miles away, and he still marvelled that he was closer to the continent of Europe than to London.

He hadn't seen Amy again since that day in the shop as he hadn't been able to pluck up the courage to go back. He worried she would see right through him and he'd feel a fool. He still found himself thinking of her often though, how her face lit up when she laughed and how she tucked her hair behind her ears when she was talking. He'd tried telling himself that fortune favoured the bold, to no avail. *Are you man or muis?* he asked himself. He answered with a squeak, much to Cat's surprise.

He had a few hours to get some work done at home before he had to go and play nice with the good people of Creative Folkestone. He was building a deck in his garden and wanted to get a few boards cut to size.

At one-thirty, Willem was showered and ready to go. He'd reluctantly put on a shirt with his jeans and boots rather than his usual T-shirt, and was already feeling uncomfortable and grumbling under his breath at Cat, who looked disdainfully at him out of his one eye. He grabbed his rucksack, which contained his drone and camera, both fully charged overnight, and set off. The email he'd received had instructed him to be at the Gasworks entrance on Foord Road, so he took the steps at the end of the cul-de-sac, swearing at the broken glass scattered down them. He passed under the viaduct, smiling at the sign which informed him it was 4.4 giraffes tall. Someone at the council had a sense of humour.

When he got to the gasworks he could see a few people milling around inside, including a couple of people wearing identical bright red T-shirts. One of them had vivid pink hair and he recognised her as Amy's friend, Jenny. Before he could chicken out he went over to introduce himself.

'Um… hello… Jenny, isn't it?' he said. 'I'm Willem, from the shop, with Amy.'

'Oh, hello, yes I recognise you. What are you doing here?'

'I've been asked to take some photographs,' Willem informed her.

'Oh, cool. Well, don't take any of me. How much does my hair clash with this ruddy T-shirt? Could they have picked a worse colour?' Jenny indicated the offending article of clothing with both hands and Willem saw 'The Plot' emblazoned across the front.

'Perhaps yellow?' Willem smiled.

'Ew, yeah, yellow would've been worse. Red it is then,' Jenny shrugged.

'Maybe you could dye your hair to go with the T-shirt?' Willem suggested.

'Sod that for a game of soldiers. Only just had it done pink.'

'Well, it was nice to meet you, Jenny. I should probably find someone who knows what I'm supposed to be doing.'

'Yeah, I should probably do the same. *Nice* to meet you too, Willem,' Jenny grinned as she turned away and he wondered why she'd put so much emphasis on the word nice. As he watched, he saw her take her mobile out of her pocket.

Willem's here. Being NICE. You should come down to the gasworks and lurk. Gaslurks. Jenny texted to Amy, chuckling to herself. She wasn't surprised when Amy texted back just two words: *Sod off.*

Back at home, Amy found she was actually considering Jenny's suggestion. She hadn't seen Willem since that day he'd come into the shop. She'd thought about popping in on a Monday, but was too shy and didn't want to make a fool of herself. She couldn't use restocking her books as an excuse as there were plenty there still. She found herself thinking about him a lot though, and it still surprised her.

Ten minutes later, having changed her outfit, brushed her hair and checked her appearance in the mirror, Amy set off to walk to the gasworks. The sign with the giraffe on by the viaduct made her smile, as it did every time.

Where are you? she texted Jenny when she got to the Foord Road entrance opposite the Tesco's.

Turn into Ship Street – I'm up the top. Look for a bright feckin' red T-shirt. Jenny texted back.

Amy soon found Jenny by another gate, which had been opened up into the gasworks.

'Nice T-shirt,' she said. 'I didn't know it was Comic Relief.'

Jenny stuck her tongue out.

'Very professional,' Amy said. 'Who can I complain to about you?'

'Just come in and look important,' Jenny hissed, beckoning with her hand.

Amy stepped through and got her first view of Morag Myerscough's 'Flock of Seagulls Bag of Stolen Chips' installation, a vibrant structural piece made up of multi-coloured panels with words and phrases on them.

'Wow!' she said. 'This is fab.'

'Isn't it great? Can I practise on you?' Jenny said. 'Pretend you're a visitor.'

'Er... I am a visitor,' Amy replied.

'You know what I mean. Don't be a dickhead.'

'How very rude. Where's your supervisor again?'

'Shut up and be my guinea pig,' Jenny said, glaring at her.

'Squeak,' Amy said, before using thumb and forefinger to zip her mouth shut.

'So...' Jenny began, 'this is a gateway or welcome pavilion for the former gasworks site, from where visitors will be able to view the whole site. Its cylindrical form and open lattice-work construction echo the gasometers that once stood on the site, while its brightly painted panels suggest a more post-industrial atmosphere.'

'Ooh! Someone's done their homework,' Amy said.

'Shush,' Jenny ordered her, 'or I'll forget.'

'I don't think you can shush your visitors, Jenny,' Amy tutted.

'You're gonna get a slap in a minute,' Jenny growled at her.

'You definitely can't slap them,' Amy admonished, shaking her head.

'Bloody hell, now I can't remember the next bit,' Jenny groaned. She dug into a tote bag Amy hadn't noticed she was carrying and pulled out a small folder. 'Crib notes,' she said by way of explanation. 'So, as I was saying, the title "Flock of Seagulls Bag of Stolen Chips" was chosen by the artist from among the dozens of key phrases that came out of the five workshops to which local residents were invited. The words painted on the other panels also came from these workshops.' Jenny stopped for breath. 'How am I going to remember all this?' she groaned. 'And this is just one of them.'

'You will. You're doing great. And it'll get easier with repetition,' Amy reassured her.

'Yeah, I s'pose,' Jenny said.

They were standing at the rail, looking down over the rest of the site. A black path for visitors to follow snaked through the grass.

'You have to stay on the path when you go in 'coz otherwise you might fall into a hole apparently,' Jenny informed Amy.

'Good to know. If you get any horrid people, you can send them off-path and hope for the best.' Just then, Amy spotted a familiar figure walking up the path towards them. She felt her face flush with colour, and wondered if she could blame the reflection off Jenny's T-shirt.

'Oh look, there's Willem,' Jenny said, waving at him.

'Oh yeah,' Amy said casually, trying to sound as though she hadn't noticed him. 'You're on waving terms now?'

'Yeah, he's *nice*,' Jenny grinned.

Willem spotted them and waved back. His heart skipped a beat when he realised it was Amy standing next to Jenny.

Amy didn't know if she was relieved or disappointed when Willem stopped and stepped off the path, taking his rucksack off his back and removing his drone and its controller. He'd been asked to get some aerial footage of the site and all its exhibits.

None of them had noticed the man standing on the opposite side of Ship Street. He was wearing a cap and sunglasses, smoking a roll-up, and quietly observing the site. He didn't hang around for long. He had places to go, exhibits to see.

Amy and Jenny watched as Willem sent the drone up, craning their necks to follow it.

'Come on,' Jenny said after a while. 'I'll show you the rest of the site.'

'Aren't you supposed to be working?' Amy said, not wanting her friend to get into trouble.

'I am. I'm showing a local celebrity and well-known author around.'

Amy made a pfft noise, but followed Jenny out and halfway down Ship Street to another gate and the start of the winding black path. Amy took in the pampas grasses and butterflies as they followed the rubberised walkway, which seemed to reflect heat up at them. The viaduct loomed ahead of them, viewed from the opposite side to Amy's house. As they got nearer to where Willem was standing controlling the drone, Amy got more and more nervous. Jenny, however, was already waving at him.

'Hello again,' she said. 'How's it going?'

Willem looked up from the screen.

'Oh, hey, Jenny. Hello, Amy, long time no see,' he said.

'Hello,' Amy said shyly, looking at her feet. *God, what is wrong with me?* she thought. *I've turned into a tongue-tied teen.*

Willem didn't seem to have noticed her discomfort though and had turned his attention back to the drone. 'Let me just bring Victor back in,' he said without looking up.

'Who's Victor?' Jenny asked.

'Victor's my drone,' Willem explained.

'Oh, okay,' Jenny said.

'As in Victor Meldrew?' Amy asked, overcoming her shyness sufficiently to speak.

'Yep,' Willem smiled without looking up.

Just then, the sound of the approaching drone made Amy and Jenny look up, craning to see the machine high above them, shading their eyes with their hands. Willem soon had Victor hovering in front of them.

'Smile,' he said, taking a photograph of the three of them, before landing the drone just a few feet away.

'That's so cool!' Jenny said. 'I've never seen one close up before. How high can he go?'

'The maximum legal height in the UK is 120 metres. He could go higher if it was allowed,' Willem informed her.

'My neighbour got one a little while ago. I was a bit shocked to see it hovering outside my bedroom window one day,' Amy said. 'I think he was just trying to get the hang of it in his garden, but it was a bit disconcerting.'

'He shouldn't have done that,' Willem said, shaking his head. 'There are rules about where you can fly in residential areas and near people. I have permission to fly here today.'

'It only happened the once,' Amy said.

'If it had happened to me, I think I'd've thrown something at it,' Jenny said.

Amy laughed at her friend's cross face. 'It does give a whole new dimension to the idea of a peeping Tom. Ooh, there's another story idea,' she said, grinning.

'You will learn, Willem, that nothing is safe around Amy. She can, and will, use anything you say or do in one of her books,' Jenny laughed.

'She's not wrong,' Amy said matter-of-factly.

'Or get on her wrong side and she might just kill you off,' Jenny added.

The colour drained out of Amy's face and Jenny realised what she'd said.

'In one of her books, obviously,' she said, laughing unconvincingly.

Amy was flustered and smiled nervously as she tried to regain her exposure. 'Ha, ha, yes, well, they haven't found the bodies yet anyway,' she said, trying to sound casual.

Amy was saved from any further discomfort by the arrival of the organisers wanting Willem.

'Goodbye, Amy, Jenny,' he said, nodding to each of them in turn. 'See you again soon, I hope.' His gaze lingered on Amy's face for a few moments before he walked away.

'He likes you!' Jenny said, nudging Amy.

'Sod off,' Amy said, not for the first time that day.

CHAPTER 11

Thief!

The next day, being a Thursday, saw Amy in the shop once more, attempting to make progress on her short story between customers. She was also thinking about Jenny, who had her first proper shift with Creative Folkestone for the opening of the Triennial, and Amy knew she was nervous.

Good luck today! she'd texted first thing, adding the crossed fingers emoji.

Thanks! I'll need it! Jenny responded, adding the green, nauseous one.

Got a paper bag if you need it. Winky face.

Too late! Vomiting emoji.

Amy sent back a laughing one. She knew Jenny would be fine once she got going. She was too conscientious not to be. Besides, she had other things on her mind. The short story for one. And Willem for another.

It was about eleven o'clock when she looked up as the door opened and he walked in, almost as if she'd summoned him psychically. Amy felt her cheeks flush and she tucked her hair behind her ears nervously as she said good morning to him.

'Good morning,' Willem said, smiling at her.

'What brings you here?' Amy asked. 'Not more lighthouses already surely?'

'No, no more lighthouses,' Willem said, revealing empty hands.

'So, you just came to buy my books then?'

Willem laughed. 'I would happily buy your books, Amy, but only if you sign one for me.'

'Oh, you don't really have to buy them! I'm sure you'd hate them. They really are written for women,' Amy said, feeling embarrassed.

'Then maybe I'd learn something from them?' Willem said, thinking how pretty she was with the pink flush to her face. With that, he went over to the book display and picked up the first of Amy's novels. He handed it to her over the desk. 'Please would you sign it... and write this...'

'Oh, God! Hang on... pen...' Amy said, burrowing in her bag. 'Okay... fire away.'

'To Willem,' he began, 'yes, I would very much like to come for coffee with you...'

Amy stopped writing and looked up at him. 'Oh,' she said, blushing even more deeply. 'Oh,' she said again.

Willem couldn't help chuckling at her discomfort, finding it very endearing.

Before either of them could say anything else, the door opened and in walked Gloria. Her usual bluster died as she took in the scene taking place at the desk. It would have been obvious to a blind man that something was going on, and you could cut the sexual tension in the air between Willem and Amy with a very blunt knife.

'What's going on here then?' she asked, trying to sound jokey. She failed.

'I was just buying one of Amy's wonderful books,' Willem said, coming to Amy's rescue.

This clearly just put Gloria's nose even further out of joint.

She made a huffy noise and then bustled off to the storeroom, slamming the door behind her.

Amy and Willem looked at each and burst out laughing, all discomfort forgotten.

'Oh my God, that was like being caught smoking behind the bike sheds by the headmistress!' Amy giggled.

'I don't think Gloria approves of me,' Willem said. 'I have made it very clear that I'm immune to her... er... charms.'

'Oof, brave man,' Amy said, raising her eyebrows. 'She absolutely terrifies me.'

'Don't let her have that power over you. She's probably very jealous of you; you're younger and, with the risk of embarrassing you further, much prettier.'

Amy went even pinker and lowered her gaze to the desk. 'You're just saying that to get a discount on the book,' she joked.

'Did it work?' he smiled.

'Yep. In fact, there's no charge. It was worth it just to see the look on Gloria's face.'

'In that case, thank you, and the coffee's on me. If it's a yes, of course?'

Amy just smiled, and finished writing in the book before handing it to Willem. 'Don't read it now,' she instructed.

Willem took the book, nodding his thanks. 'Well, I suppose I'd better let you get on. Are you writing today?'

'Yes, that short story I told you about. I have too many ideas buzzing around my head now, instead of none,' Amy groaned.

'Can I help?' Willem asked, happy to have an excuse to linger longer.

'Um... maybe... I've been thinking about the photographer who's tipped over the edge by the photobomber, and I had another idea after seeing your drone that day and talking about peeping Toms, that maybe he has an obsessive fan who stalks him while he's out photographing…'

'Funny you should say that. I've recently noticed someone almost stalking me on social media.'

'Oh? Tell me more.'

'It's probably nothing. They're just always the first to comment on my posts and they always say the same thing. It's just a bit odd.'

'You'll probably find they do it to loads of people. Might just be someone who's housebound or something and that's how they keep in touch with the real world.'

'Yes, I'm sure you're right. It's just a bit disconcerting at times.'

'I'm sure,' Amy nodded. 'You don't know who it is?'

Willem shook his head. 'No, no profile photo or obvious username.'

'Hm… I wouldn't worry too much about it. It might find its way into my story though!'

'I'll have to start charging you for all these ideas,' he joked. 'Right, I really must go, but I'll see you very soon I hope?'

Amy just smiled enigmatically and said, 'Bye, Willem.'

Willem headed to the door, raising his hand in farewell. 'I can take a hint. Goodbye, Amy. For now.'

No sooner had the door closed behind Willem than Gloria came out of the storeroom. Amy wondered if she'd been listening at the door. Amy smiled sweetly at her, refusing to be intimidated for once.

'Well, if you've finished flirting, perhaps you'll do some work now?' Gloria said, glaring at Amy.

'For now,' Amy couldn't resist. Willem had given her courage.

Gloria huffed as she rearranged a few things on the shelves and pretended to straighten a picture on the wall. She left then, without saying goodbye.

'Bye, Gloria,' Amy muttered after her. 'Don't come back soon.'

A short distance away, Willem was sitting on the wall overlooking the inner harbour, listening to the gulls screaming over something on the sand below him, and enjoying the July sun on his face. He'd just read what Amy had written in the book: *To Willem. Yes, I'd love to meet you for coffee. Amy x* She'd added her mobile number and Willem added her to his contacts before texting her. *Good. Soon. x*

Someone else was texting Amy at about the same time. Jenny. *Bloody hell. Someone nicked my bag! Great first day this is!*

Oh no! Was there much money in it?

Just my work bag, thankfully. My crib sheets, bottle of water. Nothing of value.

Oh thank goodness. Thought you meant your phone and purse and stuff.

Nah. The Plot tote bag they gave us all. Left it hanging on my chair in the gasworks. There one minute, gone the next.

Bugger. I'm sure they'll give you a replacement. How's it going apart from that?

Yeah, good thanks. Ooh, customer, catch you later.

Amy didn't give it another thought, returning her attention to her story with renewed passion.

Down at the harbour, Jenny's now-empty bag was screwed up in a bin along with the bottle of water and, in a run-down bungalow on the outskirts of town, someone was flicking through the crib notes, looking for inspiration. He'd already memorised the four-digit number scrawled on the cover, smiling to himself. *They're making this too easy*, he thought to himself.

CHAPTER 12

Murder on the dance floor

The next ten days were uneventful. The town filled up with holidaymakers, the sun shone and all was well with the world. (Apart from the ongoing pandemic, of course.) Even the body at the beach huts seemed to have been forgotten. That was until a second body turned up. Unfortunately for Jenny, she was the one to find it, working the Sunday shift at the gasworks.

'Police, ambulance! Both!' she garbled when the operator asked which service she required. 'There's a body. On the dance floor.'

The operator took some more details from Jenny and told her to stay put, help was coming. Jenny sat down on the side of the stage and texted Amy, asking her to come, pointedly not looking again at the body of the young woman in the middle of the floor. By the time a very out-of-breath Amy arrived, emergency services were on the scene. The policeman at the gate didn't want to let her through, but she pleaded with him and he relented, but only after taking her name and phone number. She rushed to Jenny's side, pulling her into an awkward hug.

'God! You okay? What happened?' As she spoke, Amy took in her surroundings. The giant black dance floor on which they were sitting was located just off the path which meandered through the gasworks. The floor was marked out in white outlines of all the dance floors of Folkestone. A large screen rose up from one side. Jenny had told her all about the installation on preview day, and she knew it was called 'Beautiful Sunday' and that the screen showed people dancing *The Slosh*, a sort of line dance indigenous to Glasgow in the seventies. Visitors could either stand and watch or join in with the dance. On this particular beautiful Sunday, however, none of the people on the stage were dancing.

'So, I got here to open up as normal and when I got down here music started playing and I saw someone lying on the dance floor… there,' she said pointing to where they were now erecting a white gazebo-like structure. 'I went over to check and it was obvious she was dead – there was an outline drawn around the body in white paint.'

Amy realised as she listened to Jenny that the song playing in the background was 'Murder on the Dancefloor' by Sophie Ellis-Bextor. Someone was yelling, 'Will someone turn that bloody song off!'

Jenny continued. 'So I rang 999 then. And texted you. That's when I saw the screen.' Jenny turned to look at the giant screen and Amy followed her gaze. The enormous white screen had a giant rip across it and, in big red letters, the words: THE SLASH. I KILLED THE GROOVE. DJ

Amy looked back at Jenny, ashen-faced.

'I know,' Jenny said, reading her friend's mind. 'It's like he's back. The Exhibitionist is back.'

'But he can't be. He can't, can he? We, I, killed him,' Amy hissed.

Jenny just shrugged. She had no answers.

The pair of them fell silent then, watching the activity taking place around them, both of them wondering what the hell was happening. Neither of them heard the faint buzzing of a drone overhead.

After a while, a police officer came over to check on Jenny and to tell her she could go. They had her details and said they'd need her to come in to the station to make a full statement the next morning. As the whole site was now a crime scene, Jenny wouldn't have to worry about work for a while. As they left the site, the coroner's van was just arriving.

'Come on,' Amy said, taking Jenny's arm. 'Come back to mine.'

'Tea? Or something stronger?' Amy asked as she unlocked her front door and led Jenny inside.

'Um... what something stronger have you got?'

'Gin? Not sure if I've got any tonic though. Might have enough Jägermeister for two shots.'

The two of them downed a shot before deciding that actually they did want tea, and Amy put the kettle on before joining Jenny at the kitchen table.

'Bloody hell,' Jenny said.

'Bloody hell indeed,' Amy agreed.

'I don't know what to think.'

Amy shook her head. 'I know, me neither. It's all scarily similar to Robert though, isn't it?'

'Yeah. It is. And don't forget it's not the first body, either – remember the one at the beach huts?'

'Someone's targeting the Triennial exhibits again, aren't they?'

'Yep.'

They fell silent for a while and Amy busied herself with making tea, adding sugar to both cups because that was what you did for shock, wasn't it? Hot, sweet tea.

Jenny took a sip. 'Yeuch! You put sugar in it,' she said, pulling a face.

'What if we got it wrong?' Amy said, absently stirring her own cup.

'What? The tea. Yeah, you put sugar in it,' Jenny said.

'About Robert. What if we were wrong about Robert? What if he didn't do it?'

'Of course he did it, Amy, don't be daft.'

'But what if he didn't? That would mean I killed an innocent man.'

'We saw the evidence, Amy. The stuff in his shed, the photos.'

'They could have been planted by the real killer though, couldn't they?' Amy was trembling now. 'He could've framed Robert.'

'No, no, I don't believe that. Robert was as guilty as hell,' Jenny insisted.

'Who's doing the killing now then, Jenny, eh? Answer me that.'

They lapsed into silence. Jenny pulled a face every time she took a sip of her tea, and Amy couldn't shake the feeling of dread.

In a quiet residential car park on the other side of the viaduct from the gasworks, a man stood unseen behind a van. If anyone saw him and was later asked to describe him, they'd probably say medium, average, nondescript; wearing blue workman's overalls, trainers and a cap. Probably. If they even noticed him at all. He was good at being invisible. What about the van? White, the van was white. No writing on that they could remember. Nondescript, like the man, they would shrug. They might remember that he was holding something and looking down at it. No, they didn't know what. Sorry.

What the man was holding was the controller for a drone. He'd got the idea on the day of the Triennial preview when he'd seen a man flying one above the gasworks. He'd later seen the footage on a video posted by the organisers. They made it so easy for him. The host whose bag he'd nicked had made it easy too. The simplest thing in the world to wait until she was busy with a visitor, walk in though one gate, lift the bag from the back of the chair it was hanging on without breaking his stride, and then leave by the other gate. He was really hoping that one piece of the puzzle would be contained in the bag, and he was rewarded with the four-digit code for the locks on the gasworks' gates. Easy. And a little bit disappointing. He was kind of hoping for a bit of kidnap and torture. Sure, he could've used bolt cutters, but where was the fun in that? Unless you were doing a bit of torture. This way, he could let himself into the gasworks any time he felt like it, suss out the lay of the land, and lock up with no one being any the wiser. One use of bolt cutters and they'd change the codes and maybe post security. Couldn't have that; spoil all his fun.

He could see on his screen that they'd erected a white tent over the body now, and it was a lot less interesting. He flew the drone away from the gasworks, keeping it as high as possible until he thought it was safe to bring it in and land it. He didn't bother to pack it away, simply got in the van and drove home. He'd enjoy the footage over a beer at home later.

As he drove, he thought back to the preparation for this particular exhibit. The planning was half the fun; the attention to detail; imagining the impact on his audience. As soon as he'd read about the dancefloor installation he knew it was the perfect piece to modify, and improve of course. He'd studied it from the aerial footage and also read all the blurb about it on the website. He would've liked to go and visit it during daylight hours, but he couldn't risk someone remembering him at a later date. He couldn't take unnecessary risks. Not when the fun had only just started.

Summer had just begun, and what a summer of fun it was going to be. Headlining here in Folkestone: The Exhibitionist 2021, a not-to-be-missed, killer exhibition; the event of the year. *No, the decade*, he thought, grinning.

The choice of soundtrack had been obvious, of course. He remembered 'Murder on the Dancefloor' well; it had been in the charts for ages and played everywhere. Couldn't believe it had been released twenty years ago though. *Must be getting old*, he thought to himself, looking back to 2001. He'd just completed his electrician apprenticeship and was going out with Gemma, who was mad about Sophie Ellis-Bextor and made him play the song constantly in the car. He had fond memories of the car: a Golf GTI which he kept immaculate, polishing it every weekend, buffing the alloys and blacking the tyres. He had some fond memories of Gemma too, but he definitely hadn't taken such good care of her and she'd broken up with him because 'he was a freak' apparently. Her loss, and he'd only blacked her eye once, and it was an accident. Sort of.

Switching the song for the dancefloor exhibit had been child's play for him. He'd let himself into the gasworks late one night, sussed out the system used and gone back the next night with the necessary kit. Rigging a motion detector which would be tripped by the arrival of the host on duty was the easiest thing in the world. He'd cranked up the volume too, chuckling to himself as he imagined the employee jumping out of their skin as the song started up. He hoped it would be the one with the pink hair; the one whose bag he'd taken. He liked the idea of the continuity.

He'd listened to the song for the first time in years, having an inkling of a lyric he'd quite like to use in his art. He'd toyed with the idea of writing the words on the screen in the victim's blood but decided that was way too obvious and this was going to be a clean corpse anyway. He could've got animal blood, he supposed, but really didn't think it would add anything of value. That's when he thought about using the blood of another victim – giving the police a little riddle to get them thinking. *Nice*, he thought. It was these little flashes of inspiration that really got his juices flowing.

He'd got his victim's juices flowing too. Before he gassed her. She'd been way too easy to pick up. Way too easy generally. Dressed like a tart in a silver mini dress, staggering out of Wetherspoon's in stupidly high heels. Easy. He'd stolen an old Golf for the job. Again, continuity, details – they mattered. He'd driven his barely conscious victim to an abandoned stone barn he'd found on one of his recces, miles from anywhere. It was then simple enough to restrain her in the car, run a hose from the exhaust pipe in and wait for her to die. He would've liked to see her exhale her last breath as she inhaled the carbon monoxide, but he had to wait patiently some distance away. He wasn't sure how long it would take. He wasn't in a hurry; it was a nice night and he had his earbuds in listening to Rammstein. He'd removed the catalytic converter from the exhaust system, which he hoped would speed things up a bit.

He was a bit pissed off with himself, if he was being totally honest. He shouldn't have given in to his baser instincts. Hard to refuse when it's offered up to you on a silver platter though. But now he'd have to bleach the body, which was a pain. At least he'd used a condom, he consoled himself, and he was quite pleased with the black eye he'd given her: a little nod to prudish Gemma from the good old days. He wondered idly what happened to her. He hadn't bothered asking his victim her name. He really wasn't that interested. He'd probably find out from the media soon enough. She'd had a little handbag with her which contained her mobile, keys and cash, along with an eyeliner and lipstick. He'd taken the makeup items – he'd thought he might use them on her body – and dumped the rest in a bin in town, just in case they could trace where her phone had been. He didn't want them tracking it to the barn and finding the murder site.

He yawned and looked at his smartwatch. Surely an hour was long enough? She was a skinny little thing and was practically unconscious before he started. He pulled a mask over his mouth and nose and made his way over to the barn, throwing open the doors and trying not to breathe. He quickly checked his passenger was dead, before going round and switching off the ignition. Then he opened all the other doors and walked away again. He thought fifteen minutes ought to do it.

He'd relive the rest of the preparation another time, he thought, as he pulled the van onto his drive. He had something in the freezer he had to deal with now.

CHAPTER 13
Tipping Point

It was a week since they'd found the body on the dance floor, with all the hallmarks of The Exhibitionist, and Amy was a bag of nerves. She'd just about come to terms with being a murderer, but that was when she'd believed the man she'd killed was a stone-cold killer. She was really struggling with the possibility that she'd killed the wrong man, an innocent man. It didn't matter how many times Jenny tried to reassure her, she felt sick to her stomach. She was barely sleeping and as jumpy as a cat on a hot dance floor. It didn't help matters that she still had two short stories to write and could barely think straight.

She'd put off meeting Willem as she didn't want him to see the state she was in and want to know why. She'd even pulled a sickie the previous Thursday when she should have been in the shop, just in case he came in. Gloria had covered for her, making it quite clear Amy was now indebted to her FOREVER.

Willem had texted her to see if she was okay.

Just popped in the shop. Gloria was there! She said you're not well. Sorry to hear that.

Just a bit under the weather, she'd texted back. *Nothing to worry about. It's not Covid.* She wondered how long it would take for people to stop saying that when they had a bit of a sniffle or a sore throat. *I expect I owe Gloria my firstborn or a blood sacrifice or something.*

Ha ha! Yes, at the very least. Although I did notice she was moving your books…

Really?

Yes, to the back corner of the shop.

OMG. The really dark corner that nobody ever looks in?

Yes, I'm afraid so.

What a cow.

A cow indeed.

She's been off with me since she came into the shop when we were both there.

With me too, Willem wrote.

They'd ended the exchange then, with *feel better, see you soon, let me know if you need anything* and so on, and Amy was left with a residual simmering anger about Gloria. While the ire was hot, she started writing.

'TIPPING POINT' BY AMY ARCHER

Another early morning, another sunrise. Kirk never tired of the sunrise, but he was struggling more and more with dragging himself out of bed to greet it.

That morning, resisting the urge to press the snooze button, he'd heaved his old, aching body up, groaning as he walked downstairs to make some strong coffee. There was no way he was leaving the house without a caffeine hit. He could really have done with a long hot shower to relieve his aching bones, but time was against him if he was to make it to the beach in time. As it was, he was going to have to take the car rather than walk the twenty minutes there. The walk there was mostly downhill, it was true, but that meant, of course, that the journey home was an uphill slog, especially with his heavy rucksack weighing down his poor stiff back.

While he waited for the coffee to percolate, he read the news headlines on his mobile, switching it off in disgust a few minutes later.

'Fucking politicians,' he swore aloud. 'All as bad as each other. Fuck the lot of them. And fuck the pandemic. In fact, fuck everything,' he grumbled. His Scots accent was always strongest when he swore, although it was more than twenty years since he'd moved from the Highlands to the south coast of England. He'd moved down for a woman. What a mistake that was. Traitorous cow had cheated on him with his best friend. He'd been off women ever since. And best friends. Friends in general really. Well, let's be honest, people as a whole. He tolerated the ones he had to, but much preferred the company of animals and a good book.

Perhaps, he thought, he should stop reading the news? All it did was wind him up and remind him what utter shits human beings were, and what a complete mess they were making of the planet. Personally he thought the planet was pretty bloody awesome and he'd made a living from photographing it for many years. He specialised in landscapes, especially coastal, and was distressed by the amount of rubbish he regularly found on beaches that had once been pristine. 'And don't get me started on the plastic in the oceans,' he muttered under his breath. Very often his trips to the beach included filling a bag with rubbish and putting it in the nearest bin. If the bin was full, he took it home and put it in his own, usually swearing under his breath about 'lazy fuckers'.

On this particular morning, Kirk's black mood was further

darkened, like adding a vignette in Photoshop, when he left his house to find rubbish strewn across the pavement. Dirty nappies and takeaway containers mingled with food waste and recyclables. Under-the-breath swearing was clearly the order of the day as he cursed his scummy neighbours for their inability to recycle and close their wheelie bins properly. He didn't blame the lone seagull sitting on his car watching him; the seagull couldn't help his nature. Same as he didn't blame the dog responsible for producing the enormous turd he almost stepped in. The dog couldn't pick it up itself. People. Are. Scum.

Getting painfully into the car (he rather fell in than got in these days) and settling himself behind the steering wheel, he turned the ignition key, saying a little prayer as he did that his ancient Vauxhall Astra estate would start. Today was not the day for his trusty old wagon to fail him. Thankfully, the engine coughed into life and Kirk set off to drive the couple of miles to the beach. The roads should at least be quiet at this time on a Sunday morning, he thought, the clock on his dashboard telling him it was five thirty-seven a.m. He took a deep breath in and tried to snap himself out of the black mood. That was when a car pulled out of a side road and he had to slam on the brakes to miss it. He jammed his hand down on the horn and gesticulated angrily at the no-doubt-oblivious moron behind the wheel of the other car.

He was still seething when he parked his car down in the harbour car park. He'd had to turn the radio off when the news came on. Otherwise he thought he might blow a gasket, much like his car had just last week, the head one at that. Years ago, he would have been able to replace it himself, but cars were different now, and he was just too bloody old and tired. So, he begrudgingly took it to the garage and forked out £670 to get it fixed. Daylight-bloody-robbery! To add insult to injury, the mechanic had told him his car was on borrowed time. 'We'll see about that,' he harrumphed as he folded the receipt ceremoniously into his wallet.

Shrugging into his rucksack, Kirk set off to walk along the esplanade to the far end of the beach. The tide was in, so he couldn't go down on the sand to photograph this morning. That suited him just fine as he had an idea for a shot and he'd been planning it for a while, checking the position of the sun in relation to the lighthouse at the end of the Harbour Arm, just across the bay. The sun should be in exactly the right position when it came up. Reaching the end of the walkway, Kirk set up his tripod and camera and lined up the shot. Everything was lining up perfectly; the sky wasn't overcast and he could feel in his old, tired bones that it was going to be a cracking shot.

Here in his element, with no one else around, his breathing had calmed and his heart rate returned to normal after the near miss with the car. And the dog shit. And the rubbish. Peace. Perfect peace.

He looked through the viewfinder just as the sun began to make its ascent and the sky took on a soft orange warmth. This was going to be stunning. He just knew it. Moments like these made everything worthwhile. Not long now... soon... yes!

Literally as he was about to press the button, a bicycle came into shot.

Kirk roared. He ran. And he shoved the man on the bicycle off the esplanade into the grey and roiling, seething sea below.

CHAPTER 14

Scouting for brownies

The only person Amy really wanted to see at the moment was Jenny, the only other person in the whole world who could understand how she was feeling. She couldn't even face going out for coffee, sacrificing their usual chocolate brownies to meet in the privacy of one of their houses. They'd met at Amy's again the day after the body was found at the gasworks and were sitting in the garden with glasses of homemade lemonade and cakes. (One of the few perks of not wanting to leave the house was that Amy had done some actual cooking.)

'Sorry, not as good as Eleto's,' Amy apologised, after taking a bite of the rather average brownie. (Maybe not such a perk, after all.)

'S'alright,' Jenny said. 'I'm just happy to be sitting in the sun doing nothing instead of being at work.'

'Giving you time off after what happened was the least they could do. You are getting paid, right?'

Jenny nodded, her mouth full of cake. 'Mm hm. For as long as I feel I need, they said. They've also offered to get me some counselling.'

'That's good of them. Do you think you'll take them up on it?' Amy asked.

'Nah. Feel fine. The initial shock wore off pretty quickly, to be honest. Totally gonna milk it though.'

Amy laughed. 'Don't blame you. I would.'

They sat quietly for a few minutes, faces tilted up to soak in the July sun. The only sounds were the chatter of sparrows in the hedge and muted voices from a neighbouring garden. The rumble of a train over the viaduct disturbed their peace.

'I haven't asked how you got on at the police station this morning. Sorry, I'm rubbish,' Amy looked apologetically at her friend.

'Yeah, you are,' Jenny agreed. 'But I'll let you off this once.'

'I should've come with you… sorry… didn't think.'

'It's okay, Amy, really. I know you've got a lot on your mind. It was fine anyway, and you've more than made up for it with this delicious brownie,' Jenny said, pulling a face.

Amy couldn't help laughing. 'What did they ask you?'

'Just asked me to describe what happened when I arrived at the site, what I saw, what I heard, that sort of thing,' Jenny shrugged.

'I don't know how you can be so casual about it.'

'Seen worse,' Jenny said.

Amy groaned. 'Thanks to me.'

'I thought I recognised her at first.'

'The dead girl?'

'Yeah, but I think maybe I'd just seen her around – in a pub or something.'

'How old do you reckon she was?'

'Um… maybe late teens, early twenties. Dressed for a night-club. Pretty tarty-looking to be honest.'

'He picked his victim carefully, didn't he? For the location I mean, the dance floor.'

'Yeah, she certainly looked the part.'

'And you said there was no blood anywhere?'

'Not on or around the body.'

'So you don't know how she died?'

Jenny shook her head. 'No, I couldn't see any obvious marks on her. I didn't hang around studying her though. I got off the dance floor to phone the police. I'd probably contaminated the crime scene enough by then.'

Amy nodded. Then a thought struck her. 'Shit, did they fingerprint you? You know, to exclude you from their enquiries.'

'Yeah, I think it's routine to do it. Took a DNA swab too. No biggie.'

'But…' Amy began.

'I know what you're thinking, Miss Marple, but they're not going to connect us to Robert's death. That's case closed, suicide, goodbye, good riddance.'

'But what if it's not? What if they reopen the case because of these new murders? What if they think The Exhibitionist is back?'

'That's a lot of what ifs. Even if they did look at Robert's death again, there's no reason it would lead back to us, is there?'

'I don't know. What if they re-examine his house and find our fingerprints or DNA?'

'We knew Robert. We're not denying that. And we can say we'd been at his house – you know, for the writing group,' Jenny shrugged.

'I s'pose. Bloody hell. I thought this was all behind us,' Amy said, still unconvinced.

'Don't sweat it, Amy. It'll be fine. Anyway, they won't keep my fingerprints and DNA on file once they've eliminated me from things.'

'God, I hope you're right.'

'I am,' Jenny said firmly.

'What actually happened to his house? Was it ever sold?'

'No, I don't think so. It went up for auction, I think, but didn't sell. As far as I know, it's all boarded up now.'

'I s'pose nobody wanted to live in the house of a serial killer?'

'Nope. I'm surprised they haven't turned it into some sort of Exhibitionist exhibition slash museum,' Jenny laughed.

'Not funny.'

'Oh, it was a bit funny, Ames,' Jenny chuckled.

Amy sighed. 'I think my sense of humour has deserted me at the moment.'

'Well, your baking's pretty funny.'

'Rude. But fair.'

'Seriously, though, it's going to be fine. This new killer will turn out to be some copycat or something.'

'Do you really think so?'

'Yeah, I do. And all this worry will be for nothing.'

'Well, it is pretty worrying to know there's a killer on the loose. Aren't you worried about being around the art installations? Maybe you should quit? They'd have to understand, given the circumstances.'

'I'm not quitting. I'll be careful though, I promise. Maybe I should get another gun?' Jenny said, all seriousness.

'No! You can't!' Amy said, a look of horror on her face.

Jenny laughed. 'You should see your face. I was only joking.'

'Very not funny, you dickhead.'

'It was a bit funny, admit it,' Jenny said, still chuckling.

'No guns. Promise me.'

Jenny held up three fingers. 'Scout's honour.'

'Were you even a scout?' Amy asked.

'Nah. Brownie.'

That sets them both off then, snorting with laughter, all thoughts of serial killers temporarily forgotten.

CHAPTER 15

Cold beers and ice queen

As Amy packed the leftover brownies in foil to go in the freezer, having decided they really were only fit for an emergency, the killer was looking in his freezer back at the bungalow.

He'd bought the chest freezer especially for this summer, setting it up in his garage. He wasn't planning to fill it with lollies and ice cream though. Currently languishing in the bottom was a rather bloody mess, and he was wondering what on earth he was going to do with it. *It* was the body of the young woman whose blood he'd used to write on the screen at the gasworks. Well, he couldn't exactly order the stuff from Inks-R-Us, could he?

He didn't have much experience of getting blood from a body and it had proved to be rather messy. He wasn't particularly fond of a messy corpse, but needs must. The question was now, however, what to do with her? Could he make her fit any of the ideas currently doing the rounds in his head? Or should he just dispose of the body? He hated to see her go to waste though – he'd become rather fond of her. She'd put up quite a struggle, so he felt she deserved her fifteen minutes of fame; her time in the sun.

He shrugged and closed the lid on the freezer. He'd think of something fitting, but not today. Today was all about crazy golf.

He went back in the house, having locked the garage door,

made himself a coffee and sat down at his laptop to look for footage of one of the new installations. They'd obligingly posted video and drone footage once again. *Too easy*, he thought, shaking his head. *You're doing all the work for me.* He read all the blurb and, to be perfectly honest, he thought most of it was a load of bollocks. It wasn't even clear what it was called, either 'Fortune Here' or 'Genuine Fake'. What he did like was the nod to the Rotunda amusements, which had graced the site when he was a kid. He had so many happy memories of the place and had been gutted when they'd demolished it. The town was unrecognisable from that of his youth; now it was all gentrified and arty-farty and full of pretentious creative twats. *If you can't beat 'em, join 'em*, he thought, chuckling, although he rather liked the idea of beating them. He would do them the honour of improving their art and making it way more memorable.

This particular installation consisted of a domed pavilion which housed some arcade games, and, on a deck at the back, a crazy golf course made up of pale pink re-creations of Folkestone landmark buildings. He'd walked past a few times now, checking out the lay of the land. The pavilion was padlocked at night, but the crazy golf platform was accessible from the beach. It would be a bit of an effort to get a body up there, but he was confident he'd find a way. He was hoping the combination for the padlock was the same as the gasworks, but he knew they might have changed them as a result of finding the body there. He'd cross that bridge when he came to it. All it meant was that he had to do all his research from a distance or from the online information, and be really organised on the night. That wasn't a problem. He took pride in his work and enjoyed the planning aspect; it was half the fun. He'd read somewhere that Benjamin Franklin had once said that 'if you fail to plan, you are planning to fail'. That good old boy knew what he was talking about, a good adage to live and work by.

Speaking of work, that was, unfortunately, where he had to go now. He had a re-wiring job in a house that was being renovated in the centre of town. He didn't actually mind too much really; he was his own boss and could quietly get on with his work, while letting his mind drift to more exciting things. Some of his best ideas, flashes of inspiration, came while he was running cables under floorboards or through attics.

He drove the short distance to town in his van, windows down, listening to Pink Floyd. It was a beautiful day. It was going to be like a furnace in the loft he'd be working in though and he was already imagining the ice-cold beer he'd enjoy the minute he got home. The thought of the unlovely corpse in the freezer holding a bottle in her cold, dead fingers made him chuckle. He definitely had to find a use for her. Inspiration would strike at some point, he was confident.

Unloading his gear from the van, he nodded good morning to the other workmen present in the house: a couple of chippies and a plasterer today. They nodded back, taking little notice of him. They knew he just liked to crack on with his work; he wasn't the chatty type. All that mattered to them was that he did a good job, and he did. Even though his attention had a tendency to drift, he was always careful with the live wires. Although he hadn't been all that careful with the one in the freezer, had he?

It took a couple of trips to get the huge lengths of cable that had been delivered to the house up the loft ladder. The heat had hit him the moment he opened the loft hatch.

'Oof,' he said. 'Think of the beers later. Think of the ice queen in the freezer.' He couldn't help laughing at his own joke as he climbed the ladder with his tools. He'd shed his usual overalls in favour of shorts and T-shirt, and had put knee pads on. 'I'm getting too old for this shit,' he muttered.

He'd rigged up a couple of work lights on a previous visit, and he turned these on now, looking around the loft space. Most of the junk had been cleared out, but he saw a few boxes at one end. 'For fuck's sake,' he grumbled. 'Why can't people take all their shit with them when they move out?' They were going to be in his way, which was a pain in the arse. Deciding the best plan of action would be to move the junk to the middle of the floor, he made his way over to the boxes. He had to hunch over as he got closer, and he cursed again at the twinges in his back. Maybe he'd have that beer in the bath when he got home. With a good glug of muscle-ease bath soak.

He reached out for the first box; it had obviously been in the attic for some time and was covered in dust and dead bugs. He hoped there wasn't a wasp nest up here. As he pulled the box towards him, the cardboard side disintegrated.

'For fuck's sake,' he cursed, waving the cloud of dust away with his gloved hand. He knelt down, and used both hands to retrieve the contents, dragging them across the boards. Once in the centre of the floor, he could see that the box was full of old games and toys. He blew the dust off a small air hockey table and was transported back to the Rotunda, his hand on the paddle, slamming the puck towards his opponent, in this case Gemma, who'd come away with a bruised hand and vowed never to play it with him again. An idea struck him and he cocked his head to one side as the idea grew legs and started to run around his head like a puck across the smooth surface of the table. *Happy days*, he thought, as he reached for the next box, which was a game called 'Hole in One' and had a couple of dated-looking golfers on the front. Idea number two struck him like a perfectly hit tee shot and he grinned. The annoying box of crap was turning into an absolute goldmine of ideas.

There was nothing else of interest in the first crate, so he retrieved the next one, which thankfully didn't fall apart but was full of useless old Christmas decorations. The final box contained what looked to be old paperwork and photographs. He thought he might have a look through them later, just in case there was anything interesting. Now though, he had to do some actual work, work which meant he could afford to buy things like chest freezers and drones for his hobby. He spent the next couple of hours happily running cables and tacking them into joists, oblivious to the sweltering heat, his mind coolly elsewhere, brewing and planning his next exhibit.

Willem was also at work on this hot July day, in the Coastal Creatives shop. It was a lot cooler in the shop though, as it wasn't on the sunny side of the street, and he was still wearing the sweater he'd worn to walk there first thing. He was wondering if Amy would come in. She seemed to have gone cold on him for some reason he couldn't understand. He was hoping he could win her back by moving her books back to their rightful place in the shop. He knew Gloria would have a hissy fit when she found out, but he didn't care about Gloria, he cared about Amy. Besides, what Gloria had done wasn't fair, and he was ready to tell her as much. Amy paid the same rental and worked the same number of shifts as the others, so she deserved the same amount of space. Willem couldn't stand injustice or the petty, spiteful behaviour of someone like Gloria. Part of him hoped she would call in today and see what he had done. He was ready to go into battle; be Amy's knight in knitted sweater.

When he'd set up the display he took a photo on his phone and sent it to Amy:

Back where they belong, he wrote.

Amy read the text and was touched by Willem's thoughtful gesture. She was also completely panicked at the thought that Gloria would think she'd done it. She didn't know how to reply to Willem.

'Bugger,' she said aloud. 'Bugger, bugger, bugger.'

Back in the shop, Willem was beginning to wonder if he'd done the wrong thing. Amy normally replied promptly to messages. It suddenly dawned on him what Amy might be thinking.

'Bugger,' he said, grateful there were no customers in the shop to hear the expletive emanating from the shopkeeper. He texted Amy again. *Please don't worry. I will tell Gloria it was me. That you had nothing to do with it.*

Amy read his reply and felt a little better. She knew he had meant well. *Thank you. That was very sweet of you*, she texted.

Willem heaved a sigh of relief, hoping he had rescued the situation and found favour with Amy once more. He wouldn't push her about meeting for coffee. Not yet anyway.

Just then, the door opened and Finn came in. Willem smiled and lifted a hand in greeting. 'Hello, my friend, what brings you here?'

'I came in to move Amy's books back. What Gloria did sucked.' He glanced round at the shelves. 'But I see someone's

97

beaten me to it,' he grinned. One look at Willem's face told the younger man everything he needed to know.

'Guilty as charged,' Willem admitted, hoping his face hadn't gone as red as it felt.

'Good for you. Are you prepared for the wrath of Gloria when she finds out though?' Finn asked, seating himself on the high stool next to the counter behind which Willem sat.

'Bring it on. She doesn't scare me. Much!'

Finn laughed. 'Changing the subject to a less scary one, what do you make of these murders? You know, the beach huts and the gasworks.'

'I honestly don't know. It's impossible not to make comparisons with what happened last year – The Exhibitionist murders – isn't it?'

'Yeah, way too similar for comfort,' Finn nodded.

'You know Amy's friend found the body at the gasworks, right?'

'I didn't. That must have been a hell of a shock. Didn't Amy know the killer? I mean the original one.'

'Yes, she told me they were in a writing group together,' Willem nodded. 'They all wrote their perfect murder stories, but this Robert character went a step further and actually started killing people in the ways his fictional serial killer had.'

'Bloody hell. She must be freaking out now then.'

'He committed suicide though, didn't he? It can't be the same killer.'

'Dunno. S'pose not. You do hear about copycats though, don't you?'

'Yes, you do. I suppose only the police can know if it is the same person.'

'Yeah, they always keep something back, don't they? They never tell the press or the public everything for this very reason.'

'I just hope and pray they catch whoever is responsible before any more bodies turn up,' Willem said, his face grim.

Finn nodded.

They couldn't know that victim number three was already on ice awaiting her grand opening.

CHAPTER 16

The right tool

At four p.m. the electrician finished what he was doing and tidied up his tools. He would never normally leave his tools at a job, but now he'd stopped working he'd realised just how hot and sticky he was. All he wanted was to get home for a cold shower and a cold beer as quickly as possible. He knew the house would be locked up by whoever left last, and he was confident nobody would need to go up in the loft for anything. Besides, he needed his tool bag for something else. He'd decided to take the contents from the box full of paperwork home to go through at his leisure, and he shoved everything in the bag, zipping it up and dropping it through the loft hatch. He followed it down the ladder, which he then hoisted back into the space above before closing the loft hatch. He knew it would have made more sense to leave the hatch open to let at least a little of the heat escape before he was next up there, but the open hatch might prove too tempting; his tools were worth a lot of money.

He called goodbye to the remaining tradesmen and headed out to his van. Hot, stuffy air hit him as he opened the door. It was like the loft all over again.

'Bloody hell. Roll on autumn,' he grumbled as he threw his bag on the passenger seat and climbed in. He didn't really mean the sentiment about autumn, of course; Summer 2021 was going to be his best ever. Better even than the one he'd spent with the lovely, if somewhat fragile, Gemma.

After a lukewarm shower to rinse off the sweat and dusty grime of the day, the killer grabbed a beer from the fridge which he took along with the bag of paperwork into the back garden. He needed some fresh air after a day in the confines of the airless attic. He sat on the bench by the back door, took a long swig of the chilled brew and leaned his head back against the brickwork, closing his eyes and letting out a sigh of pleasure.

He could smell the scent of flowers in the air. He didn't know the flowers were jasmine and honeysuckle, running wild through the unkempt garden. He had no interest in the garden as anything other than somewhere to sit and drink beer. All he ever did was give the lawn an occasional mow. Whatever plants had been put in by the previous occupants had either died or thrived with no assistance from him.

After a few minutes, he unzipped the bag and took out a handful of faded papers, which he shuffled through, finding letters both formal and personal. They held no interest for him. He grabbed another wadge, out of which fell some faded colour photographs. He picked them up and found they were mostly taken on a golf course somewhere. The men were dressed in a fetching array of houndstooth and diamond-pattern golf clothes, which he thought dated them to the 1970s. He thought they looked ridiculous, but they'd given him another idea which, if he did say so himself, was fucking genius.

Three beers later and he was burning the unwanted papers in his incinerator bin on the patio. He hadn't found anything else of interest after the golfing pics. They were safely inside on the kitchen worktop, although he would be setting them alight at some point. He couldn't wait to complete exhibit number three. He was really going to give the police something to think about. He was pretty sure no one would work out his little riddles, and it gave him a great deal of pleasure to think of them scratching their heads as they attempted to understand. He didn't mind if some bright spark – ha, bright sparky! – got there eventually; they'd be able to appreciate his ingenuity.

Before he could attend to the finer details, however, he had a somewhat messier job to attend to. He was hoping that now she was frozen, he'd be able to carve her up like a Viennetta. He couldn't decide on the best tool for the job. Should he use something like a meat cleaver and whack her, or use an electric saw? While he tried to make up his mind, he went and changed into decorator's disposable coveralls, whistling all the while.

He stood in front of his tool bench in the garage a few minutes later, looking at the impressive array of tools, each in its correct place. He might not care about the garden, but he certainly did about his garage; it was immaculately organised. He ran his fingers lovingly down a couple of his favourite saws, before deciding to go electric with the reciprocating saw. As much as he didn't want to get blood and bone and crap in its teeth, he thought it was probably the best option. *Have to suffer for your art*, he told himself. He'd give it a bloody good clean afterwards. 'Pun intended,' he chuckled. He was in good form tonight.

He spread an old sheet on the garage floor and lifted the frozen corpse out of the deep freeze, dumping it unceremoniously on top. 'Oof. You put on weight, young lady?' he asked, not expecting an answer obviously. 'I wondered where all the ice cream went. I scream, you scream, we all scream for ice queen. You shall go to the ball, my frigid little ice maiden.

You will be the belle of the ball. The golf ball,' he laughed. He was having fun.

Returning to the business at hand – chopping her hands off – he got down on the floor next to her and severed her left hand. 'That was easy,' he sounded surprised, but shrugged and repeated the process with the right. He bagged the hands up and returned them to the freezer. 'Right, what's next? Don't want to get a-head of myself,' he chortled as he turned his attention to her feet. These went the same way as the hands. He wasn't entirely sure what, if anything, he was going to do with the feet, but was confident he'd come up with something. The head was last, and proved a little more of a challenge, but soon the body parts were all safely back in the freezer. He locked up the garage, changed out of the coveralls and tossed them and the sheet in the incinerator.

After he'd washed and dried his precious saw, he thought he deserved to sit and relax for a while, maybe catch up on the local news, see what they were saying about the bodies they'd found. *His bodies*, he thought proudly. He grabbed another beer and plonked himself down on the old brown leather sofa in the front room. He flicked through the channels until he found one showing the local news. He realised as he sat there that he'd missed dinner and was suddenly starving, so he ordered a curry to be delivered. Cutting up a corpse didn't seem to have affected his appetite. By the time his takeaway arrived some twenty-five minutes later, they still hadn't mentioned the murders in Folkestone and he was getting a bit hacked off. He told himself it must have been the opening item and he'd missed it.

As he plated up his dinner, he listened to the local radio

station to see if they would say something. Surely Radio Folkestone would have plenty to say on the matter. He knew the presenter on air – Fay McFarlane – he sometimes listened to her morning show when he was working. She was very down to earth and had a really dry sense of humour. Her taste in music wasn't completely shit either. He'd often thought he'd like to meet her. He thought they'd probably get on really well. And he was quite sure she wouldn't mind a little bit of the rough stuff. He was surprised to hear her on an evening show, but assumed she was covering for another presenter.

As he listened, Fay introduced a reporter called Bella Harp, and his ears pricked up.

'So, Bella, thanks for joining me for this special segment about the recent murders that have shocked the town, just a year after The Exhibitionist killings rocked it. What can you tell us about the investigation so far?'

'Hi, Fay, well, as you can imagine, locals have been appalled and saddened by the discovery of the bodies of two women, both at Triennial art installations, in what police are calling copycat killings,' Bella began.

He bristled at the term copycat.

'So, they don't believe it's the same killer?' Fay interrupted.

'No, it's my understanding they still believe the real Exhibitionist was indeed Robert Seymour, who took his own life. The evidence they found at his home was overwhelming.'

'Isn't it possible that Seymour was framed and his murder made to look like suicide?' Fay pushed. 'And that the two killers are actually one and the same?'

The reporter paused, obviously lost for an answer. 'Um... well... I suppose that is a possibility, but I think it's pretty unlikely. I'm sure the police would know if it was the same person. Presumably there would be certain hallmarks which a copycat couldn't replicate.'

There was that term again. Bitch. How dare she cheapen him like that.

On the other side of town, Amy was also listening to Radio Folkestone. She was shaking and nauseous and she was pretty sure it wasn't Covid. Other people had already started to join the dots exactly the way she had. It was only a matter of time before the police reopened the investigation into Robert's death. She was terrified at what they might find second time round when they were trying to discount the idea that it was suicide. She couldn't keep bugging Jenny about it, and there wasn't another person on the planet she could confide in. Amy was scared, and feeling very, very lonely.

After he'd cleared up his dinner plate, the killer turned his attention back to his next exhibit: 'Hole in One'. It was going to be fantastic. It had to be, after the brilliance of 'Murder on the Dancefloor'. He prided himself on his originality. Let's see the bitch off the radio call him a copycat after this.

Jenny'd listened to Fay's show that evening too, and she knew Amy would be freaking out big time. Personally she wasn't going to worry about something that might never happen, but she knew she had to be there for Amy. Besides, she was the one who'd procured the gun that Amy had used to kill Robert. She was an accessory to it all. She was still wondering what to do about Amy when a text arrived from Pippa. Jenny felt a stab of guilt as she tried to remember the last time she'd seen her friend. Since the writing group broke up and with Covid lingering, she couldn't remember the last time she'd seen her.

Hello you two! Jenny realised she'd sent the text to Amy too. *Long time no see. How are you both? We should do lunch or something. I'd love to see you both.*

Within a matter of minutes, Jenny and Amy had agreed to meet Pippa for lunch the next day. Amy had tried to wriggle out of it, but the other two had persuaded her.

CHAPTER 17

Pippa

The next day dawned bright and sunny. July was just what summer ought to be in the seaside town. Apart from the pandemic. Oh, and the presence of a serial killer. But, it's so much easier to cope with life's little troubles when the sun is shining.

Amy, however, wasn't convinced as she took a deep breath, locked her front door and set off to walk the mile or so to the harbour, where she'd agreed to meet Jenny and Pippa. As much as she was looking forward to seeing Pippa after what seemed like an age, Amy kind of wished they were back in lockdown. Being a recluse would suit her fine right now. All she really wanted to do was bury her head in the sand and pretend none of this nightmare was happening. The nightmares were happening too; she was back in Robert's house, upstairs in his bedroom looking at the photos of his victim, running downstairs and grabbing the gun, firing a single shot into his brain. She woke shaking and sweating and very afraid.

She kept her head down as she walked, hiding behind sunglasses and sunhat. She never wore hats normally. She wasn't a hat person. But these weren't normal times, and she most definitely didn't feel like a normal person.

'Got to get it together, Amy,' she muttered to herself as she walked. 'Get it together.' If anyone saw her they would probably also conclude she wasn't a normal person.

As she neared the Harbour Arm she could make out Jenny and Pippa waiting by Bobbies Bakehouse. They saw her and waved. She stuck a smile on her face and waved back.

'Hello, you two!' she called out, hoping her voice didn't sound as shaky as she felt.

'Hello!' two voices answered.

'Are we hugging?' Pippa asked.

'Um…' Jenny said. She wasn't much of a hugger *before* Covid.

Pippa laughed. 'Okay, no hugging, but it is so lovely to see you both. It's been far too long.'

'It really has,' Amy and Jenny nodded their agreement.

'You look well,' Amy said to Pippa, taking in her friend's blonde bob and tanned face.

'Thank you,' Pippa said. 'I am well. I'll be even better after a bagel. We are getting bagels, aren't we?' she asked hopefully.

All in agreement, Pippa went into Bobbies with their orders. Bagels and drinks in hand, they made their way to a seating area on the Harbour Arm itself. It was already busy with locals and holidaymakers alike, unable to resist the lure of a sunny day.

'I see the pandemic's not keeping people away any more,' Jenny said.

'Nor the threat of a serial killer,' Pippa added. 'What do you both make of that? Did the police get it wrong last year, with our Robert?'

'Ugh… please don't call him *our Robert*,' Jenny said.

'Can we not talk about it?' Amy said. 'Tell us what you've been up to, Pippa. I want to hear everything.'

'Oh, well, that won't take long. Bugger all, really. Although I have been doing a bit of writing. That and walking the dogs, doing the garden. Nothing very exciting.'

'That actually sounds pretty idyllic,' Amy said. 'What are you writing?'

Pippa looked bashful. 'Oh, it's probably nothing but, after you seemed to enjoy my Rosie and Patrick stories last year, I thought I'd try and develop them a bit more.'

'Oh, that's brilliant. I'd love to read what you've done,' Amy enthused.

'Yeah, me too,' Jenny nodded.

'Well, if you're sure? I would appreciate the feedback,' Pippa smiled.

With that settled, Amy and Jenny filled Pippa in on what they'd been up to, in between very messy bites of smoked salmon and cream cheese bagels.

'Oh, and Amy has an admirer!' Jenny said.

Amy felt herself blush. 'No, I don't!'

'Yeah, you totally do,' Jenny nudged her.

'Ooh, tell me more. Anyone I might know?' Pippa asked.

'You might – it's the photographer guy, Willem something-or-other,' Jenny informed her.

'Oh, yes, I think our paths have crossed once or twice when I've been out early with the dogs. Have to walk them before it gets too hot at the moment. He seems nice,' Pippa said, smiling at Amy.

Amy mumbled something unintelligible through a mouthful of food, thinking she'd almost rather talk about the serial killer.

After lunch, they disposed of their rubbish and used the loos before heading for the boardwalk, which ran along the beach in the direction of Sandgate. As they passed behind one of the art installations, which featured a light-pink crazy golf course on the beach side, a man walked past them in the opposite direction. If they'd been asked to describe him later, they'd probably have said, 'medium, average, nondescript'.

The killer had just taken a final walk past the back of the 'Genuine Fake' installation. He'd studied all the available video and images of it online, but you couldn't beat seeing things for real, in the flesh so to speak, could you? He'd slowed his pace as he approached it, taking in the scaffolding supporting the decking on which the crazy golf was laid out. 'There'll soon be an extra hole up there,' he chuckled to himself. It would be easy enough to climb up, even easier now the body was in bits, and the dome hid the rear aspect from the street. As he carried on walking, trying to keep the self-satisfied smirk off his face, the killer had to step off the boardwalk to avoid three women walking abreast. He noticed that one of them had bright pink hair and was pretty sure it was the one from the gasworks. He did love a bit of continuity.

CHAPTER 18

Mad crazy golf

That night the killer had parked down the road from 'Genuine Fake' to keep watch for any security patrols who might have been employed following the discovery of the body at the gasworks. To his relief there was no sign of anyone keeping an eye on things – that would seriously have scuppered his plans. He wasn't averse to bumping off a security guard if absolutely necessary, but he preferred his victims weak and pretty defenceless and didn't fancy going up against some six-foot bruiser. He also used the time spent on the stakeout to suss out the best place to park to unload his van. All being well, he would be back the following night to complete his next exhibit. Conveniently there was a street-light out not too far away and he couldn't see any CCTV in the street.

The next night, dressed head to toe in black, he was back with the components to assemble 'Hole in One'. He'd crammed as many as possible in a huge army-style rucksack, which he hefted onto his back. Donning dark gloves and pulling his navy cap down over his forehead, he picked up the one remaining bag and walked down onto the shingle. He wanted to approach the dome from the beach at the rear rather than walking directly to it along the street. The waxing crescent moon and scattered cloud gave just enough light for him to navigate across the beach.

It was two in the morning and the only sound was the gentle soughing of the waves onto the beach at low tide and the crunch of his trainers on the pebbles. It was hard going, weighed down as he was, but in a matter of minutes he was standing at the base of the scaffolding. He climbed part way up before hoisting the heavy bag over the railing and onto the platform above. It landed with a thud and he froze for just a few seconds, listening for any other sounds. Hearing nothing, he followed the bag and climbed down onto the decking, shucking the rucksack off his back and stretching his muscles out. He listened for a few moments more, but there was no sound or sign of life other than the susurration of the sea, and his slightly heavy breathing from the exertion.

Crouching down, he opened the rucksack, ignoring the stink and bleach fumes that assaulted his nose, in spite of the plastic bags, and took out a head torch and a pair of bolt cutters. He didn't want to risk using the front entrance, which was visible from the road; he thought they might have changed the combination on the lock by now anyway. Unsure what he would find, he donned the head torch and examined the rear entrance to find it secured by simple cable ties.

He shook his head, feeling the torch wobble. *Too easy*, he thought. *They're asking for someone to break in*. He shrugged as he snipped the ties. *Happy to oblige*.

Leaving the bag on the deck, he pushed through the opening with the rucksack, seeing inside the dome for real for the first time. He'd studied the images online, but it was good to finally see it up close and personal. He was excited to finally be realising the exhibit he'd visualised.

Dragging the plastic bags from the rucksack, he slit open

the one containing the head. He wrinkled his nose at the sight and smell of it, the ragged skin of the neck and the tangled and bloodied hair. It really was messier than he would've liked, but so much the worse for whoever found it. He wondered if it would be the woman with the pink hair. Actually, looking at the blonde hair of his victim now, where blood and bleach had mingled, she did kind of look like she had pink hair herself. He smiled. He liked that.

Time to construct the first part of the installation. In the front corner of the dome was a fortune-telling machine. It was actually one of those machines you put money in a slot, turned a handle and a clear plastic ball dropped out, which contained your 'fortune' – a bit like a fortune cookie slip of paper. The first thing he did was take out nineteen balls, remove the existing pieces of paper and replace them with nineteen of his own, each containing a single letter from the words TORCHED. PHOTOS.STATED. Halfway through he was kind of regretting his decision as it was time-consuming and every minute spent on site increased his risk of discovery. He knew it was a rather pointless exercise at the end of the day. It didn't really add to the exhibit, but he liked the little quirky additions to his pieces, and he loved the idea of the police scratching their heads over the letters – if they even found them. He wondered if some bright spark would realise the letters were an anagram of the what3words for the location of 'Genuine Fake'. *Just a bit of fun*, he thought.

With all the balls back in the belly of the machine, he lifted the girl's head and balanced it on the top. He brushed the hair away from his fortune teller's – 'misfortune teller,' he chuckled – face and stood back to admire her. Nodding with satisfaction, he turned back to the rucksack and pulled out the bag with the hands.

Along one wall of the dome stood an air hockey table and he simply placed one bloody, bleached and ragged, disembodied hand at each end of it, with the puck in one of them, as if Thing from The Addams Family was about to have a game with a friend.

Satisfied with his work so far, he shoved the rucksack towards the rear opening once more. Before going back out on the deck, he located the putters and golf balls in a basket and removed one of each.

Retrieving the final bag of body parts from the rucksack, the killer looked around the crazy golf course and decided on a spot for the additional hole he was planning. Carefully removing the feet, he placed them either side of the head of the putter, which he laid on the deck. Now for the pièce de résistance: the hole. Retrieving the other bag, he manhandled the naked torso out, grimacing at the smell, and grateful for the non-slip gloves he was wearing. He positioned the torso in line with the putter, jiggling it around until he was happy. All that remained was to score the hole in one, which was simply achieved by shoving the golf ball inside the girl. Not the most pleasant task, but you must suffer for your art, isn't that right?

Standing back to admire his handiwork, the killer smiled. She wasn't quite the right shade of pink, but she'd do. This was going to be a real treat for whoever found it.

Turning back to the rucksack, he undid the smaller front pocket and took out a couple of photos with scorch marks on one side where he'd set light to them back at home, allowing the flames to partially destroy them. They were the photos of the dated-looking golfers he'd found in the attic of the house he was working in, and he thought they were a nice touch.

The finishing touch was achieved with a bright-pink permanent marker pen. Kneeling down by the torso, careful not to disturb the feet and putter, he wrote, in large capital letters, the words: TASTED. HOLE IN ONE. For the bright-spark plod, tasted was an anagram of STATED. TORCHED.PHOTOS. STATED. Job done. You're welcome.

Before leaving, the killer closed up the back flaps of the dome with a couple of black cable ties – he always had some with him. You never knew when they might come in handy. The weather forecast was for a still, calm night, but he wasn't taking any chances. He just had to hope no scavengers discovered the torso out the back. Hopefully the smell of bleach would be enough of a deterrent, and his exhibit would survive intact until it was opened up a few hours later.

Bundling the now-empty bag into the rucksack, he took a last look around. Satisfied that all was present and correct, he tossed the rucksack over the railing onto the pebbles below and climbed carefully down. His return journey over the stones was much easier without the weight of the body parts and he was soon back at his van.

As he drove home he mentally retraced his steps, looking for problems he might have overlooked. He was pretty confident he hadn't left any DNA on the body, and figured that if they did find evidence of him at the scene, he could simply say he'd visited the installation, like so many other thousands of visitors. He was pretty sure the whole place would be DNA and fingerprint soup, and he'd worn gloves at every stage of the work.

He yawned as he parked the van back at the bungalow, tired after a good night's work. If any of his neighbours ever noticed his coming and goings at all hours, he had a ready excuse. 'Night-fishing,' he would tell them, waving a rod in their direction. He thought keeping fishing tackle in the van was a stroke of genius. 'Catch anything?' they'd ask. 'Yeah, a cold!' he'd joke, before bidding them goodnight.

Tonight though, he saw no one as he walked from the van to the house, dumping his kit in the kitchen to be sorted out later. Now he needed to catch a few hours' sleep. He set his alarm for eight-thirty a.m. – he wanted to be back at the beach for the big reveal when they opened up just before ten. He thought he'd be too amped to sleep, but the killer slept like the virtuous: with a smile on his face.

CHAPTER 19

Tee time

Amy was at her desk trying to write the second short story when she got another emergency text from Jenny.

For fuck's sake! Can you come now? Please. I've only found another bloody body. The amusement installation on the beach – with the crazy golf.

Another text message binged in a couple of seconds later.

And I mean bloody. And I'm not amused.

Amy texted back at once: *On my way!*

Grabbing her bag and keys, Amy was in her car and on the way in less than a minute, torn between horror and disbelief at what had happened and slight amusement at Jenny's texts. Seeing her reflection in the rear-view mirror, she wondered if she'd actually brushed her hair this morning. She often didn't bother when she was writing. Then she ran her tongue over her teeth. 'Bugger!' she exclaimed, before reaching into the centre console for the pot of Bubblemint gum she always kept there.

A few minutes later and she was parking behind a white van just down the road from the white dome. She didn't notice the driver still sitting in it, sipping from a travel cup and enjoying the show. A drone sat on the seat next to him, unused this morning as he'd decided sending it up was too risky on this occasion. The emergency services were already there, running crime scene tape in a cordon around the structure and immediate vicinity. Amy was relieved to find the same young police officer who'd been at the gasworks manning the entrance.

'Hello! Me again!' she said, smiling at him.

The policeman looked blank for a moment.

'From the gasworks – you know, "murder on the dance-floor-or,"' Amy sang in her best Sophie Ellis-Bextor voice.

Trying not to smile, he relented and took her details again before lifting the tape so Amy could go to Jenny, where she was perched on the low wall above the beach. Her face was pale against her bright pink hair. She gave Amy a weak smile.

'Bloody hell, Jenny! I didn't think you were even back at work!'

'I wasn't. I'm not. But so many people are off sick or have quit that I agreed to cover this shift. Currently regretting that decision.'

'I'm not surprised. I can't believe it!' Amy exclaimed.

'It's bad, Ames. Really bad,' Jenny grimaced.

Amy put her arm around Jenny's shoulder and hugged her in close.

The two friends sat in silence until Jenny was finally allowed to leave, again with the instruction to go to the police station the following morning to make a full statement.

'What do you want to do?' Amy asked. 'Shall we go and get a drink somewhere?'

Jenny nodded. 'Yeah, okay.'

They walked down onto the boardwalk and set off in the direction of the Harbour Arm, arms linked.

'At least you got the day off,' Amy said, nudging her friend slightly.

'Yeah. Pretty extreme way to skive off though. I think I'd rather have worked.'

Grabbing coffees from the Harbour Coffee Co, minus the brownies on this occasion as Jenny said she felt a bit sick, they wandered back onto the beach, still quiet this early in the day, and sat down at the top of a pebble bank, looking out to sea. You could just make out France in the distance.

Neither of them noticed the man taking photographs a short distance away until he turned and waved and started towards them.

'Bloody hell!' Amy muttered, more to herself than to Jenny, and thinking of her unwashed and unbrushed state.

'Huh?' Jenny said.

'Willem,' Amy enlightened, nodding in his direction, and sticking a smile on her face.

'Hello, you two,' Willem called as he neared them.

'Hello,' Amy said, wondering if she was blushing.

Jenny smiled wanly at him.

'What's going on over there then?' he asked, jabbing his thumb back towards the police activity.

'They've found another body. Well, actually, Jenny found it. Again.'

Willem looked shocked as Amy explained it had also been Jenny who'd discovered the body at the gasworks.

'Except it wasn't a body this time,' Jenny said, finally regaining her voice.

Amy and Willem looked at her in puzzlement.

'It was bits of a body. It was all chopped up,' Jenny explained.

'Oh, God! Oh, Jenny, that's awful. You poor thing. A body's bad enough, but a mutilated one...' Amy exclaimed, leaving her sentence hanging as she considered what her friend had just told her.

'Yeah, sick fuck had used different body parts on some of the games,' Jenny said, closing her eyes on the images that were reforming. 'I didn't even go out the back to the crazy golf – I rang the police straightaway, but I heard one of the policemen saying there was more out there too.'

'Christ,' Amy said, squeezing Jenny's hand. She didn't push her for any more detail.

'That really is terrible, Jenny. I'm so sorry you've had to see such a horrific thing. And not once, but twice!' Willem said, the shock showing on his face.

'Yeah, thanks,' Jenny said, smiling that weak smile again.

'Promise me you won't go back to work again,' Amy said. 'Really, Jenny, I mean it. You can't go back.'

Jenny sighed. 'That's all very well, but I need the money.'

'No amount of money is worth that!' Amy told her.

'That's easy to say, but I kind of like eating and having a roof over my head,' Jenny replied.

'We'll think of something, Jenny, I promise,' Amy insisted.

Jenny raised her eyebrows.

'I know!' Amy exclaimed. 'We'll get you in the shop! With your sewing.' Amy looked at Willem for support. 'We could do that, couldn't we? Surely even her Gloriarse majesty couldn't object?'

'Well, maybe…' Willem began. 'It's worth a try.'

'I don't mind sharing some of my space,' Amy continued, enthused by the idea. 'And I'm sure everyone would budge up a bit to fit you in.'

'I don't know…' Jenny said, unconvinced. 'I'm not sure I could make enough stock quickly enough.'

'Yeah, you could. I'm sure you could.' Amy wasn't giving up.

'I'll think about it,' Jenny relented.

'Great!' Amy said. 'And we'll speak to Gloria about it, won't we, Willem?'

'Yes, of course,' Willem agreed, clearly unable to refuse Amy, but not relishing the prospect of speaking to Gloria, who'd been decidedly cool with him since that day in the shop when she'd seen him laughing with Amy.

With Jenny's future employment settled, the three lapsed into silence.

It was Jenny who eventually spoke.

'I think I'm gonna go home,' she said, sounding bone-tired.

'I'll come with you,' Amy responded at once, thinking her friend shouldn't be on her own after the morning's gruesome discovery.

'No, it's okay,' Jenny said, nodding her head onto Amy's shoulder as if to show her she appreciated the thought. 'I just want to be on my own for a while.'

'But you shouldn't be…' Amy started to object.

'I'll be okay, promise. I just want to go home and see the cats and rest.'

'Are you sure?' Amy asked, the worry showing in her voice and on her face.

'Yep,' Jenny nodded.

'Well, let us at least walk you home then,' Willem insisted.

Jenny mutely agreed, with a nod of her head. She really looked as though she didn't have the energy to speak, and the three of them trekked up the beach and walked up through the town to Jenny's house.

They said goodbye to Jenny on the doorstep. It was obvious she didn't want to invite them in.

'Message me later, Jenny, please. Just to let me know you're okay. Or if you need something. Anything. Alright?' Amy insisted.

'Uh huh,' Jenny responded, smiling tiredly at them as she raised a hand in farewell and closed the door.

Amy turned reluctantly away and followed Willem back out onto the pavement.

'It doesn't feel right leaving her,' Amy said.

'I know what you mean, but I'm sure she'll be okay. She's made of tougher stuff than we realise, I think,' Willem tried to reassure.

'I s'pose,' Amy sighed. 'I'll check on her later anyway.'

'You're a good friend, Amy. Jenny's lucky to have you.'

'I'm the lucky one!' Amy said. 'I don't know what I'd do without her. Go mad, probably. Madder. We've been through a lot together.'

'Well, I hope you now consider me a friend too,' Willem said. 'And I'm a good listener if you ever need to talk.'

'Thank you,' Amy smiled.

'Perhaps we can get that coffee one of these days?' Willem looked at her hopefully.

'Yes, perhaps,' Amy replied.

'How about now?'

'Oh!' Amy was taken by surprise. 'I... um... I really should get back to my writing... um...'

Willem couldn't help smiling at her discomfort. 'Okay, rain check, but next time I'm not taking no for an answer. Or perhaps.'

'Okay. Sorry. I just wasn't expecting to go out this morning. I was totally in writing mode – I hadn't even brushed my hair when Jenny messaged,' she confessed. She didn't admit to not cleaning her teeth.

'Your hair looks fine, Amy. Just fine,' Willem said, smiling at her.

'Thanks,' Amy responded, looking at the floor and nervously tucking said hair behind her ears.

'Can I at least walk you home too?'

'Yes, thanks, that would be nice.'

They made the ten-minute walk to Amy's mostly in silence. Just every now and then, though, their hands brushed as they walked.

'This is me,' Amy said, when they reached her end-of-terrace house by the viaduct.

'And that is me,' Willem chuckled, turning and pointing to his house directly opposite at the other end of the viaduct.

'No way!' Amy said.

'Yes way,' Willem nodded, smiling at Amy's look of surprise.

'Huh! We're opposite neighbours. Fancy that!'

Willem bit back the impulse to say, 'Yes, I do', instead bidding Amy goodbye and telling her he'd see her soon, very soon.

As Amy closed the door she suddenly remembered she'd driven down to the beach and that her car was still there. 'Oh, you dopey cow,' she exclaimed, heading back out to retrieve it.

CHAPTER 20
Binoculars

As much as Amy had enjoyed being in Willem's company she, like Jenny, needed to be on her own. Thoughts of what was once again happening in the town were crowding in on her and demanding her attention. She didn't think she could have hidden her feelings from Willem if they'd spent much longer together. He had a way of making her want to unburden herself, making her feel she could depend on him, lean on him, and he'd lighten the load. As decent as he seemed, though, there were some things that Amy could never share with anyone. Except Jenny. Her literal partner in crime.

Throwing open the windows and the back door to vent the stuffy air, Amy sat down at her desk once more to try and write. She soon realised that it simply wasn't going to happen, not with everything else going on in her head, and she gave up, closing her laptop with a sigh. 'Bugger,' she muttered. 'Bugger, bugger, bugger.'

Changing into shorts and an old T-shirt, Amy headed into the garden to catch up with some overdue jobs. Sometimes she found doing something physical allowed her thoughts to roam and then corral themselves into some sort of order. It often worked for writer's block too.

When the sun got too much in the back garden, Amy moved round to the front to take advantage of the shade, and was surprised to see a cardboard box on the doorstep. She knew the postman had already been and she wasn't expecting a delivery. Her name was written on the box in black marker, but no address or postage so it had obviously been hand-delivered. Feeling slightly anxious, Amy paused and looked around. There was no one in sight.

'Get a grip, woman,' she muttered to herself. 'It's just a box.' *But is it?* her inner voice argued.

Amy's head was filled with images of bloody body parts and threatening notes made up of cuttings from newspapers.

Brushing the worst of the dirt from her hands, she took a deep breath, tore off the strip of brown tape along the seam of the box and carefully opened the flaps.

'Oh,' she said, as she removed a pair of black binoculars from the box, turning them over in her hands. She checked the box, but there was no note or anything else enclosed.

Back indoors, Amy washed her hands and sat at the kitchen table with the binoculars in front of her. Normally she would have texted Jenny for her thoughts, but she didn't feel she could bother her after what had happened earlier.

'Oh!' she exclaimed as a lightbulb came on in her overheated brain. 'I wonder…'

Trotting upstairs to her bedroom, which had the window with by far the best view, Amy lifted the binoculars to her eyes and looked out. Nothing. All she saw was a hazy white blur. She fiddled around with the focus until she could see clearly and tried again. The viaduct loomed into sight and she spent a couple of minutes watching a seagull perched atop it before she swung around in search of Willem's house. It was almost a mirror image of her own. At first she couldn't see anything out of the ordinary, but when she focused on the top window, she realised there was something there:

COFFEE?

The single word was spelled out in giant black letters on a white background. Laughing, Amy disappeared down one flight to her office and hunted around for some white paper. She didn't have anything bigger than A4, so she spelled out her answer on three sheets of that and stuck them in her bedroom window, giggling as she did so and wondering if she should have added a winking face:

PERHAPS

Wondering how long it would take Willem to see her response, Amy had a quick shower and got a cold drink, which she took back to her desk. She'd placed the binoculars on the window sill and was trying to resist checking every thirty seconds. *Well, at least you're back at your desk,* she thought. *How about actually doing some work?*

Across the viaduct Willem had already seen Amy's response and was trying not to feel too disappointed. He was wondering how to respond. In the end he printed out a giant sad face emoji, but his mobile rang just as he was about to stick it in the window and he found himself agreeing to meet Finn for lunch.

When Amy still hadn't seen the sign in Willem's window change two hours later, she started to worry she'd offended him and took down the PERHAPS sign. She hastily changed it to one that read YES PLEASE and stuck that up instead. Feeling slightly better about things and admitting to a little flutter of anticipation, Amy returned to her writing with renewed determination. Imagine her disappointment when she finally checked Willem's window around teatime and saw a giant sad face staring back at her. 'Oh!' she said, not for the first time that day.

Across town, the killer was feeling the very opposite of disappointed after another successful exhibit had been unveiled. He was glued to the early evening local news, where the murder was the lead story. He was making headlines. He kind of wished people knew his identity, so he could revel in the glow of celebrity, but of course that was impossible as then there could be no more exhibits. He wasn't ready to give up yet. He was having way too much fun. They were again speculating on whether this new killer was a copycat of Robert Seymour, last year's Exhibitionist, which annoyed him.

He soon forgot his annoyance though as he had more important things on his mind. He had another idea for an exhibit. He was also a little worried that they might step up security following the latest murder and he knew he was going to have to be extra careful. He was planning to wait a couple of weeks before this one anyway, so hopefully they'd have been lulled into relaxing a bit. Besides, the planning was half the fun and he would have ample time for that while he worked to get the rewiring job finished within the fortnight too.

At home, Jenny had spent the remainder of the day lolling around the house, unable to settle to anything and generally feeling weary and upset. By the evening, however, she was starting to feel something other than weary and upset. She was starting to feel angry. How dare this dickhead upset her happy little existence like this? How bloody dare he? Well, she wasn't having it. Nope, no siree, not any more.

At about seven p.m. she messaged Amy.

Hello. Just to let you know I'm OK. Well, in fact I'm not OK, but I'm not upset any more. Need to talk. Give me a shout when you're free.

Her phone rang less than a minute after she sent the message.

'Glad you're okay,' Amy said when Jenny answered.

'Yep, all good. Just pretty pissed off now to be honest.'

'Well, that sounds more like the Jenny I know and love,' Amy chuckled, hearing the mutinous tone in Jenny's voice.

'Today was a blip, admittedly, but I'm back.'

'And bad,' Amy added.

'While you are neither black nor mad,' Jenny laughed. 'Well, you are a bit mad, I suppose. And you are a lethal weapon when you have to be.'

Amy made a strangled sound down the phone.

'Anyway, I was thinking…' Jenny began.

'Uh oh,' Amy interrupted.

'Shush,' Jenny instructed. 'As I was saying, I was thinking and I decided we should stake out the art installations.'

There was no response from Amy as she tried to process what Jenny had said.

'Amy?' Jenny prompted after a while.

'Um…' Amy began. 'Is that a good idea? Can't we just leave it to the police?'

'Nope. They're obviously clueless. Pick me up tomorrow night. At midnight. And bring coffee.'

Amy was silent once more.

'Amy?'

'Oh God, really?'

'Yes, really. I'll see you tomorrow. Don't be late,' Jenny added before hanging up the phone.

Amy stared at her phone in disbelief for a while. How had she agreed to this madness? She could barely keep her eyes open after nine-thirty p.m.

CHAPTER 21

Stakeout

The next night, just before midnight, saw Amy pulling up outside Jenny's house. She still wasn't sure how she'd agreed to this madness, but here she was.

A minute or so later, Jenny's front door opened and she stepped onto the doorstep, looking around furtively. She was dressed all in black and even had her vividly pink hair pushed up under a black beanie. She was carrying a black holdall. Amy couldn't begin to imagine what it contained.

Locking her front door, Jenny crossed quickly to Amy's car and got in behind Amy.

'Drive, drive,' she hissed.

Amy was too stunned to do as instructed. 'What are you doing?' she giggled, turning round to look at Jenny, who had both hands on the back of Amy's seat and a look of extreme urgency on her face. 'Get in the front, you muppet. This is meant to be a stakeout, not a getaway. And what do you look like?' she added.

Jenny sighed and pulled the hat off before getting out and going round to the front passenger seat. 'You're no fun,' she said grumpily.

'You look like you're off to rob a bank, not sit in a car for hours, trying to stay awake while watching for something or someone that's most likely never gonna materialise.'

Jenny sighed. 'Okay, maybe you have a point.'

'Er, yeah. A stakeout is all about *not* drawing attention to yourself,' Amy pointed out. 'And what's in the bag?'

'Just essential stakeout stuff…' Jenny began sheepishly.

'Like…?'

'Um… doughnuts.'

'Ring doughnuts? Can't stand the ones with jam in the middle,' Amy said, pulling a face.

'God, Amy, when did you *ever* see cops on a stakeout eating *ring* doughnuts?' Before Amy could respond, Jenny continued, 'Well, actually they are ring doughnuts 'coz I only like them too, but you have to imagine they're not. Think American-style Dunkin' Donuts when you're eating them,' Jenny insisted.

'Well, okay then,' Amy said, raising her eyebrows. 'I dread to ask, but what else is in the bag?'

'Um… camera, binoculars – I need to get hold of some night-vision ones before the next stakeout – notebook and pen, torch, cans of Red Bull, sandwiches…'

Amy started to interrupt, 'What's in…'

'Cheese and pickle,' Jenny said, looking crossly at Amy.

'What sort of…'

'Branston. Stop interrupting.'

Amy pulled a 'sorry, Miss' face and let Jenny continue.

'… Shewees…' Jenny said next, mentally unpacking the bag.

Amy couldn't help herself. 'Shewees?! You are kidding, right? I am not peeing in a tube for you or anyone else, Jennifer Jones.'

'Suit yourself. Don't blame me if the killer gets you while you're peeing behind a tree.' With that, Jenny buckled her seat belt. 'Let's go!'

Amy shook her head but started the engine and pulled away from the kerb. 'Where to?' she asked, having no idea where they were actually going to stake out.

'Just drive to the seafront for now, and then we'll come up with a plan.'

Amy did as instructed and soon they were parked up not far from where the gruesome discovery had been made the previous day. Turning off the engine and undoing her seatbelt, Amy looked round to where Jenny was rummaging in the bag now sitting on her lap. She pulled out a head torch, which she donned, followed by a map of the art installations, which she spread out on the dashboard.

'Right, first things first, put your phone on silent,' Jenny said.

Amy began to ask why but was silenced by the look on Jenny's face and did as she was told.

'Good. So, I've marked the exhibits that the killer's already hit – the beach huts, dancefloor and amusements – with a red X and ringed the other possible sites in green,' Jenny continued.

Amy stifled a giggle. Jenny ignored her.

'We need to do a risk assessment for each of the remaining places and try to work out where the killer might strike next,' Jenny said, all seriousness.

Amy just nodded, not trusting herself to speak without losing it. This was madness. She couldn't help wondering if Jenny had gone a little bit mad from what had happened to her.

'So, what do you think?' Jenny asked, finally looking over at Amy.

'I think you should turn that head torch off. It's blinding me,' Amy said.

'For fuck's sake, Amy,' Jenny exclaimed, snatching at the light around her head 'You're not taking this seriously.'

'Yeah, I am. Am I Riggs or Murtaugh?' she snorted.

Jenny folded her arms crossly and didn't say anything for a minute or two. Amy watched her, a bemused expression on her face.

Finally, Jenny broke the silence. 'You can be Riggs. Only because I know you really like Mel Gibson.'

There followed a conversation about the highs and lows of Mel Gibson's film career, until Jenny waved both hands and said, 'We're getting sidetracked, Amy. If you were the killer, where would you attack next?'

'I'd go back in time and bump off Patsy Kensit so she couldn't get off with Mel in *Lethal Weapon 2*.'

Jenny glared at her.

'Um… give me the map a second,' Amy said, suitably chastised. She pulled the map over, switched on the car's interior light and studied it for a while. 'Well, the easiest one has got to be the "Argonaut", I reckon. You could make a body dump there and be gone in a flash.'

'Hmm… yeah, I thought that. Plenty of scope to create something around the theme too. What else?' Jenny prompted.

'Can I have a doughnut yet?'

'No! We're not even staking anything out yet,' Jenny said.

'Then, can we go and *actually* stake out something so I can have a doughnut?'

'Oh, all right,' Jenny harrumphed. 'Let's drive to "I am Argonaut" and then we can have doughnuts.'

A few minutes later and they were parked a short distance away from the sculpture and munching on sugar-coated ring doughnuts. Amy had given Jenny a flask of coffee but wasn't having any herself in case she needed a wee.

'It wouldn't be very PC of the killer to feature this one, would it?' Amy said, in between bites.

'Why? Because the artist is disabled?' Jenny asked.

'Yeah,' Amy nodded.

'I reckon the artist wouldn't want to be treated any differently, don't you?'

'Can you hear us? This is bonkers, Jenny. We're talking about the political correctness of a serial killer, for heaven's sake.'

Jenny just shrugged and passed Amy another doughnut.

They sat in silence for a while, Jenny observing the statue through the binoculars.

'Do you actually need those?' Amy asked after a while. 'We're practically close enough to touch it.'

'That's so not the point. We're on a stakeout.'

'Oh, yeah, I keep forgetting,' Amy sighed.

Silence again.

'How long do we have to do this for?' Amy asked after a time.

'For as long as it takes,' Jenny said firmly.

'But that's crazy – we might not even be watching the right place. This could be a complete waste of time.'

'Well, what else would you be doing instead?' Jenny asked.

'Sleeping.'

'You can sleep here if you want. I'll take the first watch.'

'I don't want to sleep in my car, Jenny, I want to sleep in my bed,' Amy complained.

'All right, Amy whine-house. Have you got a better idea?'

'Other than sleeping. In my bed. No, not really,' Amy said, stifling a yawn.

'Well, what about if we drive round a bit – you know, cover several sites in the same night?' Jenny suggested.

'What about no?' Amy said. 'This is a colossal waste of time.'

'Well, I'm not giving up and I can't do it on my own. Without a car.'

Amy sighed. 'You only love me for my car.'

'Yep,' Jenny agreed.

'Well, I only love you for your doughnuts,' Amy threw back. 'Would three be greedy?'

Just then, a car pulled up next to the sculpture and the two women froze, Amy with a doughnut suspended in front of her mouth.

They watched as the back door of the car opened and a woman got out before the car drove off again, revealing itself to be a taxi.

'Phew! That was a close one!' Jenny exhaled loudly.

'What?! No it wasn't! It was a bloody taxi dropping some perfectly innocent woman off at her house, you crazy person.'

'Just getting into character,' Jenny grumbled. 'Wouldn't hurt you to get on board a bit more.'

'All aboard the ruddy skylark to Looneyville if you've got anything to do with it tonight! That's it. We're going home.' With that, Amy started the engine. Just as she was about to drive off, a man came into view, approaching them from the opposite direction. Jenny reached quickly over and grabbed Amy's hand. 'Stop!' she hissed. Amy stopped and they watched as the man, dressed in jeans and dark jacket, walked past the statue, barely giving it a glance before he carried on away from them.

'That was a...' Jenny began.

'Don't even!' Amy said as she put the car in gear and pulled away.

'That could have been the killer, Amy,' Jenny said.

'Or it could have been some bloke walking home from the pub, minding his own business. We're going home.'

Jenny realised that arguing was futile and folded her arms mutinously.

They arrived back at Jenny's at about the same time the killer was making his second pass of 'I am Argonaut'.

After dropping Jenny home, it was a very tired Amy who let herself in at home, dropping her bag in the hall and heading into the kitchen. She was feeling a little nauseous from all the doughnuts and so downed a glass of water, standing at the sink. She was glad she hadn't drunk any of the coffee from the flasks, which were still languishing in her car. She'd sort them out tomorrow.

After quickly brushing her teeth, Amy headed up to bed. She stared over in the direction of Willem's house before closing the curtains. It was too dark to make anything out and she was too exhausted to go downstairs to retrieve the binoculars anyway.

As she plugged her phone in to charge beside the bed, Amy remembered it had been on silent for the past few hours and she quickly tapped in her passcode to unlock it. The first thing she saw was a text message from Willem.

Amy, I think we got our wires crossed. I will take your final answer. Willem

Smiling, Amy hugged her phone to her chest for a moment before putting it on the bedside table, switching off the lamp and snuggling down to sleep.

CHAPTER 22

Touching base

For once, Amy's sleep wasn't filled with bloody flashbacks of Robert or the new spate of killings and she woke feeling refreshed for the first time in ages. She took it as a sign that Willem could be good for her. Good enough to meet for coffee at the very least, she thought as she threw open the bedroom curtains and let the summer sun fill the room.

'Bugger!' she exclaimed, suddenly remembering that Willem could have his binoculars trained on her this very second. She ducked back from the window, looking down at her rather skimpy nightie. 'Bugger. Bum. Arse,' she sighed.

Making a mental note to put her robe on in future before opening the curtains, Amy trotted downstairs to make a coffee, which she took back to bed, collecting the binoculars on the way. Covering her embarrassment with her dressing gown, she focused on the house across the valley. She wasn't expecting to see a new message and was praying she didn't see Willem looking right back at her, but she looked anyway. She felt a bit like her twelve-year-old self waiting by the letterbox on Valentine's Day. She'd been disappointed then. Mark Lewis, on whom she had an enormous crush, clearly didn't feel the same way about her as she did about him.

'Mark who?' she muttered, her face stretching into a grin. There in the window opposite was a big:

GOOD MORNING AMY

It was accompanied by a smiley face to match Amy's. Amy wondered if she should reply at once, or let a little time pass. The dating rules were so complicated these days. Should she play a little hard to get? She didn't think Willem was the type to appreciate games, and she wanted to reply, so off she trotted downstairs once more to get paper, marker pen and tape. There was definitely more of a spring in her fifty-two-year-old step as she bounded back up, two stairs at a time. *Haven't done that for a while*, she thought. *Haven't done a lot of things in a while, mind you*. After she'd stuck her reply in the window, Amy climbed back under the duvet to read while she drank her coffee.

She couldn't resist checking through the binoculars again before heading to the shower, and was delighted to see a response already. Clearly Willem didn't play the modern dating game either. *What a relief!*

Somehow Willem managed to upsell coffee to lunch and at twelve-thirty Amy was waiting, slightly nervously, outside Djangos Bistro in the centre of town. As usual she was early and she was feeling very self-conscious as she waited. It was a long time since she'd been on a date and the longer she waited the more filled with doubt she became. Did she even want a man in her life? After what had happened, what she'd done, could she take the risk of exposing the truth? That she'd killed a man. She was a murderer. What if she talked in her sleep? She was saved any more agonising by Willem's arrival. He grinned broadly at her and leaned in to kiss her cheek. His beard was softer than she'd expected, which was a pleasant surprise.

'Finally!' he said. 'Finally I've broken down your defences and got you all to myself.'

Amy blushed. 'Well, couldn't make it too easy for you, could I?'

'I half expected to find Jenny with you. You two are inseparable. As lovely as Jenny is, it's you I want to get to know better.'

'Well, here I am. Jenny's running late,' Amy said, straight-faced.

Willem roared with laughter, his whole body shaking.

Amy raised her eyebrows and remained deadly serious.

Willem was quiet. Thinking. No, surely not…?

Amy couldn't keep the straight face and grinned at him.

'You nearly had me there, Amy,' Willem chuckled.

Amy resisted saying any of the things that sprang to mind and turned her flushed face away. 'Shall we?' she said, turning towards the door.

All the outside tables were already taken, so they headed inside and were soon seated at a quiet table in the basement of the bistro, which was decorated in a kind of bohemian style with arty posters and cushions. It had become one of Amy's favourite places to eat; the staff were always friendly and the food never disappointed.

'I'm glad you chose this place,' Willem said. 'It's the first place I ate in when I moved here and has remained a firm favourite.'

Amy smiled at him over the menu. 'I'm afraid I'm rather a creature of habit. I always have the same thing for lunch here – jacket potato with prawns.'

'That makes two of us, although I always have the schnitzel.'

Soon they were sipping iced teas and chatting like old friends and Amy was wondering what she'd been so nervous of. It was just lunch with a friend after all. Willem was good company and easy to talk to, and he seemed to share the same sense of humour. Still at the back of her mind, though, was a little voice (it was Jenny's) reminding her she had a secret she could never tell. Could she really contemplate a new relationship based on dishonesty? Could she ever really relax and let her guard all the way down?

Inevitably, the conversation found its way to the recent murders.

'I can't believe poor Jenny found two of the victims,' Willem said, shaking his head.

'I know, crazy. I really wish she'd give up that job though. It's not safe,' Amy said worriedly.

'Why don't we go and speak to Gloria after lunch? She should be in the shop this afternoon. See if we can't get Jenny a little spot for her sewing.'

'That would be great. I know Jenny thinks she can't make enough stock, but I'm sure I can convince her to give it a go. Do you think Gloria will say yes? More to the point, do you think she'll say yes if we see her together?'

'Hm… you might have a point. Maybe it would be better if I saw her on my own,' Willem conceded.

'Brave man! Aren't you afraid she'll drag you into her lair and eat you?'

'She doesn't scare me!' Willem said, looking scared.

Amy laughed.

'Perhaps you should phone me after five minutes if I haven't come out?' Willem suggested. 'And if I don't answer, call the police. Or the pest control people.'

'I'm sure she'll be all sweetness and light with you. But I'll have Rentokil on speed dial just in case.'

After lunch – which was excellent, as ever – Amy and Willem

set off on the short walk to the Old High Street. Before they reached the Coastal Creatives shop, Amy ducked into a gift shop.

'I'll lurk in here while you face the gorgon. Good luck! It's been nice knowing you,' she said, grimacing as Willem took an exaggerated gulp and carried on a little further down the steep, cobbled street. Amy watched until he disappeared into the shop.

When Willem came out a few minutes later, Amy was lurking nearby.

'Well?' she asked. 'Any joy?'

Willem shook his head. 'She said we'll have to have a meeting with everyone, but thinks it's a non-starter.'

'Rats. Did she say why?'

'Just that people won't want to give up any space to shoehorn someone else in.'

'Did you explain what Jenny's been through?' Amy asked.

Willem nodded. 'I did. Sorry, Amy.'

'Don't apologise. It's not your fault Gloria's a royal pain in the arse. I'll think of some way of helping Jenny.'

'What are you doing for the rest of the day?' Willem asked.

'I should get some writing done. I have a short-story deadline looming. How about you?'

'Back to my workroom to get some framing done. I'm actually having my first exhibition next month.'

'What? You kept that quiet. That's so exciting! Whereabouts?'

'Do you know Touchbase in Tontine Street?'

'Yes, vaguely. That's really wonderful. Let me know if I can do anything to help,' Amy said.

'Thank you. I might just take you up on that.'

They wandered back up the cobbled street and parted company, with promises to see each other soon.

'I've really enjoyed spending time with you,' Willem said, leaning in and kissing Amy's cheek once more.

'Me too,' she smiled.

Amy smiled all the way home and was still smiling as she sat down at her laptop and began to type.

PUNCH AND JUDO

It was the day of the Folkestone Airshow but, unfortunately, God hadn't got the memo. If he did, he was obviously in a bad mood about something as the rain was lashing down and it was blowing an absolute hooley, the rain being blasted horizontal by gale-force winds.

Under a bright orange gazebo, Joe was hanging on to the metal struts of the roof for dear life and being slapped on the back by a wet canvas as the elements did their best to destroy both the gazebo and his state of mind. Saturday had been bad. Sunday, today, just got a whole lot worse. He would've packed up and gone home but it was actually too windy to even contemplate trying to disassemble the gazebo, so he just had to grin and bear it. *Grimace and bear it, actually,* he thought as the side panel slapped his back and legs once more, sticking the soaked denim of his jeans to his legs.

He was seriously regretting his life choices by this point. When he'd booked a stall at the event he'd had images of families picnicking on the grass, of Pimm's and ice cream, sunshine and strawberries. Instead of which he'd got chapped legs, ruined stock and a severe bout of grumpy-itis. At least his gazebo hadn't disintegrated or simply taken flight along The Leas as some others had. It wasn't exactly the air display people had been expecting. The first two fly-bys had been cancelled and the Red Arrows' appearance at four p.m. was up in the air. Or not. Joe resigned himself to a long, trying, fruitless day. And he didn't just mean in his Pimm's, as he thought about how much the stall had cost and how little he was likely to make selling his wood carvings.

Thinking about it now, with the wonderful power of hindsight, he should've packed up last night in the brief lull in the weather. But he'd convinced himself to hold out for another day. The weather could change at the drop of a hat here on the south coast. If you dropped a hat today it would probably take off to France. Unlike the Lancaster bomber.

A few hardy (or just plain bonkers) souls were braving the elements and occasionally took shelter in Joe's gazebo, where they exchanged a few words. Mostly about the weather. Naturally. But nobody was buying. And everyone looked miserable. Except for one man.

The Punch and Judy man was obviously on something to be quite so obnoxiously cheerful on such a cheerless day. He got on Joe's nerves with his tinny, repetitive music and regular slapstick puppet shows, performed to absolutely nobody except the seagulls. There was just something about him that wound Joe up tighter than a string of sausages. Every time the music started up, Joe felt his jaw clench as he braced himself for yet another round of 'that's the way to do it'. All through the previous day he'd fantasised about bumping the Punchman off. His favourite method had been strangling him with his own string of sausages. He quite like the idea of punch and judo too, though. Judo might mean 'gentle way', but he wouldn't go gentle. Maybe punch and Krav Maga might be more appropriate. He couldn't understand why the organisers had booked a noisy entertainer when he clashed with the bands playing on the bandstand. Joe was the filling in a sound-sandwich and he was not enjoying it.

When the wind drew breath, Joe chanced letting go of the gazebo frame, and reached for his flask of coffee. Although the air temperature wasn't all that low, he was feeling decidedly chilly – probably due to the damp clothes sticking to his body – and Joe was hoping the warm liquid would help a little. Just as he had the metal rim of the flask to his lips, a sudden gust whipped up and the gazebo budged a couple of inches, in spite of the eight sandbags and the guy ropes holding it down, and he was slapped once more by the soggy side panels.

'For Christ's sake!' he exclaimed as hot coffee sloshed out of the flask, down his chin and onto his chest. He closed his eyes and gritted his teeth. Could this bloody day get any worse?

The answer was apparently yes, as the Punch and Judy man began his next cycle. Joe was close to losing his shit. He wondered if he could just close up the front of the gazebo – shut up shop basically – and hunker down inside until it all blew over. Or off. But he was far too conscientious for that, he knew, as he looked daggers at the puppeteer and continued to fantasise about ways to bump him off. He was slightly cheered as he imagined the puppet booth being taken by the wind and the puppeteer being tangled up in a guy rope and carried off, dangling by one leg, his screams fading into the distance. Or wrestling with a giant crocodile to chants of "it's dinnertime" from the audience.

By three p.m., the horrendous weather showed no sign of improvement and Joe was miserable. Even thoughts of beating the Punchman to death with the policeman's truncheon could no longer put a smile on his face. He really had had enough. The Red Arrows were due in an hour and Joe was not optimistic.

Then, at three fifty-five p.m., as if by magic, the skies cleared, the wind and rain dying as if they'd never been born. A cheer went up from the small crowd of hardy souls present as the announcer declared the Red Arrows were on their way. Joe couldn't believe it. At four o'clock precisely, the formation of planes blasted overhead and began the most spectacular twenty-minute display over the sea, culminating in a giant red love heart. Even the dampest of spirits couldn't fail to be lifted by it.

When Joe finally packed up his sodden gazebo an hour or so later there was no sign of the Punch and Judy man, and the Punch puppet was lying on the grass in front of the booth. Joe smiled to himself as he lowered the boot of his car and set off to make the short drive home.

CHAPTER 23

Janus

The killer was really feeling spoilt for choice with the art installations, and was torn between two for his next exhibit. He'd already checked out 'I am Argonaut', a contemporary figurative sculpture which had been placed opposite and 'in conversation with' the monumental statue of William Harvey, son of the Mayor of Folkestone, Royal Physician and discoverer of the circulation of the blood. He'd been relieved not to see any increased security or cameras when he'd walked past it a couple of times late one night. He supposed there were simply too many sites for the police to cover.

Before 'Argonaut' though he was keen to do something with 'Janus' Fortress', a monumental sculptural head made of chalk and plaster, with two faces representing Janus, the Roman god of beginnings and transitions. The sculpture was located high up on the East Cliff, overlooking Folkestone's harbour, and with its two faces was able to look both towards the European mainland and towards England, connecting them, as Folkestone had always done whether as a fortress or a port. It was designed to gradually erode and disintegrate to mirror the gradual erosion of the chalk cliffs and coastline. The killer planned to speed up the disintegration and, when he went up to the East Cliff to investigate, was pleasantly surprised to find someone else had had the same idea. A large hole had appeared in the side of the sculpture that was clearly man-made rather than the gentle erosion of the elements. You could see into the hollow centre of the huge white head and to the crowned skull that had been hidden inside. He'd read that the organisers were planning to process this smaller sculpture through the town at the end of the season and were calling it 'The Day of the Crowned Death'. Well, all he was doing was bringing that day forward a few weeks.

Before leaving the site he'd stuck the boot in and made the hole even bigger. He was confident the local yobbos would have opened it up completely in no time. Legal vandalism. What's not to like?

There wasn't much planning required for this one. He wondered if it was too simple? Lacked imagination? He didn't want to let his viewing public down, look like he wasn't trying. He'd make it up to them though.

He'd already got another body in the freezer at home. A young woman he'd followed home one night. He'd had a bit of a tricky time getting her posed before she went in the freezer, but he was confident he could make it work. He had the unpleasant job of removing her head, but having had a bit of practice now, he wasn't too worried. He had some other prep work to do in his garage and was looking forward to cracking on with it now the weekend had arrived. Not for the first time, he cursed having to go to work, but the bills weren't going to pay themselves, and he couldn't have the bailiffs coming round and poking their noses in, could he?

He'd decided to link the next two exhibits and he needed to do 'Janus' first as there was something inside he needed for 'Argonaut'. He just had to hope that the other vandals didn't get to the pieces before he did. It was new moon in a couple of days and he thought the timing would be pretty much perfect: dark skies and the hollow in the sculpture made accessible. It would have been tricky to get a whole body to the site on the East Cliff as it was very close to a residential area with houses having windows facing the sea. The last thing he needed was some nosy fucking curtain twitcher spotting him lugging a corpse across the grass.

Time to get on with things. With the corpse now nicely frozen, he made short work of removing the head and putting the rest of the body back in the freezer, gratified to see it had remained in the pose he wanted. The next part of the process was going to be a bit of an experiment. Taking the head into his kitchen he hacked off most of the hair before placing the head in a huge water-filled stock pot he'd bought from a second-hand buying and selling site. He turned the gas up high and set it on to boil, wondering how long it would take for the flesh to fall away from the skull. If he was honest, he wasn't looking forward to the smell of boiling flesh, but he couldn't think of any other way of doing it. He didn't have the luxury of enough time to bury it in the garden and wait for it to decompose naturally. As an afterthought, he went round and closed all the doors and windows and turned the extractor fan up to max. Didn't want the neighbours getting a whiff of things.

While the head was boiling, he set about painting the scruffy old teak folding garden chair he'd found in a skip. He would have liked a bench to match the ones already in situ not far from the installation, but realistically he couldn't manage that, so he'd compromised on a chair. *Who was that dickhead actor who'd said 'art is no compromise'? Well, clearly they'd never tried to get away with staging a body in a public place*, he thought as he applied masking tape to create stripes down the wooden back and seat of the chair. He then used brightly coloured paints to echo the colourful kiosks and benches displayed on Castle Hill Avenue. Painting finished, he set the chair aside to dry. He really did enjoy all the preparation that went into his exhibits. He hoped the public could appreciate the time and effort he put in. He took a great deal of pride in his work and workmanship.

With the chair drying, he went reluctantly back indoors to check the state of the head. Holding a tea towel over his mouth and nose, he removed the lid of the pan and was met with a layer of steaming scum and revolting chunks of boiled flesh. He almost added chunks of his own as the bile rose in his throat. Quickly replacing the lid, he figured he'd give it another thirty minutes. While he waited, he sat in the garden with a well-earned beer and wondered how he was going to deal with the foul soup he'd cooked up.

After about half an hour he went back in and turned off the gas. Once the pan had cooled for a little, he carefully poured the contents into the sink, which he'd lined with a sacrificial tea towel. He hoped it would be easy enough to wrap up the lumps and bury them in the garden after dark. He gagged as he rinsed the skull and scraped off a few remaining bits of God-knows-what. Next it went into a solution of water and hydrogen peroxide to finish the cleaning process overnight. He would fully admit to not enjoying this particular part of the process, but you must suffer for your art, right?

Monday arrived at last and, on his way home from work, the killer had taken a quick recce at 'Janus' and was gratified to see the middle of the sculpture was now accessible. A quick glimpse inside and he smiled at what he saw there. He desperately wanted to grab the item now, but knew he'd be running the risk of being seen. He just had to pray it would still be there when he returned after dark. So far the gods had favoured him. Hopefully Janus would be no different.

Back at home, he showered and changed out of his coveralls before grabbing a bite to eat. He barely noticed what he was eating; he was buzzing and impatient to get on, but it was still hours until he could venture back to the East Cliff.

He'd deliberately left himself one job to do – he knew he'd be itching to get on – and after dinner he headed back into the garage. He pinned up an image of the object he had to try and copy and set to work using the sheet metal and tin snips he'd bought online. He hoped it wouldn't be too difficult to fashion a crude likeness of the crown. He'd already measured the skull after he'd rinsed it off and dried it after its bleaching bath. It wasn't perfect, but he was pretty pleased on the whole. At least it wouldn't attract too many flies. He hated flies. Dirty, shitty little things. It always amazed him how quickly they were on exposed or rotting flesh.

It didn't take too long to snip around the outline he'd measured and drawn of the band of the crown and the fleur-de-lis around the top. It wasn't going to win any beauty prizes, but he was happy enough. Once it was all cut out, he wrapped it around the skull to check the fit and then set to work soldering the join. As always when he worked, he was wearing his coveralls, gloves and mask. If plod thought he'd be leaving them any DNA or hairs, they could think again. They'd only ever catch him if he wanted to be caught.

After the metal had cooled he placed the crown atop the

skull and stood back to admire his handiwork, nodding with satisfaction. If he could've high-fived himself he would've. He took a few photos, something he was doing at every stage of his work. It was only right that every little thing be preserved for posterity. He was singing quietly to himself as he bagged up the skull and crown in his dark-coloured rucksack for later – 'Every little thing you do is magic... Every little thing just turns me on...' He knew they weren't the right words, but he felt entitled to a little artistic licence. He was still humming when he went back in the house, and the adrenaline was starting to rise. Not long now.

At one-thirty a.m. he set off to walk the mile or so to the site on the East Cliff. The rucksack on his back was barely noticeable. For once it was nice not to be lugging a whole corpse around. The car was an added risk whenever he set up an exhibit and tonight was all about minimising risk. The streets were pretty much deserted, as he'd hoped. Mondays were always quiet in the town. Apart from a couple of drunks winding their way home, he didn't see anyone. He was confident the two pissheads wouldn't remember seeing him and he was careful not to draw their attention anyway.

As he approached 'Janus' he slowed his pace and looked all around, checking for people, for houses with lights on, for anything that might be a problem. The only thing he saw was a fox trotting across the road. With the coast clear, he made his way over to the giant white head, hugging the path closest to the sea and furthest from the line of sight of the houses. Only when he was crouched inside the chalk head did he risk a small torch. Relieved to see the artist's own large skull-and-crown sculpture still safely bolted to the ground, it took only seconds to place his crowned skull on top of it. Once he was happy, he snapped a couple of quick photographs, grabbed the other item he wanted, shoved it into his rucksack, turned off the torch and crept quietly away.

He'd done it again! His heart was pounding and he was still buzzing when he got back home. Once safely indoors again, he took out the thing he'd stolen from inside the sculpture and smiled. The next exhibit continued to take shape in his mind.

The night of the crowned death, he thought as he drifted off to sleep. He slept the sleep of the dead, as he always did, his mind untroubled, his conscience unpricked.

CHAPTER 24
Smile for the camera

A my heard about the latest grisly discovery on the news the next day. A dog walker – as always – had found the skull inside the Janus sculpture after her dog had sniffed it out on their morning walk. Amy made a mental note to tell Jenny never to get a dog, and decided to shelve her own plans to get one to replace her Old English sheepdog, Dexter.

The woman had taken a photo of the find and obviously shared it with a reporter, as it was now being shown on the news and all over social media. Amy guessed the police would be none too happy. She couldn't help wondering where the rest of the body was. She had a horrible feeling it wouldn't be long before they found out. She tried to get inside the mind of the killer. What would she do? *Come on, Amy, you're a writer. If you were writing a book on the killings where would you go next?*

She logged on to the website for the Triennial and made a list of the exhibits for 2021. Then she eliminated the ones the killer had already hit and the inaccessible ones, like the virtual reality thing at the library. After about twenty minutes she messaged Jenny.

Morning. Have you seen the news?

Yeah. Glad it wasn't my turn to find it, Jenny replied.

I think he's going to do another one really soon. He has a headless corpse to get rid of.

Oh joy.

Seriously, though, I think it is going to be at 'Argonaut'.

Why?

Call it an educated guess. Or writer's intuition.

Is there even such a thing?

Amy wondered why Jenny wasn't getting more on board. *You ok?*

Yeah. Just wondering what to do…

What about?

Oh, you know, life. Stuff. Everything.

Amy didn't like the sound of this. *Want to catch up for coffee? Or a stakeout?* That should do the trick. Jenny wouldn't be able to resist.

Rain check? Jenny wrote.

Sure. Just let me know if I can do anything, Amy replied.

Jenny just replied with a thumbs up.

Trying to push her worries about Jenny to the back of her mind, Amy returned to her laptop. She'd had an idea for a new novel and was keen to start getting some ideas down. She found her thoughts drifting to Willem. They did that a lot since their lunch together. They continued to post messages in their windows, and checking with the binoculars was now the first thing Amy did when she got out of bed in the morning. She was careful not to do it naked though.

After a couple of hours of attempting an opening chapter, Amy texted Willem.

Don't suppose you're free for coffee this afternoon?

She didn't have to wait long for a reply. *For you, always.*

They arranged to meet down on the Harbour Arm at three o'clock and Amy admitted to a little shiver of anticipation. She already liked Willem a great deal and was eager to find out if it could be more than like. As she walked, Amy could feel the corners of her mouth lift in a smile as she hugged the possibilities to herself.

Willem was already waiting at the town-end of the viaduct when she got there and he hugged her, reaching down to kiss her cheek, before they walked over together. The tide was in and the pink holiday-home art installation was bobbing jauntily in the harbour. Amy couldn't see it without remembering the body that Robert had dumped there the previous year, and she shook the unwelcome memory away. Not today, Robert. Just fuck off.

About halfway across the walkway, Amy felt Willem's fingers intertwine with hers. She didn't object and they walked the rest of the way hand in hand. It felt right. Their hands fit well together and their steps synchronised easily.

'What would you like?' Willem asked when they arrived at one of the food vendors on the Arm.

'Oat milk flat white, please.'

Willem ordered Amy's coffee and a black Americano for himself and they took their drinks over to one of the few free tables overlooking the sea. Cormorants were sunning themselves on a nearby concrete structure, wings stretched out to dry. You could make out a ferry leaving Dover just along the coast.

Amy closed her eyes and tipped her head back, enjoying the feeling of the sun on her face.

'You're very beautiful, Amy,' Willem said.

Amy opened her eyes and looked shyly at him.

'You are,' Willem persisted. 'I'd like to photograph you one day. If you'd let me.'

Amy grimaced. 'I hate having my photo taken,' she said.

'No problem. No pressure.'

'I'm not saying never,' Amy added. 'We'll see.'

'Good enough.'

They lapsed into silence, comfortable in each other's company. Amy watched the gulls jostling for position with the cormorants. She loved living in Folkestone, in spite of everything that had happened. And she loved being with Willem. As if reading her mind, he reached over and took her hand.

Their idyll was interrupted by the arrival of a film crew, consisting of a reporter and cameraman. Amy recognised the reporter as Bella Harp. The pair set up to do a piece to camera, right next to Amy and Willem's table.

'You're joining us here on the Harbour Arm in Folkestone, where holidaymakers are seemingly determined to enjoy the summer despite the threat of a serial killer in the town. Following the announcement from police earlier today that they are reopening the investigation into the death of Robert Seymour, the man believed to be last year's Exhibitionist killer, we're here to talk to locals and tourists alike to get their reactions on the latest development in the story.'

Amy felt the colour drain from her face. This was her worst nightmare coming to life. She withdrew her shaking hand from Willem's and tried to steady herself. She could feel his puzzled gaze on her.

'Amy? Are you okay?' he asked.

'Um, yeah, fine. Somebody just walked over my grave,' she said, shuddering.

'I know. There's no escape from what's happening here is

there? It must be especially hard for you because you knew Robert.'

Amy nodded. She just wanted to get away, be on her own, but how could she explain it to Willem without telling him why she was so freaked out? Closing her eyes and taking a deep, steadying breath, Amy took Willem's hand once more and tried to push the terror to the back of her mind. She just had to hold it together for a while longer, and when she got home she'd speak to Jenny. Jenny would know what to do.

Thankfully, the reporter didn't try to speak to them, moving instead to the middle-aged couple sitting across from Amy and Willem.

'Can we go?' Amy said. 'Would you mind? Maybe walk a bit.'

'Of course,' Willem said, solicitous as ever.

They slipped quietly away and headed back the way they'd come.

'We could go and check out the gallery if you want? If you haven't got to rush off?' Willem suggested.

'I'd like that,' Amy said as they turned towards town. This time it was she who took Willem's hand.

The gallery was a white-walled space on Tontine Street, one-time red-light district with a decidedly dodgy past, that was being regenerated and reinvented along with much of the town.

'It's a nice airy space,' Amy said as they pushed open the doors.

They were met by the artist in residence, who greeted them like long-lost friends, plied them with Prosecco and explained all his abstract oil paintings in great detail. By the time they left, Amy's head was spinning. She didn't know if it was from the bubbly or the artist's own effervescence, but she gratefully acknowledged the fact of being taken out of her head for a short while.

Willem took her hand quite naturally as they left the gallery and turned up the hill in the direction of home.

'So, what did you think of the gallery?' he asked.

'I really liked it. It's a good space. The artist was a bit full on. Either he or the Prosecco have given me a bit of a headache.'

Willem laughed. 'He was pretty intense. I think we were probably the first visitors he'd had all day.'

'Yeah, maybe. All that pent-up artistic expression waiting for an audience. I can't imagine you being like that about your photography.'

Willem didn't answer at once.

'Oh God, I hope I haven't offended you?' Amy blurted. 'I didn't mean your photography is any less of an art form or anything. I just don't see you waving your arms about and making impassioned declarations about the extravagant plenitude and juxtaposition of ambiguities or some bollocks.'

Willem laughed and squeezed Amy's hand. 'I'm not offended. Not at all. I was just thinking. About my own work and how I feel about it. You're right, of course, I wouldn't be gesticulating all over the place. I am proud of my work, and I'm more than happy to talk about it, and the technicalities of photography, but I suppose I'm less eccentric than the stereotypical idea we have of artists.'

'Yes,' Amy nodded, 'you're much more normal. Thank goodness.'

They carried on walking, lapsing into silence once more.

It was only at the top of the hill, at the site of one of the 'Penthouse' art installations, and another location used by Robert during his killing spree, that Amy's dread resurfaced. She couldn't hide the change from Willem, who saw it in her face.

'What is it, Amy?'

She shook her head. 'Nothing. Just memories. Bad ones. Some things will always remind me,' she said, nodding to the silver-coloured water tower.

Willem said nothing, just wrapped her in a tight hug, as if he could glue her back together. They stayed like that for a minute, Amy feeling safe and protected for the first time in longer than she could remember. As they drew apart she tried to hold on to the way it had made her feel. She knew she had a mental battle on her hands in the days ahead and was going to need all the help she could get. Not for the first time, she wished she could confide in Willem, but she simply couldn't take that risk.

Accepting Willem's offer to walk her all the way home – he didn't want her walking alone, even in broad daylight – Amy said a reluctant goodbye on her doorstep. Willem was heading home to finish up some pieces for his upcoming exhibition.

'I'm sorry, Amy, I would love to stay a while longer.'

'That's okay,' she said. 'I should try and do some work too.'

As Willem turned to leave, he said, 'Maybe you could come to mine tomorrow. I'd love your thoughts on the photographs I've chosen.'

'I've love that,' Amy smiled.

'Great! I look forward to it.' With that, Willem was gone with a backwards wave of his hand. Amy could hear him whistling as he went. She recognised the Beatles song, which was one of her favourites.

Back indoors, Amy wandered into the kitchen. 'Alexa, play "Here Comes the Sun".'

CHAPTER 25
No doughnuts

Amy listened to the song again the following morning as she made coffee, the grin on her face making it impossible to sing along. She'd already checked for messages, the binoculars revealing the words that were responsible for the smile on her face and the temporary displacement of the thoughts that continued to trouble her:

DINNER HERE 6pm xx

She'd replied by text message, too impatient even to bother with paper and pen, that she looked forward to it.

It wasn't until lunchtime that Amy's little bubble of happiness burst, when she made the mistake of putting the local news on and saw the interviews from the previous day. People saying how terrible it was, what was happening in the town. Saying how scared they were. Or how they refused to let the killer run their lives. The reporter asked one man if he thought the wrong man had been accused last year, if Robert Seymour had been innocent, or if this killer was a copycat. Amy was asking herself the same questions. She didn't like any of the answers she came up with and couldn't shake the worry over what the police might find at Robert's house. Was she about to be arrested for murder and her embryonic happiness terminated before it had a chance to develop?

She thought about calling Jenny, but decided to grab the bull by the horns and just go round there. She'd been worrying about her friend anyway and didn't want to give her the chance to say no to a visit.

Feeling a little better just to be doing something, Amy grabbed her car keys and set off.

Jenny didn't look thrilled to see her when she opened the door a few minutes later. 'Oh, it's you.'

'Yes, it's me, don't sound so excited. I've been worrying about you.'

'You'd better come in then,' Jenny said, stepping aside and letting Amy through. 'I haven't got any doughnuts.'

'Really? Oh well I'm off then. See ya!' Amy joked, spinning around as if to leave.

Ice broken, the two friends went to sit in Jenny's conservatory with a peppermint tea each.

'How are you doing? Really?' Amy prodded gently.

Jenny sighed. 'I'm okay. Just a funny old time, one way and another.'

'Ain't that the truth?' Amy agreed, raising her eyebrows. 'What about work? Given any more thought to what you're going to do?'

'Well, it looks like they're going to have to scrap the host programme this year, close up the exhibits that need staffing. So many hosts have resigned out of fear already.'

'Can't say I blame them,' Amy said.

'I think I'll be able to get something working from home. I've applied for a couple of VA jobs.'

'VA? Victoria and Albert? Very Auspicious? Visible Arseholes?'

'Virtual Assistant, you dick.'

'Oh! That sounds good. Definitely reduces the chances of you finding a dead body when you arrive for work.'

'Indeed. Apart from the odd mouse the cats bring in.'

Right on cue, one of Jenny's cats wandered in, demanding Amy's attention for a few moments before sauntering off again. Amy used the time to pluck up the courage to broach the subject of Robert's death being reinvestigated.

'Stop, Amy, I mean it. I haven't got the energy to even think about the implications. Just keep your head down and wait for it to blow over.'

'But what if it doesn't blow over? What if they tie me, us, to his death? I can't go to prison, Jenny.'

'Nobody's going to prison, Amy. What are they going to find after all this time that they didn't find first time round? Nothing, that's what. Just get on with your life, that's my advice.'

'I don't think I can though. I'm going mad worrying about it.'

Jenny shook her head. 'What can we do? Even if we wanted to do something, what could we actually do?' Jenny persisted.

'I don't know,' Amy said miserably. But she did know, and the idea had planted itself in her brain and was starting to grow like bindweed.

Realising it was pointless to push Jenny further, Amy made her excuses, finished her tea and left, reminding her friend to call if she needed anything. She knew something had changed fundamentally in Jenny though, and in their friendship. She was on her own, divorced from her partner in crime.

After leaving Jenny's, Amy drove out of town. She avoided this particular route normally, as it was the road to Robert's old house. As the row of cottages came into view, with Robert's being at the far end of the terrace, Amy became aware of her heart beating in her ears and a feeling of nausea rising in her throat. She didn't want to be here. Didn't want to be anywhere near it. To be reminded of the terrible events of the previous year. But she couldn't do nothing. Couldn't wait to see what the fates decided for her.

Pulling the car up in a lay-by a short distance away, Amy studied the house, which had been standing empty for the past year. The front door and windows were boarded up and graffiti tags had been sprayed over them, along with a few choice words about Robert's killer status and where he could rot. There was also a board on the door giving details of the auction house who had tried, and failed, to sell the property. Nobody wanted to live in the house of a killer.

Amy figured she had two choices. She could either buy it. Or burn it down. She couldn't afford to buy it.

Turning her attention to the house next door, Amy saw a 'For Sale by Auction' sign there too. There were no curtains at the windows and the front garden was unkempt. It looked as though no one was living there either. Wanting to be sure, Amy got out of the car and trotted over to peer through the windows. It was clear that the place was uninhabited. A plan began to form in her mind. The only problem she could foresee was whether she was brave enough to carry it out on her own.

The more immediate problem at hand was deciding what to wear to Willem's for dinner, Amy thought as she drove back into town. And how she was going to pretend everything was okay in front of the world's most observant man.

Ninety minutes later she was knocking on Willem's front door, feeling a little nervous as she smoothed down the lines of her orange flowery summer dress, and more than a little distracted. Willem had a broad smile on his face when he opened the door. He took the bottle of wine Amy held out.

'Thank you. You shouldn't have though. You never need to bring something when you visit me.'

'I'll take it back then. Hand it over,' Amy joked.

'Come in, come in,' Willem said, leading the way into a house which was a mirror-image of Amy's own, except these walls were covered with breathtaking photographs of beaches and night skies, clearly Willem's own.

'Wow! These are beautiful!' Amy said, stopping to admire a particularly stunning sunset.

'Thank you,' Willem accepted the compliment gracefully, but quickly changed the subject. 'So, how's your day been? What have you been up to?' he asked as he led the way downstairs to the basement kitchen.

'Oh, nothing much. I popped in on Jenny, but I didn't feel very welcome. Feels like something's changed between us.' She didn't mention scoping out Robert's old house.

'I'm sorry to hear that. Give her time. I'm sure she'll come round. It's been a terrible time for her.'

'Yeah, I know, and I'm sure you're right. I just feel a little lost without her,' Amy said sadly.

'Well, my hair may not be pink, but I hope you now consider me a good friend too? And hopefully more?'

Amy smiled shyly. 'How about you? How's your day been?'

'Good, thank you. Finished framing the final piece for the show.'

'Oh, that's great! I can't wait to see them.'

'And you will. After dinner,' Willem promised, turning to attend to something on the hob. 'Now, what can I get you to drink?'

Over a dinner of roast chicken and all the trimmings, Amy and Willem talked about his upcoming exhibition and her new book idea. It all felt very comfortable and Amy managed to relax and put the Robert problem on the back burner of her mind for a while. She knew it was there though, simmering away, and that it would boil over if she didn't watch it carefully.

After they'd finished eating and Willem had refused Amy's offer to do the dishes, insisting he'd do them after she'd gone, they went to the top of the house, where Willem had his workroom. Amy took in the computers and printers, the enormous table and vast array of frames and mounting boards stacked on shelves.

'So, this is where the magic happens, eh?'

'Well, the magic happens where I take the photographs. Nature is the magician. I'm just there to capture her tricks.'

'And a very good job you do of it, if I may say so,' Amy said, looking at some of the images stacked around the room.

'You're very kind, Amy, thank you.'

'So, can I see the ones you're exhibiting?'

For the next ten minutes, Amy oohed and aahed over the stunning images Willem had prepared for the exhibition. She couldn't find fault with any of them and told him as much.

'Thank you, Amy. I'm really glad you like them,' Willem said, smiling as he laid the final image back down. 'Now, can I get you a coffee? Or a tea? Or something stronger?' he asked as he led the way back downstairs.

Amy was hit by a wave of exhaustion as they wound back down to the kitchen. 'Would you mind terribly if I didn't stay for another drink? I feel suddenly shattered.' Amy caught the brief look of disappointment which crossed Willem's face before he got control of it. 'Sorry,' she said.

'No, no apology needed,' Willem insisted, putting a hand on her arm. 'I'm not surprised you're exhausted, with everything that's been happening. Are you okay to get home?'

Amy nodded. 'Yes, thank you, I'll be fine. Just need my bed and a decent night's sleep. Thank you for a lovely dinner. And your lovely company.'

'You're welcome. Any time.'

Willem walked Amy out to her car and she could see him waving in her rearview mirror as she drove off. She didn't drive straight home though, instead taking the road to Robert's house once more. She couldn't help wishing Jenny was with her as she checked out the lane again, seeing how many houses had lights on at just after ten p.m.

When she finally got home about thirty minutes later, Amy fell straight into bed for another restless night, her sleep broken by vivid flashbacks of Robert. She woke feeling exhausted and alone and wondering how to face another day.

CHAPTER 26

Flamin' hot Wotsits

Amy had to face the day, as it was her day to man the Coastal Creatives shop. She was way too intimidated by Gloria to even think about phoning in sick again. Besides, she didn't want to let the rest of the group down. As she unlocked the door just before ten a.m. she was praying it would be an easy day. She really didn't feel up to dealing with any difficult customers today. Or any customers at all, to be perfectly honest.

As she went around turning on lights, Amy wondered if Willem would call in to say hello and she was smiling as she straightened his best-selling image of the Folkestone lighthouse. She noticed that Gloria had done her usual trick of inching everyone else's work along and taking the extra room for herself, and Amy took great delight in returning the space to its proper proportions. She did have a slight wobble at the thought of Gloria calling in and seeing what she'd done, but Amy couldn't stand injustice and clenched her jaw determinedly.

She'd brought her laptop with her and was planning to try and do some writing when the shop was quiet. After an hour of staring at the screen Amy sat back with a sigh. She couldn't focus on anything other than the police investigation. They could be going to Robert's house any day now, and she felt sick at the thought of a knock at her door when they found something to link her to the scene. Logically she knew that even if they found DNA traces they couldn't tie them to her

167

because her DNA had never been taken and couldn't possibly be on a database anywhere. She could, at a pinch, explain her fingerprints being there – after all, she had known Robert when he'd been in the writing group and could say she'd visited him at his house. But could she explain the presence of her prints in his bedroom? She could barely remember what she'd touched on that fateful day when she'd found the photographs of one of his victims on his bedside table. What if the police contacted all Robert's known associates and took their DNA and fingerprints for elimination purposes?

She had to do it. She had to burn the evidence. And she had to do it soon. Before the police went in and collected it. She had to do it tonight.

'Bloody hell,' Amy said under her breath, putting her head in her hands. 'I need you, Jenny. I can't do this on my own.' But she knew she couldn't count on Jenny this time. She *was* on her own.

Returning her attention to her laptop, she opened a search window and typed 'how to start an untraceable fire'. She wasn't worried about her internet searches raising eyebrows. She was a writer after all and googled all sorts of dodgy things.

Finding an article that piqued her interest, Amy discovered that arsonists sometimes used crisps as an accelerant as the 'hugely calorific and fatty' snack literally 'fed' the fire but, unlike petrol or other accelerants, was innocuous and untraceable. Fire investigators had apparently been alerted to this method of fire-starting by colleagues in the prison service, who heard about the technique from inmates. A study then showed that packets of crisps were excellent accelerants, with 'each individual crisp burning for an average of around seventy-six seconds'. Apparently it didn't matter whether you used potato crisps or the puffy maize or corn-based ones, they could all set a car seat on fire in about a hundred seconds. The firemen were amazed. So was Amy.

She was wondering if a particular flavour of crisp might be better – did spicy ones work better than ready salted, for instance? The study didn't seem to have covered that. She was thinking about bulk buying Flamin' Hot Giant Wotsits and feeling mildly hysterical when the shop door opened and she looked up to see Willem smiling at her. He'd spotted her upset in the second it took her to rearrange her face and stick a smile on it.

'Amy? What is it? What's wrong?' Amy could hear the concern in Willem's voice.

'Oh! Ignore me! Just an overemotional female today. I'm okay, really,' Amy said, trying to sound brighter than she felt. 'I just nudged Gloria's stuff back again,' she said, trying to change the subject and nodding in the direction of the shelves.

'Brave woman!' Willem said, pulling a face.

'I was just going to tell her you did it if she came in,' Amy said, all innocence.

Willem did a pretty decent impression of Munch's 'The Scream' and Amy couldn't help laughing.

'Did you need something?' Amy asked.

Willem shook his head. 'No, just popped in to say hello and see if *you* needed anything – a coffee or something?'

'I'd love a coffee actually, thank you.'

'No problem. Anything else?'

'Um… yeah, some crisps please.'

'What flavour?'

'Anything except ready salted.'

Willem ducked out again and, after thinking what a nice man he was, Amy's thoughts returned to arson. Could she really rock up at Robert's old house armed with multiple multi-packs of crisps, a box of matches and enough fire in her belly to break in and set light to it? Starting the actual fire might be the easy bit. She had to get in the house first. She knew the layout, of course, but she hadn't had to break in last time. Robert had opened the door to his killers. She would have to go prepared and hope for the best. And she would have to go tonight. Before the police searched the house. And before she lost her bottle.

When Willem arrived back a few minutes later, Amy had closed her laptop and was dealing with the first customer of the day. Having steered the woman away from Gloria's work, she was now bubble-wrapping one of Willem's lighthouses.

'Enjoy it,' Amy said as she handed the large bag over the counter.

'I will, thank you,' the customer said. 'Goodbye.'

'Goodbye,' Amy said with a smile. 'Ooh, by the way, the photographer has an exhibition coming up if you'd like to see more of his work.' Amy handed the woman one of the flyers for Willem's upcoming show.

With the shop to themselves again, Willem handed Amy her coffee and crisps.

'Thanks, Amy. You're my lucky charm.'

Amy made a strangled noise which suggested she was no one's lucky charm and reached out to take the coffee and crisps. They were salt and vinegar, baked not fried. She made a mental note not to buy baked crisps as they were presumably much lower in fat. She wondered if the study had included baked crisps. Probably not, she concluded. Maybe she should conduct a study of her own. It would be much more comprehensive than the one she'd just read about, that's for sure.

Willem had bought himself a coffee too, and he sat on the high stool on the other side of the counter.

'I do like the fact that you don't have to ask how I take my coffee,' Amy said after taking a sip from the takeout cup.

Willem smiled at her. 'I got it right then?'

'Spot on,' Amy nodded. 'Thank you.'

They sat quietly for a while, neither feeling the need to fill the silence. Amy's thoughts drifted inevitably to Robert's house.

'Sorry,' she said, 'I'm rubbish company today.'

'Not at all,' Willem contradicted. 'You have a lot on your mind. Have you heard from Jenny at all?'

Amy shook her head. 'I couldn't even bribe her with chocolate brownies. I won't give up though. I'll wear her down eventually. She'll agree to see me just to shut me up.'

'I really do think she simply needs a little time to process what she's seen, what she's been through.'

'Hopefully you're right. My world's a much duller place without Jenny in it,' Amy said sadly.

'And not just because of her pink hair, eh?' Willem smiled.

Amy managed a small smile as she pictured her friend.

'What are you up to later?' Willem asked. 'If you're free, maybe we could go for a walk or get a drink somewhere?'

'Oh, I would have loved to but I can't tonight, sorry,' Amy said, desperately wracking her brain for a suitable excuse. She could hardly say she was planning a little bit of arson with a few packets of Walkers Prawn Cocktail.

She needn't have worried though, as Willem didn't pry, he simply said, 'No problem, another time.'

Amy was saved any further wracking by the door opening and a couple of customers entering the shop.

'I'll leave you to it,' Willem said quietly. 'Have a good rest of day and I'll see you soon.'

'Yes, okay, thanks, Willem, you too. Bye.'

The remainder of Amy's day in the shop was surprisingly busy and she racked up quite a few sales, including another couple of Willem's prints and three of her books. Thankfully, Gloria hadn't called in by the time she locked up at five, although Amy might have enjoyed telling her she'd had no sales. The only other artist who'd popped in was Finn, and Amy was happy to tell him he'd sold a Scrabble set.

After leaving the shop, Amy called in to the Tesco Local and grabbed three multi-packs of crisps: Cheesy Wotsits, Walkers Roast Chicken, and Pickled Onion Monster Munch. As an afterthought she also picked up a tube of Pringles Texas BBQ. When she asked the cashier for a box of matches she had a moment of panic but, unless the woman googled the same dodgy things she did, Amy was pretty confident she wouldn't realise she was serving a wannabe arsonist.

Arriving home, Amy grabbed her car keys and drove out to Robert's. She wanted one more look in daylight before she carried out her mission.

As she neared the row of cottages, she could see at once that she was too late. The board had been removed from the door and bright yellow crime-scene tape had been stretched across it.

'Shit. Shit shit shit,' Amy banged the steering wheel and carried on driving past the houses before turning round in a farm driveway and heading back to town. A few minutes later she was parked down by the seafront eating Monster Munch and wondering what to do.

CHAPTER 27

Pickled Onion Monster Munch

When Jenny opened her front door at six-thirty that evening, she was greeted by Amy holding out a rather empty-looking pack of Monster Munch and a much fuller one of Wotsits.

'I know they're not doughnuts, but they are a peace offering,' Amy said, thrusting the bags at her friend.

'Right…' Jenny said, looking bemused as she took the crisps. 'I suppose you'd better come in.'

Amy wiped her feet on the doormat and followed Jenny into the house. They went into the kitchen and Amy sat down heavily on a chair, exhaling loudly.

'Should I ask?' Jenny enquired, holding out the open bag.

'What?' Amy shrugged. 'Can't a friend bring another friend a mostly eaten bag of Monster Munch? Pickled Onion at that. The Monster Munch of the gods.'

Jenny simply raised her eyebrows.

'Besides,' Amy continued, 'I've done you a favour by eating most of them. Think of all the calories I've saved you.'

Jenny cocked her head on one side. Still she said nothing, waiting for Amy to explain.

'What?' Amy said huffily.

More raised eyebrows. A head cocked even lower.

'So what if I was planning to set fire to Robert's house tonight. Using crisps,' Amy retorted finally.

'Er… you what now? Did you just say you were planning to set fire to Robert's house? Using crisps? Tell me I imagined that.'

Amy shook her head.

Jenny held up the bag. 'You didn't…?'

'No. The police beat me to it.'

'The police burned Robert's house down using crisps?'

'No, don't be ridiculous.'

'Oh, I'm sorry, who's being ridiculous?' Jenny said.

'It's a perfectly legitimate way of committing arson,' Amy informed her nonplussed friend.

'But not the one favoured by the police apparently…'

'The police didn't burn the house down. Using crisps or otherwise.'

'Right. Gotcha,' Jenny said, dropping the crisps on the table so she could wave her hands exasperatedly at Amy.

'To clarify,' Amy began, 'the police got to Robert's house before I could burn it down. There doesn't seem any point in burning it down now – they've probably already collected any evidence.'

Jenny was shaking her head. 'So, what happened to all the crisps?'

'Oh, I ate them.'

'Well, that explains your breath,' Jenny said under hers.

Amy blew into her hand and sniffed. 'Ew.'

'Ew indeed. You might want to use some mouthwash before you snog Willem,' Jenny said helpfully.

Amy stuck her tongue out at her. It was orange.

'Ate some Wotsits too, then, eh?' Jenny said.

'Only one packet,' Amy sighed. 'Actually I do feel a bit sick now.'

'I'm not surprised, you greedy cow.'

'It's not my fault. I was stress-eating.'

'I feel pretty stressed myself now too,' Jenny grumbled. 'What were you thinking, Amy?'

'I know, I know, I'm stupid. I've just been so terrified about them reinvestigating Robert's death.'

'Well, the main thing is you didn't go through with it,' Jenny said, finally relenting a little and smiling at Amy. 'But you are going to have to explain the crisps.'

'Oh, this is only half of them. Got a load more in the car. Much less suspicious than a can of petrol though, don't you think?'

'Oh, yeah, much,' Jenny said sarcastically. 'Are you really telling me that you can start a fire with them though?'

'Oh yeah,' Amy nodded her head enthusiastically. 'It's genuinely a thing. Arsonists use them because they don't leave a trace like petrol or some other accelerant. They did a study and everything.' She went on to explain to a bemused Jenny all about the high fat content and long burning time of each crisp. By the time she'd finished, Jenny actually looked a little bit impressed.

'I wouldn't mind trying that myself,' she said. 'Sounds like fun.'

'What? You mean…?' Amy began.

'No, I don't mean burn Robert's bloody house down. I just mean test the theory. With single crisps. In the safety of our own home. Nothing good on the telly this evening.'

It was Amy's turn to look bemused.

'What?' Jenny asked. 'You get the crisps, I'll open the wine.'

'Okay, but I haven't even been home for dinner or anything yet,' Amy said.

'You can't possibly be hungry after eating... how many... six packets of crisps?'

Amy looked sheepish. 'Ish,' she said.

When Amy returned with the rest of the crisps from the car, Jenny had lined up a selection of small earthenware dishes on the kitchen table and poured them each a glass of wine.

'I couldn't find any matches,' Jenny said.

Amy held up the box she'd brought from the car and gave it a shake.

'Get them from your arsonist's kit?'

'Yep. So, what's the plan?'

'Well, one crisp per dish, I s'pose. We can time how long each one burns on my mobile, record it and then compare them all at the end.'

'Bonkers,' Amy said.

'Hey, you started it,' Jenny retorted. 'At least I'm not planning to set fire to anyone's house.'

'Only yours if this goes wrong,' Amy mumbled.

'It's perfectly safe,' Jenny said confidently. 'They can't set fire to ovenproof dishes, can they? It's only a bit of fun.'

Amy shrugged and opened a packet of Roast Chicken. 'Small, medium or large?' she asked.

'Oh, large, definitely. Go big or go home.'

Jenny struck a match and set light to the chicken-flavoured crisp. Amy watched it burn while absent-mindedly munching on the rest of the crisps.

'Do you think we should repeat it with another one?' Amy suggested, holding out another large potato chip.

'For scientific purposes, or to stop you scoffing all of them?'

'Either. Both,' Amy shrugged.

Jenny removed the charred remains of the first crisp and set light to the second. She wrote down *37 seconds* on her notepad.

Amy continued munching. She didn't even really like chicken-flavoured crisps. 'Did you used to shrink crisp packets in the oven when you were at school?'

'Not personally, but I remember some of the other kids doing it. I was actually a bit jealous of their teeny crisp packets,' Jenny said.

'Yeah, me too. I don't know why I didn't try doing it. Apparently it doesn't work on modern crisp packets; they're too metallic or something.'

'That's a pity. That would've completed our evening's entertainment nicely.'

As they spoke, the second crisp was burning itself out, leaving just a charred scrap.

'Hm... forty-two seconds for that one,' Jenny said.

'It's quite a long time though, isn't it? You can see how a whole packet would set light to a sofa or something, can't you?'

'Yep, definitely. Is that what you were planning to do at Robert's house?'

'Yeah, scatter packets on the chairs and sofa in the lounge, and his bed. Set light to them and scarper. Thought maybe the police would just think it was kids mucking around – you know, after all the graffiti and stuff.'

'Not a bad plan. You might've got away with it,' Jenny conceded.

'Quite relieved I don't have to find out,' Amy admitted. 'Besides, this is way more fun,' she said as Jenny set light to a Pringle.

By the time they'd burned multiple crisps of all types, Amy was feeling decidedly tiddly. The Monster Munch had burned the most fiercely and the longest.

'Good to know for future reference,' she said, putting her hand up to high-five Jenny.

Her hand was met with only air as Jenny shook her head and said, 'This wasn't research, you dick, this was just a bit of fun.'

'Well, yeah, but you never know…'

Jenny's face said no, even before she voiced it.

It was gone nine by the time Amy left Jenny's, walking home as she'd had too much to drink.

'Message me when you get home,' Jenny said, after she'd failed to persuade Amy to call a taxi.

Amy was too intoxicated to think about the fact that there was a serial killer on the prowl. Luckily for her, he was busy on the other side of town, and she arrived home safe and sound. As she was texting Jenny, a message arrived from Willem saying he hoped she'd had a nice evening.

Drinks and nibbles with a friend, she replied. *Hope you had a good one too. Nighty night. x*

As Amy slept more soundly than she'd done in a while, the killer was sitting in his van a short distance from 'I am Argonaut'. It was almost one a.m. and the night sky was overcast. He hadn't seen another car for nearly an hour and all was still and quiet.

Dressed in his usual dark attire and cap, the killer knew he was all but invisible, and he felt invincible. After four successful exhibits, his confidence was higher than ever. He couldn't believe the complete absence of security, even now. Carrying the freshly painted wooden chair over to the installation site, he placed it to one side, midway between the 'Argonaut' figure and the statue of William Harvey.

Returning to the van, he got back in to wait a few minutes before carrying the headless body over. Before freezing the body, he'd pumped the blood out of it – a nice little nod to William Harvey's discovery of the circulation of the blood, he thought. He hadn't decided what to do with the blood yet, but he was confident it wouldn't go to waste.

When all remained quiet, he retrieved the still slightly frozen body from the back of the van and trotted over to the chair, flopping the corpse onto the seat. Because of how he'd arranged her limbs before she went into the freezer, she sat cross-legged on the chair. Not perfect, but good enough. The finishing touch was the six-inch-high, miniature Janus sculpture he'd taken from inside the giant one. He placed this on top of the corpse, in place of her own missing head, with one face towards 'I am Argonaut' and the other to 'William Harvey'. Now the conversation had three participants, or four, depending how you looked at it.

Looking all around and seeing no one, he jogged back over to his van and drove slowly home. His fishing gear was stashed in the back in case anyone stopped him.

CHAPTER 28

Officer Dribble

For once it wasn't a dog walker who found the body just before dawn. It was Willem. He'd gone out early to capture sunrise from The Leas, the town's clifftop promenade, and had walked up Castle Hill Avenue past Atta Kwami's brightly coloured kiosks and benches and straight on towards the sea. As he approached 'I am Argonaut' he spotted something strange. Only when he got quite close could he see exactly what it was: a headless body sitting cross-legged on an Atta-Kwami-style chair, with what looked like a miniature Janus sculpture on its ragged stump of a neck.

Willem had seen some shocking things in his life, but even so, he felt the colour drain from his face and bile rise in his throat. He swallowed it down as he dialled 999 and asked for the police.

When two uniformed officers arrived in a patrol car a few minutes later, they found Willem sitting at the base of the William Harvey statue, his head in his hands. He looked up as the two officers approached, nodding to them.

'You alright, mate?' one of the policemen said.

Willem simply nodded again before getting stiffly to his feet, silently wishing he hadn't dragged his tired old body out of bed to snap the sunrise on this particular morning. 'Over here,' he said, turning towards the body. He stood back and watched as the newcomers took in the scene. The younger of the two officers looked decidedly green around the gills, putting his hand across his mouth, much as Willem had.

The older of the two police officers was already on his radio, requesting SOCOs and the coroner. 'Yeah, send the big guns, Sarge. Looks like our killer's struck again.' He ended the call and turned to his younger colleague. 'Right, get the tape, Luke. Let's get this cordoned off before we get any more looky-loos. Lukey-loos,' he added, laughing at his own joke.

Willem scowled at him, biting back the urge to point out how inappropriate he was being. A young woman was dead, her body mutilated and dumped unceremoniously for all to see. A little more respect was in order.

The younger officer, Luke, looked relieved to step away from the scene for a moment as he went to the patrol car to fetch the crime scene tape, which he then proceeded to erect in a large square around the site, taking in the body and both statues.

The other officer took out his notebook and addressed Willem.

'So, Mr…?'

'De Groot. Willem de Groot.'

'Mr. de Groot, not from around here then?' He didn't wait for an answer. 'Can you tell me what you were doing here this morning?'

'Yes, I was on my way to photograph from The Leas,' he said, resisting the urge to exaggerate his lingering South African accent or lapse into Afrikaans, and indicating his camera bag and tripod. As Willem had waited for the police, he'd watched the most stunning orange sunrise set fire to the sky, but all he could think was that the dead woman would never see another sunrise.

'Do that a lot, do you?'

'Well, yes, it's what I do – I'm a coastal landscape photographer. Sunrises and sunsets are my bread and butter.'

'I see…' the officer said, sounding as though he didn't see at all. Willem suspected the man was immune to the beauty of the sky. 'So, when you arrived here this morning, did you see anyone else in the area?'

'No,' Willem shook his head. 'I didn't see anyone.'

'And did you touch anything at all? Did you approach the body?'

'No, I stopped within a few feet of it… of her… and I called 999 as soon as I realised what I was looking at.'

'Weren't tempted to take a few snapshots?' the officer smirked, nodding back at the corpse.

'What? No! Of course I wasn't,' Willem said, disgusted at the suggestion and at the officer who made it.

Still smirking, the officer shrugged. 'Some people might've done. You'd be surprised. It'd be all over social media if someone else had found it, you mark my words.'

Willem had already decided he most certainly would *not* mark any of the policeman's words.

By the time the scene of crime officers had arrived and started erecting a white tent over the body it was half past seven. Willem wondered if it was too early to call Amy. He really wanted to see her. More than anything he wanted to hold her, to feel a connection to a warm, living, breathing human being. Deciding to risk it, he took out his mobile, pressed call and held his breath as the call connected.

'Hello, Willem, are you okay?' Amy said. She sounded worried. Early morning phone calls did that. Willem felt a stab of guilt.

'Amy, hello. I'm sorry to call so early. It's just… I…' Willem didn't know what to say now he had Amy on the other end of the line.

'What's up? Has something happened?' Amy prompted.

'You could say that. I found a body,' Willem sighed.

Silence on the other end of the phone. Willem pictured Amy trying to process his words.

'You are joking?' she said finally.

'I wish I was,' Willem said grimly.

'Bloody hell, not you too?'

'I know. You might want to change your friends,' Willem tried to joke.

'Do you want me to come?' Amy asked.

'I… no… it's okay. I shouldn't have phoned you.'

'It's fine, really. Where are you?'

Willem told her where he was.

'Right. I'll just throw on some clothes and I'll be there,' Amy said before ending the call.

Less than ten minutes later and Amy pulled her car up as close as she could to the cordoned off area. She hurried over to where she could see Willem standing. The young officer named Luke was preventing people from entering the area.

'I'm sorry, madam, you can't…' he began. 'Oh! It's you,' he finished.

Amy smiled brightly. 'Yep, me again. We must stop meeting like this. People will talk.'

The young officer blushed to the roots of his hair and lifted the tape for Amy to go under. He didn't even bother taking her details. She rushed to Willem and pulled him into a hug.

'Oh my God, poor you! How awful! Are you okay?'

'Better now,' Willem said, feeling the warmth of her body seeping into his chilled frame. 'Thank you for coming. You didn't need to.'

'Pfft!' Amy said. 'This is what I do, don't ya know.'

'Hm… like I said… different friends.'

'Nah! I'm rather fond of the ones I've got. Even if they do have an unfortunate habit of stumbling across dead bodies.' Pulling out of the hug, Amy nodded in the direction of the white tent, now thankfully concealing the body. 'Is it bad? Sorry, that was a stupid thing to say. There's no such thing as a good dead body, is there?' Amy pulled a face.

Willem couldn't help chuckling at her rambling. 'Oh, I don't know, I could quite happily have throttled the other policeman I spoke to.'

'Who? Officer Dribble over there? That's what I call him anyway. I encountered him one time with Jenny. He's a bit of a knob, isn't he?'

'He is indeed,' Willem agreed, still smiling at Amy.

'Is it another young woman? The victim.'

Willem nodded. 'Yes, as far as I could tell. She was missing her… um… she was missing her head.'

'Oh my God! Oh, Jesus, Willem. That's horrible. Poor you, seeing that. Or not seeing that. Oh, shut up, Amy, you're wittering,' she admonished herself.

'That's not all. The killer had put one of those little Janus heads on her. He must've taken one from the East Cliff site.'

Amy was quiet for a while. Willem could almost hear her thinking, mentally joining the dots.

'Do you reckon the skull they found at 'Janus' belonged to this victim?' she said eventually.

'The thought did cross my mind,' Willem nodded.

'I wonder if the police have connected the two murder sites. I s'pose they must have. It's not rocket science, is it?'

'I'm sure if they haven't already they soon will. It would be impossible not to really, wouldn't it?'

'Yeah, you're right, of course. I still can't believe you found her, not after Jenny finding those other two,' Amy said, shaking her head. 'What are the chances?'

'It might sound weird, but I'm kind of glad it was me that found her. That odious policeman – Officer Dibble was it…?'

'Dribble, but yes…'

'Officer Dribble, he said some people would have taken photos and posted them on social media before calling the police. What an absolutely abhorrent thought.'

'I know. People can be vile creatures. There seems to be a complete lack of respect and sensitivity nowadays. She, whoever she was, was lucky you found her,' Amy said, squeezing Willem's hand and smiling up at him. 'What were you doing up here so early?'

'Hoping to catch a good sunrise,' Willem told her.

'Did you?'

'Not with my camera. But I'm just grateful to be alive to have witnessed it at all.'

At that moment, the infamous Officer Dribble came over and told Willem he could go once he'd made sure someone had all his contact details. He looked Amy up and down, his eyes resting for a few moments too long on her chest before looking her in the eyes. 'Have we met? You look familiar,' he said.

'Me or my boobs?' Amy enquired, smiling sweetly.

Dribble harrumphed. 'Well, whoever you are, you shouldn't

be here, so would you kindly get yourself to the other side of the cordon. You're contaminating my crime scene.'

Amy resisted saying the only contaminant in the area was him, and turned to walk away. As she reached the tape she heard Willem asking the policeman for his name.

'Officer Bushell. Terry Bushell.'

'And that of your superior?' Willem asked next.

'Why d'you want that then?'

'The name of your superior, if you please,' Willem repeated.

Sounding a little flustered, Dribble gave Willem the name.

'Thank you,' Willem said politely before turning to follow Amy.

'What was all that about?' she hissed as they walked away.

'I might want to complain about the delightful Officer Dribble. Tell his superiors about his complete lack of respect for the dead. And the living, come to that.'

'Really?'

'Well, no, probably not, but he doesn't have to know that. Let him sweat.'

Amy laughed. 'He is a pig.'

'He is indeed. I can see why you gave him the nickname.'

'The first time I met him he didn't make eye contact with me once. Jenny was ready to deck him. I think she would have if she hadn't been in such a state of shock.'

'Speaking of shock… could we go somewhere for a cup of tea. If you have time, of course.'

'I always have time for you,' Amy said, taking Willem's hand.

CHAPTER 29

Mark Two

Back at his bungalow, the killer was sprawled out on his sofa. The late-night expeditions were catching up with him and he'd succumbed to a snooze after another night of not enough sleep. He'd been doing a bit of research on his laptop before nodding off, and when he woke up and woke up his computer, it was still open on the Creative Folkestone website. He'd been studying the remaining art installations and wondering what to do with all the blood. He had an idea.

The installation he was interested in was inspired by the Zig-Zag Path, which wound its way down from The Leas, through rocks and grottos, almost to the sea. It was constructed in the 1920s from Pulhamite, a man-made substance that resembled natural rock and which was made from a mixture of sand, Portland cement and clinker, sculpted over a core of rubble and crushed bricks. Over time, the surface coating of the rocks wore away to reveal the inorganic rubbish used as bulking material.

The piece was titled 'Mellowing the Corners' and consisted of newly made Pulhamite boulders placed on three different sites around the town. The idea was that they were fake rocks that could be 'personified as trying to act naturally' to blend in with their environment. There was a cube-shaped one in Kingsnorth Gardens to match the topiary there, a bench at the top of The Stade steps, and a third on Mermaid Beach. The boulders contained objects donated by residents which would also begin to reappear over the next 100 years as the corners of the rocks were worn away by weather and human use.

Well, if the killer had anything to do with it, the boulders weren't going to blend in for much longer. Painted blood-red, they'd be shown up for the fakes they really were. It would be a piece of cake to decant the blood into an old paint tin, grab a nice big paintbrush and slap a coat on each of the three rocks. It would make a nice change not to have to lug a bloody body around too. Just the bloody blood. He'd do it in a couple of days' time; he needed some decent sleep before then.

Stretching and yawning, the killer got up and padded through to his kitchen to make coffee. He had a much-needed day off and was planning to spend it doing bugger all, except watching the local news and listening to Radio Folkestone for anything about his latest exhibit. It was a shame the police were always so quick to hide the body from public view. So few people got to enjoy his art as it was intended. He was quite sure the police and crime scene officers didn't fully appreciate the spectacle he created each time. What he'd really like was an exhibition – all his pieces in one place. That would really have the wow factor.

As he waited for the water to run through the coffee machine, thoughts of an exhibition kept nagging at him. Clearly this was something he needed to give some thought to. He had all his photographs of course… perhaps he could exhibit them somehow. He knew last year's so-called Exhibitionist had done something similar at the Harbour Screen. He'd killed the projectionist and treated the audience to a slideshow of all his greatest moments. They'd been expecting *The Greatest Showman*. He had to reluctantly admit that had been genius. He only wished he'd been there to soak up the atmosphere as people started to scream along to the strains of 'Enter Sandman'. He had to go one better, one bigger. He had to show the world he was no cheap copycat.

Taking his coffee back into the lounge, he sat on the sofa, feet up on the coffee table, and switched on the television to the local news channel. He put Radio Folkestone on through his laptop and sat back to wait. He didn't have to wait long.

'The Folkestone serial killer is believed to have struck again. In the early hours of this morning, police were called to Clifton Gardens, where a local man had made another grisly discovery. The victim, believed to be a young woman, has not yet been identified and police have not revealed any more details at this time. With the body being found at another Triennial art installation, we can only assume it is the work of the killer people have dubbed The Exhibitionist Copycat and The Exhibitionist Mark Two.'

He bristled at the names. He was nobody's mark 2. Fucking reporter. He'd show her. He'd make her eat her words.

'With the police making no comment at this time, speculation surrounding the murders is rife. Did they get the wrong man last year? Was Robert Seymour actually an innocent scapegoat, framed to give the real killer the breathing room to plot this year's atrocities? Did Robert Seymour really take his own life, or was he just another victim of the real Exhibitionist? We know that police have reopened the investigation into Seymour's suicide,' the woman reporter on the TV continued as a photograph of Robert's house flashed onto the screen.

He knew Robert's house had been boarded up for the past year, but it had clearly been opened up again. He wondered what police would find that they didn't the first time round. Useless wankers.

On screen the reporter was still wittering on, trying to fill the segment with very little actual information. Now she was comparing the killer to Banksy, another artist who kept his identity secret. Silly tart. He had to keep his identity secret, didn't he? Couldn't plot anything from a prison cell. Admittedly, the notoriety would be all the sweeter if he could actually take the credit for the exhibits. Maybe one day, but not yet. He wasn't done yet. And now the lovely reporter had given him another idea. Happy days.

Amy wasn't enjoying the news reports as much as the killer. After she'd had a cup of tea in a cafe with Willem, they'd parted company and she'd dropped him home before heading to Jenny's. Jenny was still in her pyjamas when she opened the door, pulling her dressing gown around her. Needless to say, everything she was wearing had cats on, right down to her slippers.

'What time d'you call this?' Jenny asked, letting Amy in.

'Um… breakfast time? What are we having?'

'Well, *I'm* having toast and strawberry jam.'

'Perfect. Count me in,' Amy grinned.

Jenny led the way to the kitchen and started gathering the bits to make breakfast.

'You'll never guess what's happened,' Amy said, plonking herself down at the table.

'You're probably right. Knowing you, it could be absolutely anything – set light to the library using Jaffa Cakes?' Jenny sighed, putting four slices of bread in the toaster. 'Tea or coffee?'

'Um… coffee please, just had a tea with Willem. Why would I set light to the library?'

Jenny turned to her and raised her eyebrows. 'Ooh, is there something you haven't told me? Tea with Willem at early o'clock.' She ignored the question about the library.

'No! It was all perfectly innocent. The thing I have to tell you is that Willem found another body this morning!'

There was silence as Jenny processed Amy's words.

'Bloody hell. You need to think about changing your friends, mate.'

Amy laughed. 'That's exactly what Willem said!'

'What are the chances?' Jenny said, shaking her head.

'That's exactly what I said!' Amy grinned.

'Is he okay? Willem?'

'Yeah, I think so. He was a bit shaken up, but he's a pretty stable character, from what I've seen. I think he'll be okay.'

'That's good. It's not a nice thing to happen,' Jenny shuddered, obviously remembering her own experiences.

'Thankfully they'd already put the gazebo-thingy over the body when I got there.'

'Lucky for you. It's hard to unsee those images,' Jenny said as she filled the reservoir for the coffee machine.

Soon the friends were munching on toast and jam, conversation halted temporarily. At one point Jenny said, 'Alexa, play Radio Folkestone,' through a mouthful of toast, to which Alexa replied, 'I'm sorry, I didn't quite catch that'. After telling Alexa to fucking listen, Jenny repeated the instruction and the radio station came on. 'Alexa, volume down!' Jenny screeched when Wham's 'Young Guns' was played.

Amy couldn't help laughing. Her friend had very particular taste in music.

'There's no need for that shite this early in the morning,' Jenny continued.

'I don't mind a bit of Wham,' Amy mused.

'Oh God! Please tell me you weren't in love with George Michael in the eighties? I bet you had one of those Choose Life T-shirts, didn't you?' Jenny pulled a face.

'Jesus, no, and if they play "Careless Whisper", Alexa's going out the window. But who doesn't love a bit of "Club Tropicana"?' Amy said, deadpan, knowing full well it was a red rag to a bull.

'Get out of my house,' Jenny exclaimed, pointing to the door.

'Can I finish my toast first?'

'S'pose so,' Jenny relented.

They ate on in silence for a while. Wham ended and UB40 came on.

'Still can't believe Willem found a body,' Jenny said after a time.

'I know. That's not the worst of it,' Amy said, grimacing.

'What's worse than finding a dead body?'

'Um… finding a decapitated one…?'

'Oh. Shit.'

'Indeed. Horrible. Poor Willem. Poor you too. That policeman was there again. You remember, the pervy one who had an entire conversation with my boobs?'

'Ugh. The repulsive Officer Dribble. How was the slimebag?'

'Slimy. I thought Willem was going to punch him.'

'Should've done. Could've blamed it on the shock.'

'He settled for taking his boss's name. Figured the threat of a complaint being made against him was enough. I don't think Willem's the violent type.'

'Me neither, but I think I could make an exception for that sleaze,' Jenny said. 'We were right though, weren't we? About 'Argonaut' being the next site to be hit. Bloody hell, Amy, we could've seen the killer when we were watching it. Remember that bloke who walked past?'

'I still think that would be a push,' Amy said, screwing up her nose. 'Helluva coincidence for him to be sussing it out at the exact time we were there, don't you think?'

'Stranger things have happened. Anyway, I love a good coincidence.'

Amy shrugged.

'I've been thinking about that night, actually. I keep feeling I've seen that man before somewhere recently. Can't place him, but something about him looked kind of familiar,' Jenny insisted.

'He just looked like a million other men. There wasn't anything memorable about him from what I can remember,' Amy said.

Jenny shook her head. 'No, there was definitely something… maybe the way he walked, or I don't know, just a feeling.'

'Probably passed him in the street or in a shop or something. Maybe he has a cat and you saw him in the cat-food aisle at Tesco's?'

'Now that I'd definitely remember,' Jenny said.

Amy laughed.

Just then, the news came on the radio and Jenny instructed Alexa to increase the volume once more. They recognised their friend Bella Harp's voice as she reported on the morning's gruesome discovery. It was Bella's report that had also been picked up by the local news channel. Thankfully for Amy, they were spared the sight of Robert's house, but the mention of it saw the colour drain from her face.

'Don't be getting any more ideas about buying crisps,' Jenny said, observing her friend.

'It's too late for that anyway,' Amy sighed. 'Any crisps I buy now will be for the sole purpose of comfort eating.'

'Good. More toast?'

CHAPTER 30
Pantone 666

The killer was thoroughly enjoying his day off. Apart from every time the reporter came on and called him 'copycat' or 'mark two'. Made him sound like a Ford Cortina. Although even that was bothering him less since it had been the inspiration for another exhibit.

He was happily mulling over this latest piece, which would involve one of the older Triennial installations, from 2008 to be precise. It was called 'The Mobile Gull Appreciation Unit' and was basically a giant hollow seagull which had originally functioned as a staffed information booth for information about gulls. Love 'em or loathe 'em, gulls were a fact of life living in a seaside town. The enormous seagull had been dusted off and wheeled out again and was currently sitting up on The Leas, serving as an information point. The hatch in the side opened to reveal an often bored-looking host who looked like they'd been swallowed by the seagull.

He knew he was moving away from his usual MO for this one. Usually his victims were random – right place, right time – but targeting the reporter who'd so maligned him meant a bit more planning. He would probably have to spend time tracking her movements, find out where she lived and worked, and where would be the best place to take her. It did increase the risk a bit, but he didn't mind; he quite liked the prospect of stalking her.

He was wondering how he should kill her, brainstorming and playing word association in his head. He felt a pang of nostalgia when he thought of the times in the past when he'd had someone else to bounce ideas off, but he quickly shook it away. He was better off on his own. You couldn't rely on other people. They didn't keep their word. Word. Words. They were key to this killing. Seagull. Words. Books. He could beat her to death with a copy of *Jonathan Livingston Seagull. Have to be the hardback,* he thought, laughing out loud. Bash her head in with a tin of Alphabetti spaghetti. As much as the ideas amused him, he was fully aware they were too uncontrolled, too unpredictable and just plain ridiculous. Nothing wrong with having a bit of a laugh while you work though, eh?

At least he had one part of the plan sorted. The seagull would eat the reporter and the reporter would eat her words. Specifically the words she'd said about him. He would've liked to have used what3words again, but with the gull being mobile, that wouldn't work. Maybe he'd pop out for a stroll later that evening – check out the locations of the three Pulhamite rocks and see how secure the seagull was.

Just then, the reporter reappeared on screen and he gave her his full attention, committing her face to his memory. He was excited about this one – a minor celebrity being bumped off would give his own profile a boost, he was sure. The reporter had nothing new to say, and he hit the off button on the remote, bored of hearing the same old story. Time to make a new one. Now he just had to find Bella Harp and see if she had a routine.

Grabbing his laptop, he typed her name into Google. He got a lot of hits. He added 192 to the search – nothing for Bella

Harp, but he figured she could be married, or Bella was short for something else. He tried Isabella. No joy. He shrugged. He hadn't really expected her address to available on the internet. Not with her occupation and potential to attract haters or weirdos. He didn't include himself in either category. He found entries for her on all the social media platforms and LinkedIn that he scrolled idly through. It was on Facebook that he finally hit potential pay dirt. She'd shared assorted photographs which he reckoned were taken from her home, most of them obviously taken at sunset looking out over the English Channel. He recognised the area of The Leas which featured in them all and from the angle he had a pretty good idea roughly where they were taken from. Shouldn't be too hard to hang around at the start or end of the day and see just what Bella Harp got up to.

By the time evening came around, he was bored of doing nothing. He remembered now why he didn't take much time off work. He'd mindlessly cooked and eaten a fry-up before grabbing his keys and heading out. There was no point taking the car right into town, as trying to park anywhere would be a nightmare and probably cost a fortune, so he left the car on a residential street some way out and set off to walk a pretty big loop.

It was another beautiful summer's evening in Folkestone and the streets and restaurants were busy with locals and tourists alike. He normally avoided the town until after dark, especially in the summer, but he wanted to check out a few things in daylight. He didn't make eye contact with anyone, not even when he walked past groups of young women flaunting themselves, wearing next to nothing. They were asking for it, silly little tarts. He indulged his imagination in a few rather tasty little scenarios as he walked on towards Kingsnorth Gardens. *Wouldn't need to pop to Homebase for blood-red paint then*, he chuckled to himself.

His first port of call was the Pulhamite bench at the top of the steps from The Stade. It would take a bit of painting, but should be easy enough. He wondered as he walked on if he would have enough blood. The idea of watering it down or mixing it with actual paint was not an appealing one – it felt like it was compromising his artistic integrity – but he would be prepared for that eventuality. Although, thinking about it, maybe it would actually be better if it *was* mixed with paint? Might actually go on better. He made a mental note to do a test at home. The image of a little tester pot like the ones you picked up for a quid in DIY stores flashed into his head and made him smile. *Blood Red, Pantone Number 666. B Positive. Rhesus Negative. Haemoglobin.* Names buzzed through his brain as he walked and he thought he might just add a little clue to each of the rocks as to the nature of the 'paint' used.

Thinking about the blood types had reminded him of something he'd seen when he'd been scrolling through the Triennial website. He hadn't thought much about them at the time as none of them seemed a fit for the exhibits he had in mind, but he was sure he'd seen sculptures of blood types and pills on walls around the town. He couldn't remember the artist's name, but the blurb had said something about an analogy between the anatomy of the body and the anatomy of a town, or some such bollocks. Well, thank you very much, whatever-your-name-is, you just made my next installation even better.

By the time he reached the park, he'd decided to make a stencil of three different blood type symbols and spray-paint them onto the rocks. It tied another two exhibits together, three if you counted the link to William Harvey. He was ticking installations off the list nicely. Didn't want any of the artists to feel left out, did he?

He walked quickly through the park, which was still full of families enjoying the unusually summery summer. The cuboid rock was easy enough to spot where it had been placed in symmetry with hedges clipped to the same size and shape. He had to admit he did rather like it. It was going to stand out like a sore thumb when he'd finished with it. A very fucking sore thumb that had been hit several times with a hammer.

Continuing on his way, the killer walked down Castle Hill Avenue, noting that the police tape was still in place around the statues. He could see the giant seagull kiosk just up ahead, parked close to the Leas Cliff Hall, and he made a point of walking close behind so he could check out how secure it was. There was a simple padlock on the door.

He paused for a moment, looking along The Leas in the direction of Sandgate. Should he check out Bella Harp's home now while he was nearby? Or continue on his way down to Mermaid Beach to find the third rock? He hated indecision so, sticking to his original plan, he set off down the Zig Zag Path, imagining the whole thing painted red and smiling to himself at the thought.

From the bottom of the path by the amphitheatre it was a short walk to Mermaid Beach. The third rock was cleverly disguised among other huge rocks on the pebbly beach, but he spotted it easily, knowing exactly what he was looking for. Very nice, he admitted begrudgingly. Won't blend in quite so easily when I've finished with you though.

There were some kids screaming in the shallows nearby and their shrieks were already getting on his nerves, so he turned tail and headed back the way he'd come. Too many fucking people everywhere. *I need a beer*, he thought as he tramped back up the steep climb to The Leas. It was busy everywhere he looked, so he headed to the Balcony bar on the roof of the Leas Cliff Hall. He didn't like their prices, but the bar itself still seemed to be a pretty well-kept secret from the tourists.

He was feeling somewhat revived after two very expensive pints, and thinking about moving on, when a woman came and sat down at the table next to him. He glanced over at her and then did a double take, hoping his face wasn't giving away what he was thinking, because it was only Bella-bloody-Harp sitting there with a cocktail, looking as though she didn't have a care in the world. She must have felt his eyes on her because she looked over at him and smiled, lifting her glass as she did so. He nodded at her in return, wishing his glass wasn't empty. What were the chances? *Fuck me*, he thought. *This is too good to be true.*

He had another moment of indecision as he tried to decide what to do. Should he stay or should he go? The lyrics of the Clash song flashed into his head… *Should I stay or should I go now?/If I go, there will be trouble/And if I stay it will be double…* In for a penny, he decided.

'Can I buy you another?' he said to the reporter, holding up his own empty glass.

'Um… I'm waiting for someone actually, but thanks all the same,' she said, smiling at him. She was pretty. Much prettier in real life than on screen, he thought.

'Another time, perhaps?'

'Perhaps,' Bella said.

Deciding to hang around – he might be able to follow her home later – he bought himself another pint and settled into a deckchair overlooking the sea. Lady Luck was smiling down on him again and there were definitely worse ways to spend an evening. The sky was clear all the way to France and he could make out the coastline of Calais quite clearly. He wondered how long it would be before the Coastguard helicopter would be out again, called to rescue yet another dinghy full of desperate immigrants. But it wasn't a helicopter that flew over, it was a Spitfire, which was a regular sight in the skies over Folkestone in the summer months. You couldn't mistake that sound, he thought, as he watched it do a victory roll over the Channel. Someone with too much money. He knew those flights cost three or four grand.

Out of the corner of his eye he saw Bella looking at her mobile and watched as she tapped out a message, before putting her phone away with a sigh. She lifted her glass to her lips and drank the remaining liquid before pushing back her chair and standing to leave. Whoever had been joining her had obviously had to cancel. Happy days. Hopefully she would be going straight home.

She smiled at him as she turned to leave. He nodded and waited until she'd left the terrace before downing the final couple of inches of his lager and following. She turned left as she exited the terrace, definitely going in the direction he believed she lived in. He still couldn't believe his luck. Maybe he should buy a lottery ticket. He kept his distance. He wasn't worried about losing sight of her. He was pretty sure she was headed to Clifton Mews.

The killer was spot on with Bella's home address and he watched her letting herself in to a building that he knew quite well – he'd done work there a few years ago. Bloody nice apartments they were. Not cheap either. Bella Harp was obviously doing all right for herself. Soon put a stop to that. The only problem was this wasn't somewhere he could gain easy access to and there was way too much risk involved in trying to grab her here. He wasn't worried. Now he had confirmation of where she lived, he could easily pick up her trail again. Might even 'bump into' her and invite her for that drink after all.

What he needed now though was a good night's sleep, so he made his way back to his car and headed home. He was supposed to be starting a rewiring job the next day, but he'd already decided to delay by a couple of days so he could focus all his attention on Bella. After all, it's important to get that work-death balance right. All work and no play makes for a very dull boy.

He dreamed of Bella that night. They were sitting on a blood-red rock on Mermaid beach, drinking. He had a pint and she had a cocktail with an umbrella in it. Sex on the beach, he decided. Well, if you insist, he grinned as he forced her down on the shingle. There were no shrieking kids in his dream. Well, it was a dream for him. Turned into a bit of a nightmare for his companion when he started shoving pages torn out of a dictionary down her throat. Swallow, you bitch. Eat your fucking words. He laughed as she choked and thrashed, but he was too strong for her, straddling her and pinning her arms above her head with one hand while the other kept on ramming screwed up pages in her mouth.

The dream was still vivid when he woke, reluctantly, the next morning. He yawned and stretched, wishing he could've enjoyed the dream a little longer. Mind you, there's only so much fun to be had with a corpse. Before making coffee he rang the project manager of the site he was meant to be working at and informed him he'd be starting in a couple of days. He assured them he'd still meet his deadline and rang off.

After breakfast and a shower, he checked his watch. It was just gone eight. He wondered what time the delectable Bella left for work. Deciding it was worth a punt, he threw on jeans and a T-shirt and jumped in his van. He had no problem parking this time of day; plenty of people had already left for work and the visitors hadn't started arriving yet. He found a space from where he could watch Bella's front door and settled down to wait. While he watched and waited, he wondered some more about ways of killing her. The trouble was, it all depended on where he was able to pick her up. It might have to be quick and clean.

It was after about an hour that he spotted movement in his rearview mirror. It was a woman jogging. She seemed to be slowing down and, as he watched, she jogged over to a bench and began stretching. Yep, you guessed it, it was only Bella-bloody-Harp. *Fuck me*, he thought, not for the first time. *I'm definitely buying that lottery ticket*. He would put money on it that she jogged most mornings and that she had a regular route. He fucking hated running, but he'd make an exception for Bella if he had to.

It was another hour before Bella came back out, obviously dressed for work. It was getting on for ten-thirty when he checked the time. All right for some, eh? Bloody part-timer. She walked a short distance to a mint-green Fiat 500 convertible and she proceeded to put the roof down, and sunglasses on, before setting off. It was the easiest thing in the world to follow her in his anonymous white van. When he realised she was heading onto the M20 motorway he hesitated, wondering where she was going. Sod it, nothing else to do today, he decided, indicating and joining the dual carriageway. She drove on past Ashford and kept going until it became apparent that she wasn't going to work at all. She was going to Bluewater Shopping Centre near Dartford.

'For fuck's sake!' he exclaimed, banging the steering wheel with the heel of his hand. He liked Bella, but not enough to spend hours trawling round a fucking shopping centre. Feeling frustrated, he headed for home. Maybe he'd go and do a few hours' work after all. And think about what the fuck he was going to wear to go jogging the following morning.

CHAPTER 31

Food for thought

The following morning saw him back at Bella's building at seven a.m. He hoped he wouldn't have to wait too long for her to appear. If indeed she did appear. He was counting on her being a creature of habit. If not, it was back to the drawing board. Still, he'd bought himself a bit of time by starting the wiring job yesterday. And, to be honest, he wasn't thrilled at the prospect of jogging. He'd found an old pair of shorts he'd not worn for about a decade, and teamed them with a plain white tee. His trainers weren't proper running ones, but they'd do the job. Besides, he didn't plan to make a habit of this.

It was about twenty past seven when the front door opened and Bella came out, wearing much more current and infinitely more stylish running gear. Her trainers probably cost ten times more than his. He watched her walk over to what was obviously her regular stretching bench and go through some warm-up exercises. He'd never done warm-up exercises in his life and he wasn't about to start now, so he waited until she'd set off and was a hundred yards or so up The Leas from him before getting out of the van and following. He hadn't thought this through properly and briefly wondered what runners did with things like phones and car keys. He left his phone in the car in the end and tried jogging with his keys in his shorts pocket, but it was hopeless so he ended up with them in his hand.

Bella was running effortlessly ahead. The killer was not enjoying himself. Did people really do this for fun? He tried to think of it in terms of stalking his prey, but even that didn't help much. Bella had taken a path down the cliff to the Coastal Park and he paused when he reached the top. *What goes down must come up*, he was thinking. *Sod this for a game of soldiers.*

'Change of plan,' he said to himself as he turned back the way he'd come and went and sat down on Bella's bench. There was hardly anyone about this early in the day and he was seriously wondering if he could actually grab her before she went back in her house. Could he get her to the van and bundle her in without anyone seeing or would he be taking a crazy risk? He'd have to restrain her and shut her up. He trotted over to his van and opened up the back.

It was about thirty minutes later when he saw the reporter heading back to the bench to stretch. He pulled his cap down over his eyes a bit and stood looking around as though he'd lost something. As Bella made her way back to her front door he called out to her.

'Excuse me… Miss…'

She looked over.

He called again. 'I don't s'pose you've seen a dog on the loose?' He didn't speak overly loudly and it had the desired effect.

'Sorry, what?' Bella said, making her way over to him.

'My dog? You haven't seen a black Labrador?' As he spoke he looked all around. There was no one in sight. He held out his mobile. 'Here, I've got a photo of him…'

As soon as she was close enough, and her attention on his phone, he grabbed her, one arm round her body, the other over her mouth. She was in the back of the van with him before you could say 'Ford Cortina'. She was strong. He'd underestimated how strong, and it took every ounce of his strength to subdue her. He smacked her head down hard on one of his tool chests a couple of times and that seemed to stun her enough for him to shove an old rag in her mouth and bind her hands and feet with electrical cable. He was in the driver's seat and pulling away seconds later, heart pounding and head rushing with adrenaline.

'Yesss! Fuck! Yesss!' he slammed the heels of both hands on the steering wheel. He couldn't believe what he'd just done. The only trouble was he didn't know quite what to do next. Could he get her back to his place and inside without anyone seeing?

Pulling up a few minutes later, he reversed the van up to the garage, figuring the best bet was to open both back doors and get her straight into the garage. Once she was safely inside and secured, he'd work out what to do next.

With Bella safely tied to a chair and gagged in the garage, he went into the house. He chugged down a cold beer from the fridge and tried to think. This was all happening rather faster than he would ideally have liked. It was a hell of a rush though and he felt more alive, higher, than he could ever remember. He sat on a bench in the back garden and tried to formulate a plan. He knew what the final exhibit would look like, but it was the time between now and then that he had no clue about. What the hell was he going to do with her?

After a second beer he went into the garage and set a chair opposite Bella. He could see the terror in her eyes. It made him feel powerful. She was trying to speak through the gag, but all he heard was an annoying series of muffled grunts.

'Shut up,' he said, leaning towards her. 'Shut. The fuck. Up.'

Bella did as instructed, the look of terror increasing.

'That's better. Much better. If you'd shut up a bit sooner you wouldn't be sitting here now.'

Bella just stared at him and kept quiet. Silent tears rolled down her cheeks and dripped off her chin.

'Calling me a copycat and "mark two" is what got you into this mess. Should learn to keep your trap shut. Except, of course, you won't have the opportunity now, will you?' he grinned. 'No more lessons for Bella.'

A faint whiff of something hit his nostrils.

'You dirty bitch,' he said, looking down at the damp patch spreading across her lap.

Bella sobbed though the gag, unable to hold back the sheer terror.

'Well, I guess my dream won't be coming true now,' he said, more to himself than to her. 'Soiled goods now, aren't you? And I have to clean up your mess.'

He sat back in his chair and just watched her. He still couldn't decide what to do with her. Had to get it done tonight though. Couldn't risk anyone hearing her. What if she toppled her chair or got loose? No, he had to do it tonight. A thought flashed into his head of lying her down on the Pulhamite bench and slashing her so that her blood painted the rock for him. A sort of sacrificial altar. As much as he liked the idea, he'd definitely made up his mind about the seagull 'eating' her. Besides, getting her to the bench unseen was fraught with risk and difficulty. Better to stick with Plan A.

Realising he was starving hungry, the killer left Bella to go in search of food. 'Don't go anywhere,' he said as he left the garage, locking the door behind him.

He'd think more clearly on a full stomach.

He threw some rashers of bacon under the grill and put some bread in the toaster and was soon demolishing bacon sandwiches with plenty of HP Sauce and scrolling idly through his phone for inspiration. There were quotes for everything on the internet and he flicked through a whole load of them about the power of words to hurt. He stopped on one which was supposedly from Proverbs 18:21: *Words kill, words give life; they're either poison or fruit – you choose.* He googled the actual verse, which was: *The tongue has the power of life and death and those who love it will eat its fruit.*

Hmm… definitely food for thought. Not as tasty as bacon, but still, it had given him another idea.

After he'd eaten he made a coffee, which he took back into the garage.

'I thought we'd have a bit of a chat,' he told Bella. He thought he could actually smell her fear. Maybe he should've waited until she'd had a shower after her run before grabbing her. 'Obviously going to be a bit of a one-sided conversation,' he said, shrugging with his face before taking a mouthful of coffee. 'Sorry, how rude of me, you must be thirsty.'

Bella nodded and more tears squeezed their way out of her eyes.

'Oh well, not for much longer, eh? So, anyway, what shall we talk about? How about the fact that you were not very flattering about me in your reports?'

Bella struggled against her bonds and tried to speak, shaking her head.

He put up his hands. 'No, no, it's too late to apologise now, the damage is done. People think I'm second best thanks to you, so you've really left me no choice, have you? No one to blame but yourself, Ms. Bella Harp. Signed your own death warrant, didn't you? I'm just the executioner. Just can't make up my mind how to do it. The killing bit, that is.' He ignored her gasping and struggling and carried on the monologue. 'It's a shame, really, 'cause you could've been an ally. And you're pretty fit, too. And I don't just mean from all that running. Do you recognise me from the bar? We could've had a couple of drinks together, made a night of it. Would've been nice. Finish up with a bit of erotic asphyxiation – not a bad way to go, eh? Instead of which, you're tied up in my garage, stinking of piss and waiting to die.'

He ignored the sobs coming from the young woman.

'You shouldn't have called me "mark two" like that. You don't know the first thing about me. Think I'm just some cheap imitation of the infamous Exhibitionist? If only you knew. I'm the original. And the best. But you won't be around to realise that now, will you? You've fucked it right up. They'll have to find some other bimbo to report on my exhibits. Let's hope she doesn't make the same mistakes as you, eh?' He paused for a few moments. 'Maybe I should have made it clearer who I was right from the start. Signed my pieces like that traitorous shit Seymour did. Shame he topped himself though. I'd have liked to have taken him out myself. Chickenshit probably knew I'd be gunning for him and took the easy way out. What do you think I should call myself then? The Master maybe? The Grand Master? Nah, that sounds like chess, doesn't it?'

He was interrupted by a low buzzing noise. It seemed to be coming from somewhere on the reporter's person. Her eyes grew wider than ever and she flinched as he approached her. He found the iPhone in a pocket in her leggings. He pulled it out and looked at the screen. It was a text message from someone called Jenny asking if they were still on for lunch.

'Fuck,' he exclaimed, smashing the phone to the concrete floor and stamping on it for good measure. He was angry with himself for not searching her in the van. Would they be able to track her mobile to his street? To his house? Fuck. What a fucking mess. He sat back down on the chair and put his head in his hands. 'Stupid, stupid, idiot,' he muttered. He should have replied to this 'Jenny' that lunch was off instead of smashing the phone like that. *Can't be helped now*, he thought. *Just got to deal with it*.

Taking a deep, steadying breath, the killer tried to get his thoughts in order. He knew what he had to do.

Taking a piece of cable from a reel on his workbench, he went behind Bella and looped it over her head. She thrashed as he tightened the wire and cut off her air supply. It was over quickly. He cut her ties and laid her down on a tarpaulin. No time to lose now. Wrapping her in the tarp, he tossed her back into his van, pushing the body right up behind the seats, as far from prying eyes as possible. He then shoved a load of tools, reels of cable and other work stuff in front of it. Locking the van, he then removed any trace of Bella from the garage, stuffing the broken phone, ties and gag into a bag, which also went into the van to be dealt with later. He cleaned the chair and the floor where Bella had been seated and looked around the garage, nodding to himself.

Feeling a little calmer, the killer changed into work clothes and drove to the site. If the supervisor was surprised to see him, he didn't say anything. It was the best alibi the killer could come up with. He would say he'd arrived earlier if the police asked. He doubted anybody would remember the exact time he'd arrived if they were asked. If only he'd found that fucking phone before taking the reporter back to his house. Rookie error. He was angry with himself and found it hard to focus on the job at hand. He kept thinking of the body in his van, waiting to be dealt with later that night. Thankfully, he was working alone and able to avoid any of the banter that normally went on on a job like this.

He worked through lunch and on past four p.m. when the other trades clocked off, rejecting calls to go for a beer. 'Another time,' he said. 'Just want to get this room finished.'

He finally stopped at six, realising he was tired and hungry, his back hurting and his head pounding. He blamed the reporter for the way he was feeling and wished he'd had more time with her and hadn't had to rush her death. He hated feeling out of control and, for the first time, was genuinely worried about being found out. He knew she would have been missed by now and possibly reported missing, although he was pretty sure the police wouldn't do anything for at least twenty-four hours. He couldn't guarantee that though, not when there was a serial killer on the loose. He wanted to remain on the loose too; he wasn't ready to stop yet. And he wasn't prepared to compromise any more. He *would* complete this latest exhibit. But he had some time to kill before he could do so, and he was reluctant to go home. He knew he couldn't put it off forever and that it was entirely possible the police might come calling if they tracked the reporter's phone and, for once in his life, he was at a loss.

CHAPTER 32

No show

Amy's phone rang just as she sat down at her desk to continue writing. For once the words were flowing and she hated anything that interrupted that flow. Glancing at her phone, she saw it was Jenny. Wondering briefly if she could ignore it, Amy sighed and answered. Jenny was the one person she could not afford to ignore.

'Yo. Wassup?' she said.

'Hello. Well, nothing, hopefully. It's just I was meant to meet Bella for lunch and she didn't show up. No missed call or message to cancel and now she's not answering her phone.'

'Reporter Bella? The one I met at the radio station?'

'Yes. I'm worried.'

'Okay, well I'm sure there's a perfectly innocent explanation. What time were you meant to meet her?'

'Half twelve. It's gone two now.'

'Still, probably too soon to panic. There may have been an emergency, or something came up at work. She might not have had a chance to call you.'

'I'm sure you're right, but…'

'Yeah, I know, but…' Amy sighed. She could feel the muse slipping away.

'I don't know what to do. Can you come?' Jenny pleaded down the phone.

Closing her eyes for a moment, Amy took a deep breath and heard herself saying, 'Yes, of course.'

Twenty minutes later and she was at Jenny's, trying to reassure her friend and come up with a plan of action.

'Let's start by trying her phone again,' Amy said.

No answer. The message they got said that the number was not currently in service. This didn't help Jenny calm down any.

'Okay, does she have a home phone?' Amy asked next.

'No. At least I don't think so. I've never noticed a landline at her flat,' Jenny responded.

'So you know where she lives?'

'Yes. Should we go round there? You don't think she's fallen over or something, do you?'

Amy shrugged. 'Well, it's a possibility. Let's not jump to conclusions though. I still think there'll be an innocent explanation. What about work? Let's try phoning the studios. Do you know where she was working today?'

'Um... I think she's mainly working from home at the moment, when she's not actually reporting from the scene of something.'

'Well, it's worth a try – they might have heard from her. It may be that she's simply been called away to report live from somewhere, mightn't it?'

'Oh God! Maybe they found another body? We should put the local news on.' Jenny scrambled for the remote and turned on the TV. The two of them sat in silence as they waited for the local news to come on. When it did, there was nothing about the killer having struck again.

Jenny heaved a sigh of relief. 'Well, that's something at least, but where could she be?'

'Let's call the radio and TV stations,' Amy suggested.

A few minutes later and they were no more enlightened. Neither studio had heard from Bella.

'What now?' Jenny asked, pressing her fingers into her temples.

'Now we go round to her flat.'

'And if she's not there?'

'Then I don't know,' Amy admitted.

'Try the hospitals?' Jenny looked worried.

'Or the police?'

'Yes, or the police,' Jenny agreed. 'Oh God, Amy, what if something awful's happened?'

'Try not to think the worst,' Amy soothed. 'Come on, let's go round to her flat.'

They arrived at Bella's building a few minutes later and there was no answer when they rang her bell. Amy tried the other doorbells and waited for someone to answer.

'Hello,' a voice said.

'Oh, hello, um, I'm looking for Bella, Bella Harp – she lives at number four.'

'Yes, I know Bella. I presume you've tried her bell?' the female voice continued.

'Yes, no answer. She's not answering her mobile either and we're just a bit worried in case something's happened to her,' Amy explained.

'You'd better come in, dear. Number three,' the woman said and the door buzzed.

Amy and Jenny were greeted by an elderly lady wearing a lilac twinset that matched her hair, standing in the doorway of number three when they reached the top of the flight of stairs. She pointed to the door opposite. 'I've tried knocking, no answer I'm afraid. Do come in,' she said, turning and leading the way into a sunny lounge, which overlooked The Leas.

'Um… thank you,' Amy said. 'So, have you seen Bella today?'

'Yes, dear, she went out for her run as usual this morning. I heard her door.' She frowned. 'I don't remember hearing her come home, but my hearing's not what it used to be, and if I have the radio on, I sometimes don't even hear my own bell.'

'Did you have the radio on this morning?' Jenny asked. She was decidedly agitated now.

'Er… let me think… yes, I believe I did.'

'Well, did you or didn't you?' Jenny pushed impatiently.

Amy put her hand on her friend's arm and apologised to the older woman. 'Sorry, we're just very worried in case something's happened to Bella.'

'Well, I'm not sure I can be of any more help, dear. Unless, well, I do have a spare key for Bella's apartment… We could check…'

'Why didn't you say so sooner?' Jenny exclaimed. 'Let's go. Now! She could've slipped in the shower or something!'

Amy mouthed a silent apology to the neighbour and waited for her to produce a key from a hook in the kitchen. They let themselves into number four and found everything in order and no sign of Bella. They were none the wiser and didn't know what to do next. Thanking the neighbour, Amy returned the key and she and Jenny left.

'Bloody hell! Where is she?' Jenny said. She sounded scared and upset now. 'I've got a really bad feeling about this, Amy.'

'Look, the neighbour heard her leave this morning – her usual time to go jogging, by all accounts. Maybe she slipped or something, banged her head or, I don't know, found a lost dog and is trying to find its owner.'

Jenny just shook her head.

'Come on, Jenny, it's unlikely anything really bad happened to her in broad daylight. Do you know where she goes running? We could check her route.'

'Only roughly,' Jenny said.

'Well, it's got to be worth a try, don't you think?' Amy said, smiling encouragingly at her worried friend.

'Yeah, I s'pose so. If she banged her head, she might be unconscious or have amnesia or something.'

The friends set off walking along The Leas.

'I know she runs towards Sandgate and cuts down to the Coastal Park at some point,' Jenny said as they walked. 'I'm not sure exactly which path she takes though.'

'Okay, well, let's think like runners,' Amy said, pulling a face that suggested this might be beyond her. 'If you were a runner, which way would you go?'

'Well, I'd avoid the steps. Take the most gentle slope, I s'pose,' Jenny said.

'Well, let's do that then. If we don't find her, we can always come back up a different way.'

They continued on in silence, turning left when they reached the path that sloped most gently down to the sea. They passed plenty of people, but there was no sign of Bella.

'Someone would've found her by now. If she was anywhere to be found, that is,' Jenny said.

'Well, I don't know what else to suggest,' Amy shrugged. 'Let's complete the loop anyway. We can ask people if they've seen her.'

'That's a good idea. Why didn't I think of that?' Jenny said, pulling out her mobile to find a photo of her friend. 'Here's one. I'll WhatsApp it to you.'

Amy heard the wobble in Jenny's voice. She reached her arm around her shoulder. 'We'll find her, Jenny, I'm sure of it.' Inside though, Amy was feeling less and less sure of her own words as the day wore on. It was now nearly five o'clock and there was still no sign of the missing woman.

By the time they were back at Bella's building, both women were feeling hot and tired and decidedly worried. They sat on a bench to get their breath back. Unbeknownst to them, it was Bella's stretching bench.

'What now?' Jenny asked.

'I'll ring the hospitals with A&E departments.'

After several aborted attempts to get an answer from the hospitals, Amy finally managed to check all the possible places Bella could have been taken if she'd had an accident. There was no sign of her, or anyone matching her description.

'Police?' Jenny asked. 'Do we have to wait twenty-four hours to report her missing?'

'No, I don't think so, but I'm not sure how much notice they take for the first twenty-four to forty-eight hours. I think most people turn up within that time.'

'Well, I can't wait that long. Can we just go to the police station now?'

Amy sighed. 'Yep, let's go.'

They walked back to Amy's car and set off on the short drive to the police station.

'Not gonna lie, Jenny, I'm feeling pretty anxious about going into the police station and voluntarily putting myself on their radar,' Amy said as she parked the car.

Jenny was already opening her door. 'What? God, Amy, I can't do this on my own. Just come on.'

'Oh Christ,' Amy muttered, but she undid her seatbelt and got out all the same and followed Jenny up a flight of steps and into the ugly concrete building. There was a uniformed policewoman on the front desk, who looked up and smiled as they approached her.

Amy took a deep breath just as Jenny began to speak. 'Hello, we'd like to report a missing person please.'

CHAPTER 33
Time to kill

The killer had time to kill. He drove around for a while, wondering what to do to pass the hours until he could dump the body. After a while, he went to the drive-through McDonald's on Park Farm and then headed down to the seafront to eat his Big Tasty with Bacon Meal. It wasn't as tasty as it should have been though as the retard who'd assembled it had forgotten to put the bacon in. He cursed them under his breath but ate it anyway.

By the time he'd finished eating, it was still early, and sunset was a couple of hours away. He couldn't just sit here and do nothing, but he was anxious about going home just in case the police were already looking for Bella.

'Oh fuck! The blood!' He'd suddenly remembered the container full of blood, defrosted and waiting to be employed as paint. He started the engine and drove home, carefully obeying the speed limit and trying to stay calm. He hated how all this was making him feel. He was usually so in control. It felt like he was spiralling.

All was quiet in his road when he arrived home. He hurried into the garage and removed the blood, grabbing the paint tins and brushes too. This could be the only chance he had to paint the Pulhamite rocks. For the first time since he'd begun his summer exhibition he was feeling panic that he might actually get caught. He was angry with himself for not finding the phone, but taking over from that emotion now was fear, fear of the police catching up with him before he was ready. If he got caught, he wanted it to be on his terms. He wouldn't mind too much then – he could revel in the fame, the admiration. He'd be a celebrity. They'd make a movie about him. A documentary. What a legacy! But it had to be on his terms. He had to prove he was smarter than the police. That was the only acceptable way this ended.

Just got to get through tonight, he told himself. *Then I can collect my thoughts and work out a plan.*

Just as he was getting into the van to leave once more, he was struck by another thought. Locking the van, he went into the house and to his computer. Opening a Word document, he typed out the words: MARK TWO and COPYCAT in a large font and hit 'print'. He was careful not to get any fingerprints on the page when he collected it from the printer tray. As an afterthought, he grabbed some more paper and a marker pen, along with the ancient Scrabble set he'd inherited from his mum. He was wondering about signing this piece. He needed his public to know that he was number one.

Still with time on his hands, the killer drove to a local beauty spot on the cliffs over Dover and parked his van facing the sea. There were always cars parked there as people took in the view or watched the cross-Channel ferries through a pair of binoculars. Nobody would bat an eyelid at his anonymous white van. And if they did, it wouldn't hurt to have been seen in a different town, a good few miles from the scene of the crime. Well, impending crime.

He had mixed feelings as he watched the ferries coming and going. He'd worked on them when he was younger and had a jumbled assortment of memories associated with that time. It seemed like another life now, looking back. They'd worked week on, week off and the weeks spent on board had been pretty boring. Once your shift was over there wasn't a hell of a lot to do besides read, watch rubbish TV or chat with your mates. He'd had a couple of good friends back then. He'd lost touch with Andy when he left the job but he and Bob had stayed friends for years afterwards. They'd had a shared interest that had bonded them, for life, he'd thought, but you can be wrong about people, can't you? Well, he'd have the last laugh, the last word. That reminded him.

Pulling on a pair of thin rubber gloves, he reached over for the Scrabble box and took out the bag of letters. It took a while to shuffle through them to find the ones he wanted. He needed a second M and was starting to wonder if there was only one and he'd have to improvise with an upside-down W. He hated improvising. This whole bloody exhibit was proving to be a huge pain in the arse. He'd be glad when it was over and he hated that he wasn't getting the usual thrill from it. The planning was usually half the fun: the thought that went into it, the attention to detail. This was just rushed and sloppy. That wasn't how he liked to work.

Eventually he found all the letter tiles and set about cleaning each one using wipes he always had in his glove box. It was actually quite soothing working slowly and methodically and he started to feel a little calmer about things. After that he wiped the actual game-playing board over to remove any DNA or fingerprints from that too. Then he sat back in his seat and closed his eyes, letting his thoughts drift out to sea with the ferry just leaving Dover.

He must have fallen asleep because when he woke up it was getting dark. The sun had set and the other cars had all left. He stretched his back as he stifled a yawn. He'd been dreaming about his P&O days – a remembered conversation with Bob – but he couldn't quite retrieve it now. He shrugged. He had other, and certainly better, things to focus on now.

Deciding this was as good a place as any to prepare Bella for her grand opening he got out and went round to the back of the van and climbed in.

'Hello, gorgeous,' he said. 'Sorry to have kept you waiting so long. It'll be worth it, promise. You'll soon be the leading story on the news. Other side of the camera of course, but still the starring role. No, no need to thank me. You're most welcome. Just got a little bit of preparation to do before you make your appearance. Just think of it as hair and makeup.'

As he talked, he was pulling Bella's tarpaulin-wrapped body by the feet so that she lay lengthways down the centre of the van. Straddling her body, he peeled back the tarp from her head.

'Well, this isn't quite as sexy as I'd imagined it would be, Bella. Not so bellissima now, are we? Shame really. We could have had some fun. Different time, different place,' he shrugged. 'Now, how the fuck do you cut out a tongue?' he asked her as he tipped her head back, forced his fingers into her mouth and tried to get hold of hers. It wasn't as easy as expected, but he eventually managed to get a grip on it long enough to saw it off with his trusty Stanley knife. He didn't remove it from her mouth, instead shoving it as far into her throat as it would go. Next he took the words he'd printed earlier, screwed up the piece of paper and shoved that into the gaping wound of a mouth.

'Well, I think you're nearly ready for your close-up, Bella Bellissima. What's that? Speak up. Cat got your tongue? Ooh, I missed a trick there, didn't I?' he laughed to himself. He was once more enjoying the process of making his art.

Wrapping the tarp back over her face, he climbed out of the van and checked the time. Nine p.m. He was hungry again. Starting the engine, he drove slowly down the winding road towards the castle and then took the road to Whitfield and the KFC there. Ignoring the drive-through, he parked up and went in, figuring it wouldn't do any harm to be seen miles from Folkestone again. He was soon tucking into a three-piece meal, fries and beans, washed down by a Pepsi Max. He hated diet cola. Why did every fucker drink diet cola now? He took his time eating and then went back for a chocolate muffin, making a point of smiling at the young woman who served him. 'Thanks, love,' he said as he turned back to his table.

It was almost ten when he left the fast-food restaurant. Still too early. For fuck's sake. He had to admit he was sick and tired of hanging around now. He sat in the car park for a few minutes, wondering what to do.

Five minutes later and he was on the A2 heading towards Canterbury. He figured there must be cameras somewhere that would pick up his van. He drove the fifteen-or-so miles into the city and parked up at a pub called The Old City Bar, which he'd watched footie at a few times in the past. He'd have a pint and maybe chat the barmaid up a bit, make sure she remembered him. Kill some more time.

He made sure he was still there at closing time and made a point of telling the young woman who'd served him that he'd see her again. He didn't mention the fact that the circumstances might not be quite so warm and friendly next time. She'd make a nice corpse.

Leaving Canterbury, he pointed the van in the direction of Thanet and took a slow drive to Margate. The seaside town was still buzzing when he arrived at eleven-forty p.m. He wondered idly if he might have his next exhibition there. The Turner Contemporary had brought a bit of culture to the town. Maybe he could take it to the next level. *Food for thought*, he nodded to himself as he watched a group of girls wearing next to nothing crossing the road ahead of him, giggling and unsteady on their feet. He shook his head, grateful he wasn't one of their fathers. He pulled up alongside them and opened the window.

'You be careful tonight, girls,' he said. 'Stick together – there are plenty of perverts out there preying on young girls like you. Take care, get home safe, eh?' The girls just giggled all the more and he closed his window and drove on. Silly little cows think they're invincible.

He drove on down Marine Drive and onto Canterbury Road, past the flashing lights of the Flamingo Amusement Arcade he remembered from day trips to Margate with his mates from school. Back then, when Folkestone still had its own share of seafront amusements and nightclubs, Margate had seemed to them like their hometown on steroids. Margate's Dreamland made Folkestone's Rotunda seem small and kind of pathetic. He wondered idly why Margate had retained the tacky British seaside resort feel while Folkestone had taken a wrecking ball to it. He shrugged. He didn't much care. The gentrification had brought money to the town and Londoners who wanted their cheap-as-chips houses rewired or updated. He didn't feel much gratitude to his parents, but at least he owned his house thanks to them dying young. He probably couldn't afford to buy property in the town now.

As much as he was enjoying the trip down memory lane, the killer was getting tired, so he set off on the journey home, careful to take the back roads between Canterbury and Folkestone.

It was gone one a.m. when he arrived back in Folkestone. All he wanted to do now was dump Bella's body and crawl into bed. There was no way he was going to paint the rocks tonight. He was knackered, too knackered to worry about the police coming and knocking on his door.

He parked the van a short distance from where the seagull stood on The Leas and watched. There was no one in sight so he drove the van as close to the bird as he could get. It only took seconds to break the padlock with his bolt cutters and open the door. Back at the van, he checked all around again before hefting the body out. He held his breath until he was safely inside the cramped interior of the seagull, and dumped the body unceremoniously on the floor. One more trip to the van to fetch the Scrabble board. It was only by luck that he spotted the screwed up piece of paper on the ground by the back of the van.

'For fuck's sake,' he grumbled, picking up the paper which he'd thought was safely lodged in Bella's mouth. 'You're a royal pain in the arse. If you weren't already dead, I'd fucking kill you!'

Back inside the gull, he stuffed the paper back in Bella's mouth and set about composing the letters on the Scrabble board, using the torch on his phone to see what he was doing.

O R I G I N A L
U
M
B
M A E S T R O
R   N
E

He felt rushed and uncomfortable as he checked around him before climbing out and pushing the door closed, and he was glad to be back in his van and pulling away in the direction of home.

CHAPTER 34

No news is bad news

After they left the police station, Amy and Jenny were both feeling a little lost. The police had tried to reassure them that Bella would turn up soon, but the friends couldn't shake the nagging feeling that something was badly wrong. With nothing left to do but wait and hope, they went back to Jenny's house to feed the cats and have a much-needed cuppa.

'How long's it been now?' Jenny asked, taking a sip of the tea that had turned into gin.

'Six minutes since you last asked,' Amy said.

'Shall I try ringing her again?'

'I don't think there's any point, is there? You've left messages; I'm sure Bella will get back to you when she can.'

'If she can,' Jenny said glumly.

'Are you hungry?' Amy asked, trying to change the subject as much as anything.

'Dunno. Maybe. Not sure I could eat though. Feel sick.'

'Yeah, I know, me too.'

'Could maybe manage some biscuits,' Jenny relented after a while.

'Yeah, I could go for some biscuits,' Amy agreed.

Jenny trotted off to the kitchen and returned with the biscuit tin. It had cats on it.

'Chocolate Hobnob?' she said, holding out the tin to Amy.

'Don't mind if I do.'

They sat in relative silence, the only sounds the soft crunching of biscuits and one of the cats purring.

'We've eaten all the biscuits,' Jenny said a while later.

'Oh.'

'Yeah, oh.'

'Crisps?' Amy enquired, looking hopefully at her friend.

Jenny just shook her head.

'Bad times,' Amy said glumly.

Silence resumed once more. The cat hadn't got the memo and Amy stroked it absent-mindedly, increasing the volume of the purring. It was really quite soothing until she realised that the purring noise was actually coming from her stomach. And it was more of a rumbling.

'Will you be okay if I go home?' Amy asked. 'I can stay if you want.'

Jenny looked up, almost surprised to see Amy sitting there with her cat. 'What? Oh, sorry, I think I was elsewhere for a minute.'

'Somewhere nice hopefully?'

'Depends on your definition of nice. It was actually a very tacky disco I went to with Bella and Fay once. We had such a laugh.' Jenny smiled at the memory. 'It was so bad it was good, if you know what I mean.'

Amy nodded. 'I think I do. One of those discos that's like stepping into a 1970s time warp or something, all glitter balls and sequins.'

'Yes! That's exactly it! I'm very afraid I won't get the chance to go to another bad disco with Bella.'

'Don't say that,' Amy said. 'No news is good news.'

'Not in Bella's profession,' Jenny smiled sadly.

'Well, no, but good news in this case.'

'Hm… maybe. What were you saying before?'

'Just wondering if you want me to stay?' Amy said. 'I don't mind.'

'Um… no… I'll be okay.'

'If you're sure? Phone if you need me though, won't you? Any time.'

Jenny nodded.

They hugged on the doorstep and Amy turned to go. 'Remember… any time,' she called over her shoulder, but Jenny had already closed the front door. Amy really hoped she would be all right on her own. At least she had the cats. Amy suddenly felt sad at the prospect of going home to an empty house. Taking out her mobile she pinged a quick message to Willem and ten minutes later she was pulling up outside his house.

'Hello,' she said as he opened the door. 'Are you sure this is okay? I'm not interrupting?'

'No, no, of course not, it's lovely to see you. I was ready to stop for the day anyway. Come on in.'

'Thank you.' Amy followed Willem downstairs to the kitchen.

'Can I get you a drink?'

'I've already had a gin with Jenny and I'm driving, so better make it a soft drink.'

Soon they were sitting in Willem's lounge with glasses of elderflower cordial. Amy leant back with a sigh.

'That was a big sigh,' Willem said. 'What's up? Anything I can help with?'

'Probably not, but thank you. It's just been a bit of a day.'

'There seem to be a lot of them around at the moment,' Willem said.

'You're not kidding,' Amy agreed, sighing again.

'Please tell me it doesn't involve another body?'

'No, no body, not this time. Well, not exactly...'

Willem looked confused.

'One of Jenny's friends has gone missing. She was meant to meet her for lunch and she didn't show. She's not answering her phone and nobody's seen or heard from her since seven o'clock this morning.'

'Do you think there's cause for concern? She could just have forgotten and gone off for the day or something. There's probably a perfectly rational explanation.'

'I know, but, well, it's apparently very out of character for Bella to go off like this. And she's normally glued to her phone by all accounts – she's a reporter.'

'I take it you've informed the police?'

'Yes, we've done everything we can think of. Jenny's out of her mind with worry.'

'I can imagine. This on top of everything else she's gone through lately.'

'I feel bad for leaving her. I should probably have stayed.'

'She'll call you if she needs you, I'm sure,' Willem reassured. 'Are you hungry? Have you had any dinner?'

'My stomach keeps telling me I'm hungry. I had some biscuits at Jenny's.'

'You need some proper food. Let me cook you something,' Willem said, getting up and heading back into the kitchen.

'No, really, don't go to any trouble,' Amy began to object.

'It's no trouble, really. I have to eat too. It won't be anything fancy.'

'Thank you. Can I do anything?'

'Yes, you can come and keep me company while I cook.'

While Willem rustled up a stir-fry, Amy told him about the day she and Jenny had had.

'Of course, neither of us wanted to say what the other one was thinking... What if the killer's got her? It's just too awful to contemplate,' Amy said, resting her head in her hands. 'God, I feel knackered. And my head hurts. Sorry, I don't mean to whinge.'

'It's fine. Let it all out. I have broad shoulders.'

Amy looked up and smiled at him.

'Speaking of shoulders, I give a mean massage if you're ever in need of one,' Willem said, waving a fish slice over his shoulder.

'Um... thanks, I'll pass if it involves kitchen implements,' Amy laughed.

Willem laughed too. 'Your loss,' he said as he served up two steaming bowls of chicken, noodles and vegetables.

As they ate, Amy realising how hungry she was and making appreciative noises, Willem just smiled. He loved being in this woman's company and, perhaps even more, he loved the fact that she'd reached out to him in her hour of need. He hadn't felt needed for a long time. He liked how it felt.

After they'd eaten, Willem refusing Amy's offer to wash the dishes, they'd gone back to sit in the lounge.

'Do you want to watch something? Or listen to music?' Willem asked.

'Um... I'm not sure what I want, to be honest. Apart from to sleep for about a week. Preferably in a hammock on a tropical island,' Amy said, stifling yet another yawn.

Willem smiled. 'Hammocks aren't all they're cracked up to be, you know.'

'No? Well, I'd quite like to find out for myself anyway. Happy to switch the fantasy to a sun-lounger if need be.'

'Have you got any holidays planned?'

'Nope. Sadly not. Between dire finances and the lack of a travel companion…' Amy let the sentence hang.

'Well, I can help with one of those,' Willem said.

Amy felt her cheeks flush, knowing full well what he meant. 'Thank you kindly. Million pounds should do it,' she joked.

Sensing her slight discomfort, and cross with himself for being the cause of it, Willem didn't pursue the offer. It was way too soon to be offering to go on holiday with Amy, but he knew he'd hop on a plane with her at the drop of a sun hat.

The pair lapsed into silence, Willem watching Amy as her eyelids drooped and she fought the urge to let sleep claim her.

'Sorry, I'm being a rubbish guest,' she said eventually, sitting up and stretching her back. 'I think I need my bed.'

'Of course,' Willem said, trying not to let the regret show in his voice or on his face. He really hoped he hadn't scared Amy off by being too forward. 'Will you be okay getting home?'

'Mm hm,' Amy nodded, 'I'll be fine. It's not far. Thank you for feeding me and looking after me.'

'You're welcome, Amy, any time.'

He walked Amy out to her car and watched as she drove away. He'd forgotten to ask her to text him when she was safely home. Knowing he wouldn't be able to settle and not wanting to bother her again tonight, he went upstairs and stood at the back window. He waited and watched until he saw a light go on in her house before heading back downstairs to clear up and prepare the house for sleep.

CHAPTER 35

J.T.

When Amy woke the next morning after another fitful night, the first thing she did was check her phone for messages from Jenny. Nothing. She tapped out a quick WhatsApp before getting up and heading to the bathroom. As she washed her hands she studied her face in the mirror, not liking what she saw there very much. 'Getting old, girl,' she informed her reflection, touching the furrows between her brows and the lines beside her eyes.

Plodding to the kitchen to make her first coffee of the day, Amy vowed to take better care of herself: do more exercise, drink more water, eat less junk. She wasn't optimistic, but the thought was there and that was what counted. She scooped a heaped teaspoon of sugar into her mug, ignoring the voice in her head telling her sugar was bad for her. She'd cut down from two to one, but any more and she'd rather give up coffee. And that was never going to happen.

Taking her mug into the lounge, Amy thought about the day ahead. It was her turn in the shop and she wasn't really in the mood. Couldn't be helped though. Calling Gloria was an even worse prospect than coffee without sugar.

When her mobile alerted her to a message she assumed it would be Jenny and quickly opened the app.

'Bloody hell, the old witch is psychic,' she muttered when she saw the message was actually from Gloria.

Just to inform you an electrician will be in the gallery today, installing new sockets and lighting. Do be a dear and make him a coffee or two, won't you? G. Amy read the message aloud, imitating Gloria's voice. She followed it up with some pretty childish nose-wrinkling. 'It's not a fucking gallery, you pretentious old cow, it's a shop. And he can get his own fucking coffee,' she declared mutinously. Gloria really did bring out the worst in her. 'Unless he's fit,' she added as an afterthought. 'Then I might consider making him one.'

She sent a quick reply: *No problem, will do*, groaning about being a chicken as she hit 'send'.

With still no word from Jenny and time ticking on, Amy headed back to the bathroom for a shower. Twenty minutes later and she was dressed and thinking about breakfast. Finding nothing except the dusty end of a bag of granola, she scrapped the idea of eating. She'd pick something up later. Just before she left the house to walk to the shop, she sent another message to Jenny.

I'm in the shop today. Come and keep me company. Please!

The walk to the shop was an easy one and Amy let her thoughts drift. She was wondering about Bella and hoping she'd turned up. If only Jenny would answer her bloody messages, she might actually find out. It was as she was unlocking the shop that Jenny's reply pinged up.

What's it worth?

Million pounds. Willem's giving it to me, Amy chuckled.

I bet he is. Jenny sent back, followed by the vomiting emoji.

Don't be a dick. I'll buy breakfast/lunch/cake.

Yeah, OK. See you later.

Feeling a bit better about the day, Amy set about opening

up, turning on display lights, straightening cards in the racks and generally making the shop look its best. She was pleased to see that her books hadn't been relegated to the darkest depths of the shop again, although the copies in the window weren't looking their best and there was actually a dead fly hanging off the cover of one. Amy removed the offending bug and replaced the books with fresh copies. These sun-damaged and dog-eared ones would go to the Oxfam bookshop next time she was passing. They did pretty well out of Amy's display copies. She could only dream that one day she'd get a mainstream deal and her books really would be available in all good bookshops. She'd settle for even bad ones at this point in her writing career.

She'd just switched the sign in the window to 'open' and settled herself behind the desk when the door opened.

'Good morning,' Amy said brightly, assuming it to be a customer before she took in the dark blue overalls and cap, and the toolbox.

'Electrician.'

A man of few words, Amy thought. *Well, suited her just fine. She didn't really want to spend the day making small talk with some random man.* 'Oh, yes, Gloria said you'd be coming in,' Amy said, getting up and coming out from behind the desk. 'What do you need? Oh, will you have to turn the power off?' she asked, wondering how she was going to manage without electricity.

'Maybe. Not for long though. Should be able to isolate the circuits I need,' he said, in a low voice and an accent that identified him as most definitely local.

'Oh, okay, that's good.' At this point, Amy hadn't quite decided if he was attractive enough to warrant her coffee-making skills or not. He was an ordinary-looking sort of man, medium height and build, no real stand-out features or anything that would make him memorable. She guessed him to be around forty, but he could easily have been a few years either side. He had a sewn-on badge on the left breast of his overalls which read 'J T Electrical'. Amy wondered if they were his initials. He didn't look like a Justin or a Jordan. Maybe a John? She shrugged. 'Well, let me know if you need anything.'

'I won't,' came the reply. Jeff Teller wasn't happy about having to do this job today. He wanted to be at home, watching the news and waiting for them to find the body. It was only because fucking Gloria had called him asking for a favour that he was here at all.

Amy felt an involuntary shudder run down her spine at his curt response. She didn't say anything more, simply returned to her seat and pretended to look at her phone, willing Jenny to arrive soon.

The electrician disappeared into the storage area where the fuse box was. He seemed to know his way around the shop so Amy hoped he was right about not needing her for anything. He definitely gave her the creeps. An image of Robert flashed into her mind. That was who he reminded her of. She got the same vibe from this 'J.T.' that she'd got from Robert.

The shop was pretty quiet and Amy sat tensely in her seat, praying for customers, as the electrician worked quietly and efficiently. When Jenny finally arrived at about ten thirty, Amy heaved a sigh of relief, her face lighting up at the sight of her friend. Jenny's expression did not match hers. She looked close to tears in fact.

'Hey you. What's up?'

'They found another body.'

'Shit. Really? Whereabouts? Do they...?' Amy couldn't bring herself to ask if they knew the victim's identity. She didn't notice the electrician stop what he was doing to listen.

'They haven't released a name yet, but it's Bella. I just know it is.' Jenny stifled a sob.

'You don't know that. Don't assume the worst,' Amy tried to reassure, but she had the same feeling in her gut too. 'Where was the body found?'

'In that seagull – you know, the big mobile thing that's parked on The Leas at the moment,' Jenny said, wiping tears from her cheeks. She was about to say more when the door opened and in walked Gloria. She stopped in her tracks when she saw the scene in front of her.

'Well, if you two are trying to scare customers away, you're doing a fine job of it,' she said, hands on hips and head shaking. 'Is that any way to welcome people into the gallery? For heaven's sake.'

Amy bit back the urge to tell the older woman to fuck off, and it wasn't a gallery. 'There haven't been any customers to scare off,' she said instead.

Gloria huffed a bit and waved her hands to express her general dissatisfaction with the pair of them. 'Well, anyway, is Jeff here?'

Amy looked at her blankly.

'The electrician,' Gloria clarified.

'Oh, yes, he's over there,' Amy said, pointing.

Jenny, who had up until that point been wholly unaware of the man crouched in the corner of the shop, turned her gaze to him as he rose to greet Gloria. He didn't look especially pleased to see Gloria either but his glower turned to a small smile that most definitely didn't reach his eyes.

'Gloria,' he said, his eyes flicking to Jenny and a flash of recognition appearing in them. Their eyes met and held for a few moments and Jenny was frowning when Amy looked at her friend.

'Oh, Jeff, there you are. How are you getting on? I hope Amy made you coffee.'

'I didn't, he didn't…' Amy began to explain, but Gloria wasn't listening as she joined Jeff at the back of the shop and proceeded to check on his work so far. Once she was satisfied that Jeff's work was satisfactory and all proceeding according to plan, Gloria rejoined Amy and Jenny at the desk.

'I used to babysit for Jeff when he was little,' Gloria began, nodding at the electrician who was back to glowering once more. 'Our parents were friends, so of course I got asked to look after him when they went out for dinner together. I know, I know, you're probably thinking I don't look old enough to have babysat him…'

Amy raised her eyebrows, but said nothing as Gloria continued.

'He was such a sweet little boy. Do you remember, Jeff? Sometimes I used to bath you before bed, then read you a story.'

Amy glanced over at Jeff, who looked like he wanted to kill Gloria at this point. He said nothing, but Gloria needed no encouragement.

'Remember that book you always wanted me to read? What was it called? *Oi! Get Off Our Train*? Yes, that was it! You loved that book. Used to make me read it over and over again. You'd be all tucked up under your dinosaur duvet, with your thumb in your mouth. Still sucking your thumb when you started primary school, weren't you? Adorable.'

Amy snuck a look at Jeff and could see by the tension in his jaw and the clenched fists at his sides that he wasn't enjoying the trip down memory lane nearly as much as his former babysitter. There was something scarily sinister about the man, any trace of the adorable thumb-sucker long gone. But then, what grown man would enjoy being reminded of his baby days in front of two strangers? When she looked at Jenny, she found her friend studying a spot on the floor. She didn't look up.

Gloria was oblivious to the tension and carried on wittering on about her adventures in babysitting for a while longer. Eventually, Amy could stand it no longer.

'Well, we should probably let… um… Jeff get on with his work, shouldn't we? And I could do with a decent cup of coffee rather than that instant stuff we have round the back. Jenny? You up for a coffee run?'

Jenny finally looked up from the floor and nodded. She looked only too happy to have an excuse to get out of the shop and a couple of minutes later was on her way to the cafe just up the street. Jeff had actually declined the offer of a drink, saying he was nearly done anyway. Amy hoped he didn't see the sigh of relief that escaped her lips. Thankfully, Gloria had also declared herself far too busy to be standing around drinking coffee and had also left. Amy had half expected her to go and ruffle Jeff's hair before taking her leave and she was convinced it would have resulted in Gloria being stabbed through the eye with a screwdriver.

As much as Amy didn't relish the prospect of being alone in the shop with the surly electrician, she had told Jenny to take her time. She retreated behind the counter and willed customers to come in and browse, but the shop remained eerily quiet, bar Jeff working away unobtrusively in the corner.

Jenny still wasn't back after fifteen minutes and had texted Amy to apologise.

Sorry but that man gives me the creeps. Text me when he's gone.

So, Amy toughed it out on her own, saved only by the interruption of a sole customer who came in and bought one of Willem's lighthouse prints. Amy tried to engage the customer in conversation to get them to stay a little longer, but they made their excuses and left too. By the time Jeff tested the sockets and lights and declared himself finished, Amy had a tension headache pounding behind her eyes, no doubt made worse by the lack of caffeine.

She watched the electrician pack his tools away. He seemed calm again, but this was still somehow equally unnerving. He was almost too calm; there was a controlled fury going on behind the stony expression, which gave Amy the chills. She exhaled in relief when he finally closed the shop door behind him.

It's safe to come back. The psychopathic sparky has gone. Don't forget the coffee. Stonking headache.

Jenny was back in just a few minutes and Amy took the offered cappuccino gratefully, taking two big glugs of the froth before sighing with relief. 'Thank you, I needed that.'

'Sorry for abandoning you,' Jenny said sheepishly. 'I couldn't be around that man another minute. He seriously creeped me out.'

'You and me both, to be honest. I thought he was going to kill Gloria.'

'He still might,' Jenny said, raising her eyebrows.

Amy studied her friend's face to see if she was joking, but there was no trace of humour there. She cocked her head to one side and frowned. 'Nah. Don't be daft. He's just some lame electrician who didn't like being reminded of the days when the girl next door got to see him playing with his rubber ducky.'

Jenny shook her head. 'There was something about him. I feel like I've seen him before somewhere, but I can't put my finger on where.'

'You've probably just seen him around town if he's local – buying ready meals for one in Sainsbury's or something.'

'No, that's not it. Besides, when did you ever see me eat a ready meal?'

'Oh yeah, that's my sad single existence. Cat food then? Maybe he has a cat?'

Jenny simply shook her head again as she rooted around in her memory bank for sightings of the man.

For a while they sat quietly, drinking coffee and thinking their own thoughts. Amy's were mainly of Willem. She was pretty sure Jenny's were all far less pleasant.

CHAPTER 36

Big red rock

It wasn't until the next morning that the police released the name of the serial killer's latest victim. Jenny rang Amy in tears and Amy dropped everything and went round to try and comfort her friend. It had obviously rained overnight and Amy automatically thought that was good as the parched gardens really needed it. Then she mentally reprimanded herself; the gardens really didn't matter a shit in light of what was happening. She would sacrifice every flower and blade of grass for it not to be.

Jenny was still in her pyjamas and dressing gown when she opened the door, her pink hair dishevelled and her face blotchy as she dabbed at her puffy nose.

They went to the kitchen and Amy put the kettle on for tea, getting two mugs ready and retrieving the milk from the fridge. She wondered whether to put sugar in Jenny's mug. As if reading her mind, Jenny spoke through the snot: 'Don't do it.'

Amy couldn't help laughing. 'Okay, okay, no sugar. I'll have yours,' she said, spooning sugar from the jar into her mug.

Taking the two teas over to the kitchen table, Amy saw a photograph in front of Jenny. Picking it up, she saw it was of Jenny with two other women she recognised as Bella and the radio presenter, Fay. They were grinning and holding drinks, looking like three friends without a care in the world. Only now one of them was dead. Amy felt tears prick her own eyes.

She hadn't known Bella well, but it was still shocking and painful to think of what had happened. She reached over and squeezed Jenny's hand. 'I'm so sorry.'

Jenny nodded and fresh tears erupted from her eyes. Amy grabbed the box of tissues from the counter and passed them over.

'Thanks. I still can't believe it. Why Bella? She was the sweetest person; she'd never hurt anybody.'

'I know. I don't think it was personal though, do you? Just wrong place, wrong time?'

'It feels fucking personal!' Jenny exclaimed.

'Sorry, bad choice of words. I just meant… well… you know.'

Neither of them spoke for a while. Amy didn't know what to say and Jenny was clearly lost in thoughts of her friend.

'I wonder who's reporting on Bella's death?' Jenny said after a while. 'At least she could say she was the first reporter on the scene,' she smiled sadly. 'She really loved her job, you know. It was her life, really. Her parents were older and both died a few years ago. At least they're not around to witness this.'

'Does Bella have any other family? Brothers and sisters?'

'No, not really. She was an only child. I think she's got an aunt and uncle somewhere, and cousins, but no one she was close to as far as I know.'

Amy couldn't help wondering who would arrange Bella's funeral and take care of her flat, her possessions. It was sad to think there was nobody to tie up the loose ends of her life.

'Do you want to get some fresh air?' Amy asked after a while. 'Blow the cobwebs away?'

'Um… yeah… could do, I s'pose,' Jenny said with a sigh. 'I feel drained.'

'I know,' Amy said. 'Do you good though.'

'I don't have to have a shower first do I? I really can't be arsed.'

'No, you can be stinky. I just won't walk downwind of you.'

'Okay, I'll get dressed,' Jenny said with another sigh.

A few minutes later and the two of them were headed out, an unspoken agreement to avoid The Leas and surrounding area. They found themselves at the gate to Kingsnorth Gardens.

'Can you believe I've never actually been in here?' Amy said as they paused at the entrance.

'Really?' Jenny sounded surprised. 'It's lovely, a bit of a hidden gem – gets a bit busy but worth seeing. Do you want to go in?'

The park was still relatively quiet at ten in the morning and the overnight rain was still dripping off the trees and plants. The parched grass had soaked up the rain that had fallen on it and turned a darker yellow. They followed the path into the formal gardens and Amy exclaimed in delight. 'How have I never been here before? It's lovely.'

There were several cube-shaped topiary hedges lining the path ahead, with ornate ponds either side. The summer planting was bright and the gardens beautifully maintained. It was hard to imagine the horror that was happening elsewhere in the town, faced with such beauty.

They hadn't gone much further when a red stain appeared on the path ahead. The two friends looked at each other in confusion but walked on, looking for the source of the mark across an otherwise pristine walkway. They didn't have to go far.

In the place of one of the topiary cubes sat a large rock. It was the same size and shape as the hedges and it was painted bright red but the paint had obviously run due to the rain that had fallen overnight and the rock was now a patchy red.

'What the hell…?' Jenny began, looking in puzzlement at Amy. 'You know this is an art installation, right? The cube-shaped rock, I mean.'

Amy shook her head.

'There are several dotted around town – I forget how many – and they're made of Pulhamite like the Zig Zag path. One's a bench. Another is on Mermaid Beach I think.'

'I take it they're not normally painted red?'

Jenny shook her head. 'No. Definitely not. This is weird.'

'Kids? Vandals, d'you reckon?'

'Honestly, with what's going on, I don't know what to think, but I've got a bad feeling…' Leaving the sentence unfinished, Jenny crouched down by the red stain and proceeded to run her finger through it, lifting her finger to her nose and sniffing.

Amy grimaced. 'What?'

Jenny wiped her finger as best she could on the grass and got back to her feet. 'I don't know…' she wrinkled her nose. 'It smells like paint… but… Amy, I think it might be blood.'

'Oh God! Really? Jesus,' Amy pressed her fingers into her eyes.

Jenny proceeded to walk all the way around the rock, examining it from all angles. At one point she stopped and gestured for Amy to come and look.

'Does that say B+?' Amy said, squinting at some smudged lettering at the bottom of the rock.

'Yep, I think it does. B positive. It's a blood group.'

'It's my blood group. Christ.'

'Do you think we should phone the police?'

'I don't know. What if it is just paint and it's just kids muck-ing about with too much time on their hands?'

'And what if it isn't?'

'Bloody hell. Why us?' Amy groaned.

'Let's go and check out the other rocks and then decide,' Jenny said.

'That's quite a trek.' Amy didn't look thrilled at the prospect.

'Best we get going then.' The discovery seemed to have reinvigorated Jenny and she set off towards the exit at quite a pace.

Amy followed her, grumbling under her breath, and they didn't talk until they reached Mermaid Beach about twen-ty-five minutes later. Jenny had paused briefly at 'Argonaut' when they'd walked up Castle Hill Avenue, frowning as though she was trying to recall something, but she didn't say a word. When they arrived at the beach they didn't need to get close to the rock to see that something was definitely amiss. A small crowd of people was gathered around it and they could see the pebbles on the beach nearby were looking decidedly pink.

Jenny stomped over the pebbles and pushed her way to the front, examined the base of the rock and returned to where Amy was waiting on the path, before turning determinedly towards the town and setting off at a fast pace once more, beckoning Amy to follow.

'Well?' Amy asked, jogging to catch up.

'AB negative.'

'Shit. Not kids then?'

'No, not kids, Amy. The killer.'

They set off along the boardwalk on the beach, pausing

only when they reached 'Genuine Fake' and Jenny stopped and screwed up her eyes again. When Amy tried to speak to her, she just shook her head and set off walking again. It was another fifteen or so minutes' walk to The Stade, followed by a steep climb up the steps to the location of the Pulhamite bench. They couldn't see how many people were gathered around the bench. Because there was a white tent erected over the top of it.

'Oh fuck,' Amy said, standing at the top of the steps with her hands on her hips, trying to catch her breath.

'Oh fuck, indeed,' Jenny agreed.

They walked towards the area which had already been cordoned off with the now familiar tape. Amy and Jenny both recognised at once the young policeman standing next to it holding a clipboard. He looked up as they approached and was opening his mouth to speak when he recognised them too, blushing slightly as he recalled his earlier run-ins with Amy.

'Hello again,' Amy began. 'Fancy meeting you here.'

'Well, I... um...' the flustered young policeman said, looking at his clipboard and shifting uncomfortably from one foot to the other, clearly lost for words in Amy's presence.

'What's happened here then?' Jenny asked, ignoring the officer's obvious discomfort.

'Well, I... um... I can't really tell you anything, of course. Protocol, you know,' the officer said.

'Protocol shmotocol,' Jenny said, waving her hand. 'You know us, we're practically family after everything we've been through together. You can tell us. We won't breathe a word. Honest,' Jenny said, crossing her heart as she spoke.

'Well, no, even so, I can't...'

'What if we guess then? And you just nod if we're right?' Amy suggested. Before the officer could answer, Amy spoke again. 'Was the rock bench painted red?'

The policeman didn't need to say anything to confirm Amy's suspicions, his face said it all. 'How did you...?'

'Ah! We're actually private detectives,' Amy said conspiratorially. 'We've been on the trail of the killer this whole time – that's how we're always at the crime scenes so fast. He's just been one step ahead of us the whole time.'

'Yeah, but we're closing in,' Jenny said, joining in. 'Think Miss Marple meets Cagney and Lacey.'

'Miss... who meets who?'

'Oh for fuck's sake. The youth of today,' Jenny said, shaking her head sadly. 'Never mind. So, the bench had been painted red. With blood?' She didn't wait for an answer. 'And there was a body on the bench? A woman?'

'Yes, no, I...' he mumbled, clearly not knowing how to handle these two obviously barmy middle-aged women.

'Was it a young woman?' Amy pushed, watching his face closely for any telltale signs. 'Not a young woman?'

'I didn't say...' the officer tried to get a word in.

'A man then?' Amy queried.

'No, not a man or a young woman, eh, officer? It was an older woman, wasn't it?' Jenny interrupted.

Amy and the policeman both looked at Jenny with matching quizzical expressions.

'An older woman with curly grey hair,' Jenny continued.

The policeman just stood there with his mouth open. Amy continued to look puzzled. And then the penny dropped and she tugged Jenny's arm and pulled her away from the scene.

'Oh my God. Gloria! You think it's Gloria!' Amy hissed.

Jenny nodded solemnly.

'Fuck,' Amy said.

'Fuck indeed.'

CHAPTER 37
The bloody Mona Lisa

Back at his bungalow, the killer was enjoying a well-earned rest after literally painting the town red overnight. He was a little bit peeved that it had rained in the early hours of the morning and somewhat ruined his handiwork, but such is life. Such is art.

The blood/paint mixture had gone on pretty well and it hadn't taken too long to drive between the sites and roller it on. He'd used the blood-type stencils, a different one on each rock, although he didn't know how legible they'd be after the rain. He hadn't planned to leave a body on the bench. He hadn't planned to kill Gloria. But the bitch had to die after embarrassing him in the shop like that. How fucking dare she belittle him like that? And in front of those two other women. Of course he'd recognised the one with the pink hair, and he was pretty sure the other one, the brunette, had been with her on at least one occasion. It was a small town though – you were bound to bump into the same people from time to time. He got a funny vibe from the one with pink hair. He'd caught her eye and felt a flash of recognition on her face.

Killing Gloria had been a piece of cake. He knew where she lived and that she lived alone. It was the easiest thing in the world to turn up at her house on some pretence, knowing she'd let him in, probably only too happy to embarrass him some more about the good old days when he was little.

He didn't have much contact with her these days, but when she needed electrical work done she always called him and he always obliged out of some weird family-friend loyalty thing. He'd fitted in the job at the shop as a favour. Well, no more favours for Gloria, eh?

He would've liked to kill her at the actual site, using the bench as a sort of sacrificial altar, and letting her blood spill onto the rock, but transporting a live body was simply too fraught with risk, so he'd had to be content with bumping her off at the house.

When he'd rung her bell at about nine-thirty that same night, Gloria had answered the door wearing a long, flowing multi-coloured kimono. Her grey curls were loose around her shoulders for once.

'Oh! Hello again. This is a nice surprise,' she'd said.

Was it his imagination, or did she let her robe slip open a little more?

'Gloria. Sorry to bother you so late.'

'Not at all. Come in, come in. Let me get you a drink.'

He followed her through to the kitchen.

'What can I get you?'

'Oh, nothing for me, thanks anyway.' The last thing he wanted to worry about was washing his prints and DNA off a glass or mug and faffing about any longer than he needed to. He had a busy night ahead of him.

'Well, you won't mind if I have a teeny gin?' she simpered.

She made him feel sick. Did she really think he'd find her attractive? As soon as she turned her back on him, he stepped behind her, the electrical cable in his hands went round her throat and he choked her to death. The glass she'd been reaching for smashed at her feet. She barely put up a struggle at all and he laid her on the kitchen floor while he went to look for something.

He'd seen her work before – the bizarre collage recreations of paintings by the Old Masters and he rather thought he'd like to place one at the scene. He wasn't surprised to find the walls of Gloria's lounge covered with her own works. Vain cow. He was hoping for a da Vinci and wasn't disappointed when he found the Mona Lisa herself hanging above the fireplace. Only Gloria would dare recreate the world's most famous painting using pages torn from a gaudy magazine. Well, he'd give her her fifteen minutes of fame, her and her 'art'.

He stashed the picture in the van and then came back for the body, which he wrapped in one of Gloria's own duvet covers from the airing cupboard. He'd burn it when he was done. *Best thing for it anyway*, he thought, looking at the psychedelic swirls and vivid colours of the fabric. *Imagine waking up under that with a hangover*. No more hangovers for Gloria though. No more anything for Gloria. Especially no more embarrassing him.

Checking the street outside was clear, he loaded the body into the back of the van and drove home. It was way too early to complete this installation. He was still anxious about going home after the incident with the reporter's phone, but he couldn't face driving round for hours, so he decided to chance it. Luck had been on his side so far. He'd find something to watch on Netflix and set an alarm for one a.m. in case he fell asleep. The paint was already in the van and the only other thing he needed to do was sign the Mona Lisa with 'THE MAESTRO'. He wondered briefly if he should sign it with

254

Gloria's blood, but decided that was more effort than it was worth. He'd use some of the ready-mixed paint. *Was he getting lazy?* he wondered.

Nah, you're just knackered, my old son. Not for the first time he wondered what this whole experience would've been like if he'd had a partner to share it with: all the highs and lows, the adrenaline rushes, the fear, the exhilaration. Well, he'd never know now, would he?

The exhibit had gone off without a hitch. The rocks were painted and Gloria dumped unceremoniously on the rock bench with the Mona Lisa propped up against the fence at the back, clearly signed in big, red letters by 'THE MAESTRO'. Hopefully they'd get the message that he was no understudy.

As the killer settled in for a few hours in front of the television, back at Jenny's house the two friends were sitting at the kitchen table, deep in thought. They'd been talking themselves around in circles all day.

'What makes you think the body was Gloria?' Amy had asked.

'Gut feeling. I think she signed her own death warrant yesterday in the shop,' Jenny said grimly.

'What? So...' Amy screwed up her eyes as she tried to make the connections, 'you think that electrician bloke is the killer? Fuck.'

'I do. As soon as I saw his face, I knew I'd seen him before. And more than once. It wasn't until we walked from the park yesterday that I knew exactly where I'd seen him.'

'And...?'

'I'm sure he walked past 'Argonaut' the night we were there, and he walked past us on the boardwalk behind 'Genuine

Fake' that day with Pippa. Not only that, I'm pretty sure I saw him hanging around the gasworks more than once when I was working. He could easily have taken my bag.'

'Yeah, but that doesn't prove anything. They could just have been coincidental sightings.'

'Yeah, they could, but I just know it's him, I'm sure of it. I got such a strong vibe from him when I saw him in the shop. And you must have seen the way he looked when Gloria was talking about bathing him and stuff. If looks could kill and all that.'

'He was embarrassed; any man would've been,' Amy insisted.

Jenny just shook her head. 'Nope. He's a psycho, Amy, take my word for it.'

'So, what do we do? We can hardly go to the police based on a hunch. They won't take us seriously.'

'No, I know. They probably already think we're a right pair of neurotic old ninnies.'

'Ninnies. I like the word ninnies,' Amy chuckled. 'And nincompoops. Do you think ninnies is short for nincompoops?' she mused.

Jenny raised her eyebrows. 'Focus, Amy.'

'Sorry. So, what do we do then? If we can't go to the police with our suspicions.'

Jenny sighed. 'I suppose we have to try and find some proof.'

Amy screwed up her face.

'You got any better ideas?' Jenny shrugged.

'Um… bury our heads in the sand. Preferably in the Caribbean somewhere.'

'No can do, Amy. This got personal when he took Bella.'

'Lordy. I s'pose you're right. And, as much as I couldn't

256

stand Gloria, she was one of our own too. Bloody hell. Where do we start?'

'Did you get his full name when he was in the shop?' Jenny asked.

'Um… no, I don't think so. Just Jeff. But his overalls had J T Electrical on them. I remember thinking he was no Justin Timberlake.'

'Glossing over the fact that you shouldn't ever be thinking about Justin Timberlake, that's actually a good start.' Jenny reached for her mobile and tapped 'J T Electrical Folkestone' into the search bar. 'Got him. J T Electrical with a mobile number. No address or website though.'

'Hm… I s'pose if he's a one-man band he might not have a shop or anything. What about Yellow Pages? Do they even still exist?'

'Only one way to find out.' Jenny typed into Google again. 'Seem to get redirected to Yell… Hang on… Yep, here he is. Bugger, no address.'

'Ooh, I know,' Amy said after a minute or two. 'The company address must be registered with Companies House and all that stuff is in the public domain. Hang on…' she tapped out a search for 'j t electrical company address uk' on her own mobile and sure enough was rewarded with a residential address on the other side of town. 'Bingo!'

'Nice one,' Jenny said, nodding with satisfaction.

'Now what?'

'Now we check out where he lives.'

Amy groaned. 'Please tell me we don't have to do it at night?'

Jenny shook her head. 'No, be better to do the initial sweep during daylight hours. Hopefully he'll be at work and we can check out the lay of the land, neighbours and stuff.'

'What if he's not at work and he sees us? He's bound to recognise us and get suspicious. I really don't fancy being on his radar,' Amy said, looking worried. 'You'll have to dye your hair. Or at least wear a hat.'

'Well, I'm not dyeing my hair for anyone, but I s'pose I could wear a hat if it would make you feel better.'

'It would, thank you. And not a really standy-outy hat either. An unremarkable hat, please.'

Jenny raised her eyebrows and shook her head. 'Right, I'll wear a really boring hat. Can you lend me one?'

'My hats aren't boring,' Amy responded with a frown. She paused. 'Are they?'

'If the hat fits, my friend…' Jenny grinned.

'I'm wounded. I think. I might have to take my hats to the charity shop now.'

'Good idea, but not until we've completed our surveillance mission.'

'Oh God, we're on a mission. Do you happen to remember what happened last time we went on a mission at all?'

'Oh yes, I remember, Amy. Not likely to forget in a hurry either.'

'No gun this time, so we'll be fine,' Amy said, trying to reassure herself.

'No gun,' Jenny conceded. Amy didn't catch her muttering 'not yet, anyway' under her breath.

CHAPTER 38

Special delivery

The killer was starting to feel the strain a little after the unplanned shenanigans with Gloria. He was wondering if he needed to wind things up with one grand finale. He also needed to get the wiring job finished before he started getting into strife about that too. When both were finished he'd disappear for a while. Maybe hire a camper van and head north for a few weeks. He could keep an eye on the news down south, see how far the police got with their enquiries and play it by ear a bit. He had plenty of savings and could afford to stay away for quite some time. Maybe he should actually buy a camper van instead of renting one? That would definitely give him more flexibility. Feeling good about his plan, the killer turned his thoughts to his last exhibit.

Amy was starting to feel the strain too. For different reasons. The feelings of déjà vu were making her decidedly anxious and she had tried telling Jenny she didn't want to stalk the man they suspected to be the killer. It had been madness with Robert last year and this was just plain insanity. Wasn't the definition of madness doing the same thing again and expecting a different result? Well, look it up in a dictionary and you just might find a picture of Amy holding a gun. She felt sick with fear just at the thought of it. Making up her mind, she messaged Jenny to say she absolutely couldn't do it, sorry. Jenny had simply replied with one word: *Fine*.

Please don't do anything stupid, Amy had responded. No reply from Jenny. Bugger.

And that's how Amy found herself walking past Jeff's bungalow later that same day with Jenny, who was wearing a black beanie over her pink hair which, to be honest, on a hot summer's day, probably attracted as much attention as Jenny's hair would have done.

'We should have borrowed a dog,' Amy said as they walked past Jeff's house on the opposite side of the road. There was no vehicle on the short drive at the front of the house, much to her relief.

'Er… why?' Jenny asked, looking quizzically at her friend. 'As a guard dog, you mean? Or an attack dog? Not sure they have dogs like that on borrow-my-doggy-dot-com. Don't think your average Shih Tzu or Cockerpoo looks terribly menacing. Although a Jack Russell can be pretty scary when it wants to be.'

'What? No! Just so it looks like we're innocently walking our dog, rather than casing the joint of a suspected serial killer. Christ, I can't believe I caved. Again.'

'Oh,' Jenny said. 'Nah. We're fine. Just two normal people out for a stroll on a lovely summer's day.'

'Nothing normal about us or this,' Amy muttered under her breath. 'Or wearing a woolly hat in eighty-degree heat.'

Jenny either ignored her or pretended not to hear. Maybe the hat blocked out Amy's lowered voice? 'Let's carry on to the end of the street and then walk back on the other side.'

Amy said nothing, just kept walking and tried to look normal.

As they approached the house again, Jenny hissed at Amy:

'Stop and bend down as if you're tying your shoelace.'

'What? I'm wearing slip-ons,' Amy hissed back.

'For fuck's sake, woman, improvise!'

Grumbling to herself, Amy bent down and tried to balance on one foot as she removed one shoe and shook it upside down as if she'd got a stone in it. As she did so, Jenny focused all her attention on the bungalow and she wasn't prepared for a decidedly wobbly Amy to suddenly grab her as she tried to regain her balance, her shoe half on, hopping about on one foot. Jenny lost her balance too and the two of them came close to falling into an undignified heap on the pavement. Jenny's hat came off in the process, her pink hair falling to her shoulders as it was released from its woollen bonds. Anyone watching would have had no trouble describing the two madwomen in the street that day.

Shoe on and back on two feet, Amy marched back down the road, refusing to look at where Jenny remained standing on the pavement, looking at her hat and wondering whether it was worth putting it back on again or not. Deciding not, she followed Amy back down the road.

'That went well,' Amy glared at Jenny when she caught up with her.

'Not my fault you can't balance on one leg,' Jenny shrugged.

'Well, I'm not as young as I used to be. I actually had very good balance,' Amy said, 'about twenty years ago. Getting old sucks.'

Ignoring her, Jenny said: 'We need to come back after dark and have a proper look around the back. And see if we can peep in the garage window.'

'Er… no, we absolutely do not. No way no how, Jenny. This

has to stop. Right here, right now.'

'Right here, right now/right here, right now... da da da da da da da da da da da da da...' Jenny sang, Fatboy-Slim-style.'

Amy growled at her. 'I'm serious, Jenny. Let the police deal with this.'

'But they're not even on to him, are they?' Jenny insisted. 'It's our civic duty to point them in the right direction.'

'Then take your suspicions to them. Don't get any more involved. No good can come of snooping.'

Jenny said nothing, but Amy knew full well she wouldn't give up. When the killer had chosen Bella, he'd marked his card as far as Jenny was concerned.

They walked on in silence and parted company when they reached the town once more.

'Catch up tomorrow,' Amy called out after Jenny's departing back. 'Don't do anything stupid!'

Jenny just raised her hand in reply and kept on walking.

The bad feeling didn't leave Amy all the way home and she couldn't focus on writing when she sat down at her desk a short while later. Giving up any pretence of working, she took a book into the garden, but found herself re-reading the same paragraph over and over again, unable to take anything in. She simply couldn't shake the feeling of impending doom.

Jenny had no such qualms as she phoned her dodgy ex in London.

'Hello, I need another favour,' she said when he answered.

'Alright, bird, straight to the point as ever,' the dodgy ex said.

'You know me,' Jenny replied. 'So, can you fix me up?'

'Yeah, I s'pose so. What happened to the last one?'

'Don't ask,' Jenny said. 'Can you deliver to Folkestone this time? My lift isn't available and getting to Chatham on the train's a right pain in the arse. I'll buy you a pint.'

'Well, how can I refuse an offer like that?'

'Good. Phone me when you leave,' Jenny instructed.

'Er… might take me a few hours to lay my hands on what you want. I don't have shooters lying around the house.'

'No? Getting soft in your old age?'

'Fuck off. Right, leave it with me and I'll give you a shout when I've got one.'

Jenny hung up without saying goodbye. Didn't want to encourage him too much. He was an ex for a reason after all. Multiple reasons, come to think of it.

It was actually less than an hour when the dodgy ex phoned her back.

'Right, meet you down at the Pilot Bar on the beach about six,' she instructed him. She toyed with the idea of inviting Amy to join them for a drink, but decided against it. Better to do this on her own. Couldn't have Amy freaking out and giving the game away.

After doing a few little jobs at home, Jenny took a slow stroll down to the Harbour Arm and walked up the old railway platform to the beach. The Pilot Bar was busy. If she'd stopped to think, it would probably have been better to meet somewhere a bit quieter, but she loved this bar right on the beach with its old Waltzer cars and deckchairs, palm trees and sea views. She hovered for a few minutes, glancing about in the hope of grabbing a couple of seats from people leaving. She couldn't believe her luck when a young couple got up to vacate one of the Waltzer cars, a sparkly purple number right next to where she was standing. Without even waiting for the woman to step out of the car, Jenny slid into her spot, much to the indignance of another couple who were also hovering nearby.

Jenny shrugged her hands and shoulders at them by way of apology. 'Have to be quicker than that,' she muttered through gritted teeth, smiling disingenuously at them. Ordering a couple of pints on the app, Jenny waited for the beers and her dodgy ex to arrive.

She was halfway down her pint of lager when he turned up, looking all around for her. He hadn't changed. Still the slightly overweight, ageing skinhead she knew and had once loved. Edward by name; Eddie to his friends; Spud to his close friends. Partly to do with King Edward potatoes, but mostly his resemblance to one. She raised her hand and called out.

'Spud! Over here.'

A smile crossed the skinhead's face as he spotted her. 'Alright, slapper,' he said, sliding into the car next to her, picking up the pint and downing half of it in one. 'Oof! Cheers, thanks for that. Needed it. Fucking hot again. No air con in the van.'

'Least I could do. So, you got it?'

'That's my girl, straight to the point. No small talk, no messing,' Spud laughed. Nonetheless, he reached into the olive-coloured canvas messenger bag he had with him and brought out something wrapped in a tea towel, which he passed across to Jenny.

'Wondered what happened to that tea towel,' Jenny said, looking at the familiar item that was covered in images of cats in wigs, before transferring it to her own shoulder bag. 'Thanks for that. Cheers!' Jenny said, reaching for her own glass and clinking it against Spud's.

'Nice here,' Spud said after a while. 'Can see why you moved down.'

'Yeah, it is. I like it.'

'Apart from this fucking nutter who's going round killing people. Didn't you have someone doing that last year too?' Spud asked, squinting across at Jenny.

'Yup,' Jenny nodded. She didn't meet Spud's eyes, but she could practically hear the cogs turning in his brain. Spud was many things, but he wasn't stupid.

'Hold on a cotton-picking minute…' he began, 'please don't tell me *this* is anything to do with *that*?'

Jenny just shrugged and took a glug of her beer.

'Fuck me. There's me thinking you've left the excitement of the big city behind you, living a dull life in a sleepy seaside town, and here you are involved with not one, but two serial killers. It is two killers, right?'

Jenny shrugged again and gazed out to sea.

'No,' Spud said a few moments later. 'No. Please tell me it's not… you're not…?'

Finally, Jenny turned to look at him. 'Not what? Oh for fuck's sake, you don't think I'm the killer, do you?' She burst out laughing. 'Oh my God, that's hilarious. Do you really think I could murder anyone?'

It was Spud's turn to shrug. 'Well, I reckon you thought about murdering me once or twice over the years,' he said, winking at her.

Jenny thought for a moment. 'You're not wrong,' she said, nodding. 'But no, I'm not Folkestone's serial killer. Sorry to disappoint.'

'Then why…?' Spud began, nodding towards her bag and the gun inside.

'Protection. Precaution. Nothing more.'

Spud studied her face. But, finding nothing there, simply nodded and took a mouthful of beer. 'Cool.'

It wasn't long before Spud got up to leave. 'Well, much as I'd love to stay and drink beer on the beach, I've got a gig in Camden tonight, so I need to make tracks. Be safe, Jen. Good to see you. Don't do anything stupid.'

'Thanks again,' Jenny said. 'See ya!' Don't do anything stupid. It was what Amy had said to her too. What a low opinion her friends had of her. Of course, they weren't wrong, she smiled as she finished her drink and got up to leave.

CHAPTER 39

Strike a pose

Later that night, Amy was pacing up and down her living room. She hadn't been able to settle to anything all day. She just knew Jenny was going to go back to Jeff's house after dark, with or without her, and she was wracking her brains trying to think of a way to stop her. Jenny hadn't answered her phone when Amy had tried to call her and she felt sick to her stomach with worry. Even a call from Willem hadn't made her feel better. Normally he was such a calming influence on her.

'Sorry, Willem, I wouldn't be very good company tonight,' she'd said in response to his invitation to watch a film or something at his house.

'That's okay. You sound stressed. Anything I can help with?'

'No, I don't think so. It's just Jenny… She… I… It's nothing, really, don't worry. Just a difference of opinion. You know me, don't like to fall out with anyone. I'm sure we'll be back to normal tomorrow.'

'Well, if you're sure. You know you only have to phone if you need me,' Willem said, not convinced by Amy's attempt to reassure him.

'Yes, absolutely. And thanks, Willem. Catch up soon.'

Willem had hung up the phone, but he too now couldn't shake off the feeling that something was wrong. He began pacing up and down his lounge.

Back at her house, Jenny was also pacing. Impatiently. Now she'd made her mind up on a plan of action, she just wanted to get on with it. The cats had picked up on the tension and were winding around her legs, threatening to trip her up, so she sat down on the sofa and mentally paced instead. She'd ignored a call from Amy earlier. She knew her friend would only try and talk her out of it again and she didn't need that kind of negativity. If Amy didn't want to come with her, so be it. She was going anyway. And she had her accomplice safely in the pocket of her jacket. Just in case. Of course she didn't plan to use the gun, but it was reassuring to know she had it and could wave it around threateningly should the need arise. Ooh, actually, come to think about it, *could* she wave a gun around convincingly? She'd had a little practice at Robert's house last year, but it couldn't hurt to have a little dress rehearsal, could it?

Retrieving the gun, she went upstairs to her bedroom and the full-length mirror there, and struck a pose – a two-handed stance like the ones you saw on telly. She tried with one hand, but didn't feel as confident. And her hand shook rather more without the support of the other one. Then, thinking that she may, of course, be shooting in the dark, she went in search of a torch. A rummage in the odds and ends drawer in the kitchen revealed a thin hand torch, also known as a dead-battery holder.

'For fuck's sake,' Jenny grumbled as she hunted around the house for replacement batteries. Eventually, having had to remove the batteries from the TV remote, she got the torch working and headed back upstairs, where she proceeded to try the shooting stance once more with the gun balanced on the torch. It definitely wasn't as easy as they made it look in the movies and, to be perfectly frank, she looked a bit of a twat.

Giving up on the whole thing, Jenny plodded back down-stairs feeling slightly despondent. Well, hopefully she wouldn't even need to produce the gun and, if she did, adrenaline would kick in and release her inner badass. Although she wasn't confident she even had such a thing these days. She was more likely to produce an anxious fart nowadays. For a moment, she wished she wasn't a vegetarian. And that Amy was coming with her.

Amy was still pacing, but had come to a decision. She wouldn't give in and go with Jenny. She was adamant about that. But she'd decided she would be lurking nearby in her car, just in case. Just in case of what exactly, she wasn't sure, but she'd be there if Jenny needed to make a quick getaway.

Willem was still pacing and had an uneasy feeling. Something was going on with Amy and Jenny, he knew that much. He'd heard the anxiety in Amy's voice over the phone and he wanted to be her knight in shining armour. Although she'd have to make do with his less-than-shining Volvo for any rescue mission. But then, did she even need, or indeed want, rescuing? What if she was a bit of a feminist in that department? He was sure Jenny wouldn't want rescuing by a man, but he thought perhaps Amy wouldn't mind. And he was pretty sure she did like him more than just a bit now. Mind made up, Willem grabbed his car keys.

When Amy drove away from her house at just after eleven p.m., she didn't notice the Volvo estate pulling out after her. She drove the short distance to Jeff's road and turned the car around before parking up several houses back, killing the engine and sitting back to wait. She was confident she'd beaten Jenny there. There was no vehicle parked on the drive again and Amy hoped that meant Jeff wasn't at home. She was sick with worry about Jenny getting caught snooping.

Willem followed Amy at a distance. He had no idea where she was headed as she drove to a residential street on the other side of town. There was a hairy moment when she stopped and did a three-point turn in the road and he thought she might have spotted him, but she showed no sign of having done so as she pulled her car over to a stop. He carried on past her some way before making a similar turn and parking on the opposite side of the road where he had a clear line of sight to Amy's car. He yawned and wished he'd brought a flask of coffee. He had a feeling he could be in for a long night.

There was no movement in the street apart from a wandering fox until just after midnight. Amy had been fighting sleep and was crunching her way through a packet of Extra Strong Mints to keep herself awake. She was starting to wonder if Jenny had come to her senses and stayed at home and how long she should wait. There was still no sign of life at Jeff's bungalow. It was at about twelve fifteen when the darkly dressed figure came into view, head down, hands in pockets. Amy could tell right away that it was Jenny.

'Bugger. Why couldn't you have stayed at home, Jenny?' she cursed under her breath.

Sliding down in her seat, Amy watched as her friend approached the house, looking all around before she jogged up the drive and went round behind the garage, disappearing from view. It was only a matter of seconds before a set of headlights half blinded Amy as a car arrived in the road. Amy ducked down and held her breath, willing it to continue on past. No such luck. The white van to which the lights belonged turned onto Jeff's drive.

'Fuck! Fuck fuck fuck!' Amy exclaimed, panicking and wondering what to do. Should she message Jenny? Or call her? What if Jeff heard her phone and caught her? Making her mind up, she tried phoning Jenny but the call went straight to voicemail. 'Shit!' Amy quickly texted *Get out, he's home!* She didn't know what else to do. Her heart was beating out of her chest as she watched Jeff get out of the van and let himself into the house. She just hoped Jenny had heard the car. All she could do now was sit and watch and hope.

Back in the Volvo, Willem was also watching and waiting and wondering. Had that slight figure all dressed in black been Jenny? He thought it probably was. What the hell was she doing skulking around the houses in the middle of the night? When he saw a white van pull onto the drive, the bad feeling he'd had ever since he spoke to Amy intensified.

Amy really thought she might be sick. There'd been no sign of Jenny since Jeff had arrived home. Lights had gone on downstairs in the bungalow, that was all. *What if he'd got her?* Amy thought. *It would be all her fault.* Before she could agonise any further, the passenger door swung open and someone got in next to Amy. She squealed, half expecting to find Jeff there brandishing a knife.

'Oh my God, Jenny, you nearly gave me a heart attack!' Amy said when she realised who it actually was. 'How did you…? Where did you…?' she stumbled over the questions, a mixture of fear and relief pounding in her chest.

Jenny lowered her hood and turned to her friend. 'I think

I should be the one asking the questions, don't you?' she said, raising her eyebrows.

'Well, I, um... I was worried...' Amy began, but before she could finish her sentence the back door behind Jenny opened and someone else got into the car. Both women jumped and Amy squealed again. They turned, fully expecting to see Jeff grinning insanely at them.

'Willem!' Amy and Jenny exclaimed in unison.

Leaning between the two front seats, a hand on either back support, Willem looked from Amy to Jenny and back again. 'Fancy meeting you two here,' he said. 'Come here often?'

'We... no... I ... oh God!' Amy mumbled, putting her face in her hands.

'Jenny?' Willem asked. 'Care to explain? Clearly the writer lady is all out of words.'

Jenny shrugged. 'Can't a girl go for a moonlit jog?'

'Even you're not that strange, Jenny,' Willem said.

'Oh, she is, aren't you, Jenny?' Amy said helpfully.

Jenny just smiled sweetly at Willem.

'Amy?' he tried again. 'What's going on?'

'Nothing, really...' Amy began. She mouthed a silent apology at Jenny before continuing. 'If you must know, we were just checking out the man who lives here,' she said, nodding towards the bungalow.

'Because...?' Willem pushed.

'Because we... um... have our suspicions about him,' Amy clarified.

'Will one of you please tell me *exactly* what is going on. What suspicions? And why are you skulking around in the middle of the night dressed like a cat burglar, Jenny?'

'Well, as you know, I am mad about cats…' Jenny began, smirking at Willem.

'Enough!' he roared.

'Shh!' Amy urged. 'The psycho killer will hear you!'

Willem stared at Amy, his mouth hanging open in disbelief.

'For fuck's sake, Amy,' Jenny tutted.

'Sorry,' Amy said.

'Well, you might as well tell him everything now,' Jenny said, crossing her arms mutinously.

'Really?' Amy asked, raising her eyebrows.

'Well, edited highlights perhaps, don't you agree?' Jenny said.

'Just tell me!' Willem groaned. 'Before *I* turn into a psycho killer.'

And so, Amy told him. About Bella and Gloria and their suspicions about Jeff.

Willem listened intently, not interrupting, until Amy had brought him up to speed.

'So why don't you just go to the police with your suspicions?' Willem asked. He resisted adding, 'like any normal people'.

'Dur! Because we don't have any proof,' Jenny informed him, uncrossing her arms and holding both palms out.

'So that's what you were doing? Looking for proof? And?'

'And nothing,' Jenny said. 'Tried to see in the garage window but couldn't make anything out. Then I heard a car pull onto the drive so I scarpered – there's a little alleyway running along the back of all the gardens.'

'Ah, so that's how you managed to creep up on me!' Amy nodded.

'Yep. I'm a regular ninja. Um… are we actually going to

address the elephant in the back seat at all?' Jenny said, nodding in Willem's direction.

'Rude,' Willem said.

'More of a grizzly bear than an elephant,' Amy giggled.

'Whatever. What *are* you doing here, Willem?' Jenny asked.

'Stopping you two getting yourselves killed, by the look of it.'

'Oh! We can look after ourselves, Willem, honestly…' Amy began.

'You'd better believe it,' Jenny nodded. 'Say hello to my little friend.' As she said the words, Jenny pulled the gun from her pocket and waved it in front of two shocked faces.

'What the hell?' Willem exclaimed, jerking backwards as if he'd been shot.

'Oh good grief, Jenny, really?' Amy said. 'Spud?'

Jenny nodded.

Amy nodded too.

'Who or what is Spud? And can you please stop waving that thing around, Jenny,' Willem said.

'Spud is Jenny's dodgy ex from London,' Amy enlightened a baffled-looking Willem. 'He has contacts,' she added with a wink.

'So I see.'

Amy laughed. 'See what you did there…? Contacts. See. Very good.'

Willem shook his head in disbelief. 'None of this is funny, Amy.'

Amy looked abashed. 'No, I s'pose not. Sorry.'

'What are you apologising for, Amy? That sorry isn't from me. Nobody asked you to get involved,' Jenny said mutinously, looking back at where Willem was still pressed against the back seat.

'Well, forgive me for being worried about you both. I'll leave you to it then, shall I? Whatever *it* is.' At that, Willem opened the back door and began to slide out. 'And if you're going to quote Tony Montana, you're gonna need a bigger gun.'

With that, he got out of the car, slammed the door and disappeared. A minute or so later, they watched as he drove away. Only when his tail lights had disappeared from view did the friends speak again.

'Good riddance,' said Jenny.

'Oh God,' said Amy.

CHAPTER 40

Our Jeff

A my drove Jenny home after the aborted mission.
'Well, as you're here, you might as well give me a lift,'
Jenny had said. 'Really not a fan of this middle-of-the-night
jogging. Or any jogging for that matter.'

Amy was currently speechless. She was still trying to come
to terms with what had just happened with Willem. Had she
blown it with him by getting involved in Jenny's hare-brained
plan? And why on earth had Jenny produced the gun? What
must Willem be thinking?

'What were you thinking?' Amy said, finally finding her
voice.

'Just now? That I really fancy a bowl of Coco Pops.'

Amy looked at her in disbelief. 'What?'

'Coco Pops. Can we detour to the twenty-four-hour Tesco's?'

'Um… two things… no and what the actual fuck? Besides,
Tesco's don't open twenty-four hours any more. Because of
Covid.'

'Fucking Covid,' Jenny said. 'Still ruining our lives. I s'pose
I'll have to make do with Nutella on toast. Want some?'

Amy was parking the car outside Jenny's as she considered
this question. It was nearly one a.m. and she should really be
heading home to bed. She knew perfectly well that she was way
too wired to sleep any time soon though.

'Yeah, why not,' she sighed.

Soon they were seated at Jenny's kitchen table with two slices of toast and Nutella each. Amy had watched Jenny wrap the gun in a tea towel – was that really a cat version of Marie Antoinette? – and stuff it inside a box of cereal while waiting for the toast to pop up. They weren't speaking, each lost in thoughts of what had happened and, indeed, what might happen next. Eventually it was Amy who broke the silence.

'Who's Tony Montana?' she asked, toast paused midway to her mouth.

Jenny looked at her in surprise. 'What?! You don't know who Tony Montana is? Are you even human, Amy Archer? Or have you arrived on planet Earth from some dim distant galaxy where they never showed *Scarface*?'

'Oh. I have heard of *Scarface*, but I've never seen it,' she said. 'That gangster stuff really doesn't appeal.'

'Might wanna rethink that, Ames. You're practically one yourself now,' Jenny chuckled.

'Ahem. It wasn't me waving a gun around earlier. What the bloody hell were you thinking? And what will Willem think?'

Jenny shrugged. 'Does it matter?'

'It does to me,' Amy said.

'Okay, I'm sorry. I s'pose I was just on a bit of an adrenaline high. It won't happen again,' Jenny said, trying to keep a straight face.

'Well, that's no sodding help at all. The cat-in-a-wig's well and truly out of the can of worms already, isn't it? How am I ever going to look him in the eye again?'

'Do you want me to apologise to him?' Jenny asked, looking a little bit penitent at last.

'Yes. No. Oh, I don't know.' Amy took another bite of toast

and chewed thoughtfully.

'Penny for them?' Jenny asked after a while.

'Better make it a… whatever currency they use in the Maldives… I was just wondering where to run away to. Maybe the Caribbean somewhere. I always fancied taking a leaf out of Ian Fleming's book and writing on a sun-drenched island,' Amy said wistfully.

'Didn't he die in Canterbury? Ian Fleming,' Jenny said.

'Um… yeah, I think he did actually. Good knowledge, my learned friend,' Amy said, nodding.

'Came up in a pub quiz once,' Jenny said.

'Ooh, we should join a pub quiz team.' Amy looked enthusiastic at the idea.

'Well, running away to the Caribbean and joining a pub quiz team aside, don't you think we should talk about what to do next? About Jeff.'

'We could think about it on Antigua. I think much better in the sunshine of a tropical island. And what sort of name for a serial killer is Jeff anyway? Do you really think he's it?'

'We can pop down to the Pilot Bar tomorrow if it helps. Park ourselves next to a palm tree, order something with an umbrella in it…' Jenny said sarcastically. 'Also, Jeffrey Dahmer.'

'Oh yeah, forgot about him. Do you think our Jeff's a Jeffrey?'

'Probably,' Jenny said, shaking her head in despair. 'And he's not our Jeff. And stop avoiding answering the question.'

Amy sighed. 'I don't know. Do you remember *Rainbow* from when we were kids? He was a Geoffrey too, wasn't he? The presenter. Couldn't imagine him being a serial killer.'

'Amy!' Jenny exclaimed. 'You're doing my head in now, shut the fuck up.'

Amy then proceeded to do her best impersonations of George and Zippy from *Rainbow*, at which point Jenny got up and dumped her plate unceremoniously in the sink. 'Out,' she said, one hand on her hip, the other pointing towards the door.

Only too glad to obey, Amy pushed her chair back, picked up her jacket and made to leave. Jenny followed her to the front door.

'Sorry,' Amy said as she stepped out. 'We will talk about this. Just not tonight, okay?'

'Okay,' Jenny relented. 'Now fuck off.'

Amy laughed. 'Night.' As she reached the front gate, she suddenly turned and pretended to point a gun at Jenny. 'Say hello to my little friend,' she said in her best bad gangster voice.

Willem was still awake too. He couldn't believe what had happened. Had Jenny really produced a gun? Was it even a real gun? Was it loaded? And what the hell were she and Amy doing stalking some bloke they believed might be the killer? He shook his head for the umpteenth time as he tried to get it around the events from earlier in the night.

He was sitting on his sofa nursing a good measure of whisky. Normal people didn't behave like Jenny had. And Amy, sweet, sensible Amy of all people, why would she go along with such madness? He knew he needed an explanation, but he also knew it would have to wait until tomorrow. Downing the rest of his drink, he took himself off to bed, not optimistic he'd be able to sleep. Cat, who'd been eyeing him from the window sill, jumped on the bed and curled himself into the curve of Willem's body. Willem could feel the animal breathing against him and allowed himself to be lulled by Cat's purring and, finally, he slept.

Jeff, or Jeffrey as he had indeed been christened, was still too wired to sleep at two a.m. He'd actually given himself the night off and gone back over to The Old City Bar in Canterbury in the hopes of chatting up the barmaid again. He was in luck and had spent a very pleasant few hours on a bar stool chatting to Elisa when she wasn't serving customers. He'd jokingly asked her if she fancied running away in a camper van with him. She hadn't looked too enthused at the idea though, and he'd laughed it off. At least he'd pretended to. He didn't do well with rejection. At that point, he'd taken his drink to a table, ostensibly to watch the football match that was showing on the big-screen TV, but in reality he was brooding and thinking of what he'd like to do to the barmaid before he slit her beautiful throat. At the end of the match, he couldn't have told you what teams were playing, let alone who won. Still, it was better than being at home and wondering when the police might come calling. He needed to crack on with his final exhibition of the summer and plan his getaway.

After the pub closed, he took a walk into Canterbury city centre. The streets were buzzing with tourists and students, spilling out from bars and fast-food restaurants. It had a different feel to Folkestone. There's something about a British seaside town that is quite unique. As a teenager he'd loved his home-town in the summer when it was bursting at the seams with visitors, vibrant with life and flashing amusements; loud and raucous and so alive. It was funfairs and hot dogs, getting pissed on the beach with your mates, and going on the pull every night. So many teenaged girls, giggling in their miniskirts and make-up, looking to have a holiday fling. He and his mates had been only too happy to oblige. Then the long, bleak winter months when the town was dead and he felt dead with it.

His feelings had changed as he'd got older. Now the influx of summer visitors got on his nerves and he actually preferred the winter months when the locals got their town back. Although nowadays of course the locals had been joined by a ton of DFLs, sending house prices soaring. Maybe he should cash in while the town was still on the up. He'd make good money on his bungalow now. His parents had paid off the mortgage before they'd died – the only good fucking thing they did. Maybe he'd sell up and buy a decent camper van that he could actually live in for a while.

With thoughts of hitting the open road and leaving his hometown behind him, the killer drove slowly home. He was always careful to obey the speed limits these days and he'd only had one pint at the pub before switching to Coke. He wasn't in a hurry anyway. To be perfectly honest, the less time he spent at home at the moment, the better.

He was starting to yawn as he pulled into his road. He couldn't help noticing there was a car parked a few houses down that he didn't recognise. He knew all the cars in the street and a new one always stood out. As his headlights hit the car he thought he could make out the shape of someone sitting in the driver's seat, but after he blinked the shape was gone. He pulled his van onto the drive and went indoors without looking back at the car. He didn't bother taking off his jacket or boots before he flicked on the light in the lounge and then jogged upstairs to the front bedroom and, moving the curtain just a fraction, peered into the darkness. As he scanned the street, he thought he could make out another strange car under a streetlight.

'Fuck,' he said under his breath. *Were the police onto him? Was he being watched?* 'No, not yet,' he said through gritted teeth. 'I'm not finished, not yet.' As he continued to watch, he caught sight of a dark figure approaching from the other end of the road, behind the cars he'd spotted. From the build and the way it moved, he thought the figure was probably a woman. She reached the car closest to his house and got in the front passenger side. As the interior light came on he squinted, trying to see more, but it was too far away and the light only on for a second. He continued to watch, wondering if he could get any closer, and swore when he saw someone get out of the second car and go and get into the back of the first one. 'Fuck,' he hissed again. This one was definitely a man. As the back door opened and the car's interior light came on again, he could swear he saw a flash of pink in the front seat.

It wasn't long before the man got out and walked back to his car. The killer watched as he drove off. He couldn't make out anything more than the car was a Volvo estate. He needed to get closer to the first car and see who the two occupants were. Jogging back downstairs, he grabbed his keys again and kept watch from the lounge. When the car's headlights came on and it drove away a couple of minutes later, he jumped in his van and followed at a safe distance.

'I fucking knew it!' he said a few minutes later as he watched the two women get out of the car. It was that pink-haired bitch and her friend. *Were they onto him?* He sat in the car watching the house for a while. At least it wasn't the police watching him, but what the fuck were these two doing parked in his road in the middle of the fucking night? And, more to the point, what was he going to do about it?

He sat and waited and eventually his patience was rewarded when the brunette came out and got into the blue hatchback and drove off. He ducked down in his seat as she drove past him, before swinging his van round and following. They didn't go far and he watched the woman let herself into an end-of-terrace house next to the viaduct. Now he knew where they both lived. Whatever he decided to do next would be so much easier now. He'd just have to hope the man in the other car didn't get in his way. He looked like a big bloke and he didn't fancy taking him on.

CHAPTER 41

The grand finale

The killer had a restless night and awoke when his alarm went off at seven a.m. feeling groggy and bad-tempered. He had to be on site today or questions would be asked, but hopefully he could get the bulk of the wiring finished if he cracked on and worked late. He didn't bother showering or making breakfast, opting to grab a coffee and a bacon and egg roll from the van in Wickes' car park on the way.

He was at work by eight and trying to focus on the job at hand, but his thoughts kept drifting to the two women he'd followed last night and what he was going to do about them. It was just as well the other trades weren't working in the same part of the building as him because there was no way he could've held up his side of a conversation. Besides, he didn't particularly enjoy the banter that was normally heard on jobs like these.

By the time the other trades clocked off at four, the killer had made solid progress and he reckoned he could get the job finished by about seven. His back was aching and his knees hurt from crawling on floorboards, despite his knee pads. *I'm getting too old for this shit*, he thought more than once as the day went on. Maybe it was time to rethink his job? Look for a cushy little number sitting behind a counter somewhere, none of this hands-and-knees bollocks. Before that though, an idea was forming in his head involving the little bitch with the pink hair… if he could pull it off.

The plan for his grand finale was really taking shape. As the idea grew, so did his excitement. The idea had spawned when he'd been walking through town, past the old Debenhams building, which had been turned into a vaccination centre during the Covid pandemic and was now standing empty. The huge shop windows had been filled with vinyls of photographic images of the local area – much nicer to look at than a depressing empty space. Well, it just so happened there was another large empty shop on the same stretch of Sandgate Road in need of a similar facelift.

The BrightHouse store had been closed for some time after the company went into administration and it would be a perfect venue for the killer's exhibition. He'd found a service entrance to the rear of the property where he could gain access easily enough with a pair of bolt cutters.

He'd had to fork out a bit of money for a bloody great printer. Couldn't exactly pop along to Happy Snaps and get his photos printed, much as the idea amused him. He'd managed to pick one up second hand on eBay from someone down in Brighton, which had meant a trip down in his van, but he thought it was worth it. Besides, who doesn't love a trip to the seaside? He'd set up a fake account to buy it and paying cash meant there was no paper trail as such. Fucking thing weighed a ton and the bloke he'd bought it from had to help him get it in the van. Unloading it when he arrived home had been a pain in the arse, but he'd achieved it with determination and a sack trolley. Thankfully it came with a roll of paper so he didn't have to faff about ordering that.

He had all the images he'd taken at every stage of his summer killing spree in a password-protected file on his laptop. He'd spent many a happy hour looking at them when there was nothing on television. And when there *was* something on television. No matter how often he looked at them, he never stopped appreciating the art and the originality. Fucking awesome. He deserved a bigger audience. Well, this was the first step. Hopefully once the images got onto social media, they'd go viral. Got to love the internet.

The first print he did was disappointing. He'd gone large – A1 – without realising that the quality of the photo, which he'd taken on his mobile, was too low-res to print large without losing sharpness. Refusing to give in at the first hurdle, he'd coughed up for some expensive software which allowed him to increase image resolution a bit. He was pissed off at having to compromise, but it was a learning curve. Next time he'd use a decent camera. If there was a next time. He wondered again how close the police were to finding him. He was angry with himself for not searching the reporter properly when he'd grabbed her. Rookie error. Lesson learned.

In the end, he had to settle for printing the photos as A3 size and, although it was smaller than he would've liked, by making a collage of before, during and after shots, he produced an impressive display for each exhibit. He gave the images twenty-four hours to dry and then rolled them into cardboard tubes. What he really would have liked was top to bottom vinyls that filled the windows like the ones in the Old Debenhams building, but he would just have to be satisfied with the compromise. He wanted the exhibits to be on show for as long as possible, which meant he needed to prevent anyone from gaining access to the building once he was done. While he didn't know a great deal about explosives, he did know about wiring and motion sensors and he was pretty confident he could rig front and back doors and all the windows to blow if the police or fire services tried to get in. It would take time to get explosives experts to the scene and by then, hopefully, Joe Public would have done their worst. *Maybe he should suggest some hashtags*, he thought with a chuckle: *#themaestro #killerexhibition for starters.*

He'd ordered the cabling and sensors to be delivered to the job site he was working at rather than to his home address. No one would bat an eyelid, as they had supplies delivered direct all the time, and the packages had been waiting for him when he'd arrived this morning. He'd stashed them in his van before getting started. The only problem he had now was that he had no frigging idea where or how to get explosives.

As he worked, he began to think that maybe he didn't actually need explosives. He just had to make people think they were there. If he placed all the wiring and some sort of warning on the door, that would probably be enough, wouldn't it? They'd have to assume the threat was real. It would also mean he wouldn't have to destroy all his beautiful images. Add in his new genius idea about the interfering cow with the pink hair, and he was confident he could pull it off.

By the time he finally screwed in the last socket it was almost seven thirty and he was knackered. Hungry, thirsty and aching all over. Before he could do anything else he needed food and a soak in a hot bath. Hopefully then he'd be able to summon up the energy for what he needed to do next.

He stopped to pick up a large cod and chips on the way home which he swallowed down with a cold bottle of lager. Feeling marginally better, he ran a hot bath with a good glug of muscle-relaxant foam and sank into the bubbles with a sigh, a second bottle of beer on the side of the bath within easy reach. He leant his head back and closed his eyes, letting his thoughts drift.

They drifted inevitably to the woman with the pink hair and her friend. He was still trying to work out in his head how the plan would go and something just wasn't sitting right with it. He wanted to make the one with the pink hair part of his final exhibit by sitting her in the shop window wearing a suicide vest and wired into the 'explosives' on the doors and windows. Up the urgency a bit by having her holding a dead man's switch maybe? Drop a note through the brunette's door telling her where to find her friend and then stand back and watch the action. There was one fatal flaw in his plan however. Fatal to him. The two women could identify him. He sighed and reached for the beer. Time to come up with a Plan B, where B was not for bomb.

Closing his eyes again and trying to come up with an answer, he was lulled by the warmth of the water and his exhaustion and fell asleep. When he jolted awake some time later, the water was lukewarm and he was starting to feel chilled.

'Fuck.' He climbed out of the bath and dried his hands before checking the time on his mobile. Ten p.m. He dried himself roughly off before wrapping the towel around his waist and heading into his bedroom to get dressed. When he opened his wardrobe he saw the old fishing vest he'd been planning to rig with fake explosives and wires along with an old mobile phone to make them think he could remote detonate. It was a shame he'd had to scrap that idea, but he'd decided what he was going to do. The idea must have formed when he was sleeping.

Before he could deal with Miss Marple and her mate, he

had to complete his exhibition. It was going to take a bit of time to rig all the wiring and hang all the images. It was going to be a long night.

Just before midnight, he parked his van around the back of the old BrightHouse shop. He quickly dealt with the padlock using a pair of bolt cutters and let himself in to the store. It smelled a bit musty, the way buildings do after they've been standing empty for a while. Returning to his van he grabbed his bags of cables, sensors and tools and the cardboard tubes containing his precious images.

There was just enough light to make out the layout of the shop and he crept silently along the side wall to the front of the shop so he could peer into the shopping street. All was quiet and there was nobody around. He'd been worried about a homeless bloke who sometimes kipped in the doorway, but there was no sign of him or his sleeping bag. He knew that chances were someone would walk past while he was there so he'd need to keep his wits about him. Hopefully though, anyone walking past would think some homeless person had broken in and was dossing down for the night, or they'd be too drunk to even notice.

The first thing he did was to lay cabling all along the base of the four large windows to the left of the front door, with motion sensors at regular intervals. He continued the wiring round to the door itself and around the handles before finishing it in the window to the right of the door. He then connected it all up to a package of fake explosives he'd fashioned out of brown tubes, gaffer tape, a circuit board and a digital timer. He reckoned it was convincing enough to buy his exhibition some time. He was just sad he wouldn't be around to witness people's reactions. He wondered, not for the first time, how Banksy could bear remaining in the shadows after all this time, and not want to bask in the glory of his art. But then, of course, once your identity is known, the mystery and intrigue that brought such success is destroyed. He hoped, at the very least, that he would be able to bask in the glory of his exhibition on the internet. It was just a shame he didn't have anyone to share it with. It shouldn't have been like this, a solo endeavour, but Bob had other ideas, didn't he? So be it. He didn't need anyone else anyway. He was The Maestro.

Checking the street was still quiet, he took out all his carefully printed and prepared exhibits and laid them in order on the floor. Once he'd decided how high they should be placed, it didn't take long to peel off the almost invisible double-sided tape he'd already applied and secure them to the glass. One final artistic touch was to attach the cartoon-style image of an explosion with the word BOOM! in the door. Once he'd finished, he quickly gathered up his bags, tools and the now-empty cardboard tubes and loaded them back into the van before taking one last look around the store. He'd worn gloves at every stage of preparation and wasn't too worried about DNA being found, as he could easily say he'd been a customer in the past or even worked in the building. Hopefully, if the next bit of business went smoothly, he'd be able to come back as a spectator later in the morning. After he pulled the back door closed, he locked it with a replacement padlock he'd brought with him and stuck another BOOM! sign on it. He hadn't bothered wiring the inside of the solid door as it couldn't be seen from the front windows. He was confident this would buy his exhibition enough time.

As he climbed into his van, the killer was feeling bone-weary. He would have killed to go home and crawl into bed right now, but some things just couldn't wait. Time was of the essence when he had no idea if the two women had already gone to the police. All he could do was hope they hadn't and that his actions tonight would prevent them from ever doing so. Or ever doing anything for that matter.

CHAPTER 42

Cereal killer

Amy was dozing fitfully when the text message arrived. Reaching groggily for her mobile she saw it was three a.m. and the message was from Jenny.

Emergency! Please come. My house. Now!

'Oh Christ, what now, Jenny?' Amy mumbled as she pushed her hair out of her eyes and sat up in bed, fumbling for the bedside lamp as she tried to wake up properly. Her head ached and she felt exhausted. What could possibly have happened that Jenny needed her so urgently? Making a decision, she tried phoning, but the call went to voicemail. 'Bugger,' Amy sighed. She texted: *What's up? Can't it wait 'til morning?* No response. Feeling she had no other option, Amy dragged her jeans and a sweatshirt on and headed downstairs, where she shoved her feet into trainers, found her glasses and grabbed her car keys.

It was still dark outside and Amy was grumbling to herself as she opened the front door. She gave a little scream when she saw there was a tall figure on her doorstep.

'Willem! God, you nearly gave me a heart attack. What on earth are you doing here? It's three o'clock in the sodding morning.'

'I could ask you the same thing, Amy. What are you doing leaving the house at three in the morning? Has something happened?'

'Would you believe me if I said going for a run? No? Thought not. It's Jenny,' she sighed.

'What now?' Willem asked.

'Honestly? I have no idea. I just got a text message from her asking me to come and that it was urgent.'

'Did you try calling her?'

'Yes, of course. No answer. I can't ignore it.'

'No, I s'pose not. Why did you even have your phone on?'

Amy shook her head. 'You wouldn't understand. It's just something Jenny and I promised to do – always have our mobiles on.'

Willem raised his eyebrows. 'What is it with you two?'

'I have to go,' Amy said, not offering an answer to his question.

'Then I'm coming with you,' Willem said firmly.

'What? No. You can't. Jenny'll have kittens.'

'Well, we both know how fond she is of cats, so I don't think that'll be a problem, do you?'

Amy sighed. 'Okay. Your car or mine?'

'Let's take mine,' Willem said, leading the way to his car.

As they drove the short distance to Jenny's house, Amy asked again what Willem had been doing at her house in the middle of the night.

'Keeping an eye on you, Amy. I knew something was going on and I couldn't just do nothing. Watching you and keeping you safe was the only thing I could think of. I was starting to worry about how I was going to stay awake mind you. Then I saw a light go on in your bedroom, and I was just about to ring the bell when you opened the door, and here we are.'

'Yes, here we are,' Amy sighed. She was actually secretly rather chuffed that Willem had been looking out for her, but she didn't want to go all damsel-in-distress. 'I hope Jenny's okay. I can't imagine why she would be messaging me at this time of night.'

'I don't know, but I guess we'll find out soon enough,' Willem said as he parked the car in Jenny's road.

The downstairs lights were on in Jenny's house but there was no answer when Amy knocked and rang the bell. She looked at Willem as if to ask, 'What now?' He reached past her and tried the handle. The door was unlocked and they went into the hall. The house was quiet.

'Jenny?' Amy called out. No answer.

Amy led the way through to the kitchen at the back of the house. As she stepped into the bright little room, she gave a gasp. Jenny was sitting at the kitchen table wearing what looked like an old fishing vest, a drab green thing with lots of pockets that seemed to be stuffed with something and had wires protruding from them. Her arms were tied to the arms of the chair with long black cable ties and there was grey tape across her mouth. Above it, her eyes were as wide as saucers and filled with terror, tears and snot mingling on her face.

And, standing behind her, was the killer. He was holding one hand out and in it was a small black barrel with a wire coming from the bottom which was connected to the contraption Jenny was wearing. His thumb was pressing down on a round, white button on the top of the device. He looked pleased to see Amy. He looked less pleased when Willem appeared in the doorway.

'Don't come any closer!' the killer exclaimed, holding the device out towards them. 'One false move and I lift my thumb and we all get blown to smithereens.'

Amy was speechless, tears streaming down her own face now as she took in the tableau before her. She met Jenny's eyes with her own and tried to send her a message of strength, but she'd gone completely blank.

Willem started to move past Amy, but she put out her arm to stop him.

'No!' she told him, but she could feel the anger rising in him at the scene before them. Willem stepped back reluctantly. 'It's okay, Jenny. It's going to be okay,' she said, desperately trying to work out what to do. 'Let's all just stay calm,' she said, raising her palms. As she spoke, she moved slightly to her right, where the boxes of breakfast cereal were lined up on the work surface. 'Willem, why don't you sit down?' she said, getting eye contact with him and nodding at the chair opposite Jenny. Willem frowned but obeyed and the killer followed Willem's movements as he pulled out the chair to sit down. Then, hearing a rustling noise, the killer quickly spun his head back to Amy, who was pulling something out of one of the cereal boxes. She shook it and what looked like a tea towel fell to the floor, revealing a gun in her hand which she pointed at the killer.

The killer thrust the dead man's switch at her and Jenny squawked behind the tape. 'Don't fucking do it,' the killer said. 'If I die, we all die.'

Amy, who hadn't actually thought past this moment, carried on pointing the gun at him. And that was when Willem got calmly up, took the gun from Amy's shaking hand and walked round the table to where the killer was standing.

'Do it,' Willem said, holding the gun to the killer's temple. 'Go on, do it. I dare you. Drop the switch.'

'Willem! No, what the fuck are you doing? Are you insane?' Amy screamed. Jenny was still squawking away behind the tape covering her mouth, her eyes now the size of dinner plates.

Willem held the gun steady and waited. 'Do it,' he said again.

The killer was shaking and sweating, but his thumb remained firmly on the switch.

'Willem!' Amy exclaimed again. 'What the hell are you doing?'

'He's bluffing,' Willem said, not taking his eyes off the man in front of him.

'What?! How do you know? And what if you're wrong?' Amy sounded frantic.

'Trust me, Amy. The vest is a fake. Nothing's going to blow up.' As if to demonstrate his point, he knocked the switch out of the killer's hand and in one swift movement had kicked his legs out from under him and brought him to the floor.

Amy screamed. Jenny tried to scream. The killer gasped as he hit the floor.

But nothing went BOOM!

'Oh my God, oh my God!' Amy exclaimed. 'I thought we were all going to die! But how did you know the explosives weren't real?' she asked Willem who was now kneeling with his knee in the killer's back.

'Army training. I did two years' National Service back in South Africa when I was eighteen. Stayed on and became a specialist in explosives.'

'Huh. Well, you learn something new every day,' Amy said, sounding impressed.

'Oh, there's a lot you don't know about me, Amy Archer.'

'Clearly. Maybe I'll have to take the time to rectify that,' Amy said, smiling at Willem. She was brought back to the here and now by grunting noises and wriggling coming from Jenny. 'Oh God, sorry, Jenny,' she exclaimed before tearing the tape off Jenny's mouth.

'If you two have quite finished flirting!' Jenny said. 'Could you free my arms?'

Amy found a pair of scissors in the drawer and proceeded to snip through the cable ties binding her to the chair.

'I'm getting rid of these fucking chairs and buying some with no arms,' Jenny said as she rubbed the circulation back into her hands.

Behind her Willem was still kneeling on Jeff's back. 'Before you plan a trip to IKEA, have you got something I can tie this dickhead up with?'

Jenny got up and rummaged about in the drawer the scissors had come out of, producing cable ties similar to the ones that had been used to bind her.

'I'm not going to ask,' Willem said as he forced Jeff to his feet and onto the chair Jenny had just vacated. He secured Jeff's arms before turning to Amy, who appeared to be in a bit of shock. 'I don't know about you two, but I could do with a cuppa right about now,' he said. 'Shall I put the kettle on?'

Amy nodded mutely.

'Knock yourself out,' Jenny said.

A few minutes later they were all sitting round the kitchen table with steaming mugs – with cats on, naturally – of tea.

'Fuck's sake, not you too,' Jenny complained when she tasted the sugar Willem had heaped in.

They sat quietly for a while, sipping their tea and watching

Jeff, the serial killer, who was glowering at them from his side of the table.

'Can we gag him?' Jenny asked after a while. 'Seems only fair after he did it to me. Mind you, I won't have to wax my 'tache this week, so maybe he did me a favour,' she shrugged.

That seemed to bring Amy to her senses. 'You wax? Huh. Never knew that.'

'I think we should see what he has to say for himself, don't you?' Willem said.

'Hm, s'pose. Can I put tape across his mouth and then pull it off first though?' Jenny asked.

Amy and Willem looked at each other. 'Don't see why not,' Willem said, and Amy shrugged.

Jenny got up and went to the same drawer, producing a roll of black duct tape. 'What? Doesn't every kitchen have an abduction-and-serial-killer drawer?' she asked innocently when Willem raised his eyebrows as she cut a length of tape off. She then proceeded to stick the tape over Jeff's mouth, pressing it down hard. 'Give it a couple of minutes,' she said as she sat down and took another mouthful of tea, grimacing at the sweetness. 'Anyone for more tea? Jeff? You'll have a cup, won't you?'

Amy and Willem just stared at Jenny, neither knowing quite how to handle this version of their friend.

Jenny refilled the kettle and made another mug of tea. She didn't bother putting sugar in it. Or milk. Or, in fact, tea. She then threw the mug of boiling water at Jeff, scalding his abdomen and crotch. He screamed silently behind the tape and wrenched his body upwards. The other two watched as Jenny then got up and ripped the tape off Jeff's face as hard and fast as she could. 'Oops,' she said, 'clumsy me.'

'You crazy bitch!' Jeff spat at her.

'Now, now, I don't think you're in any position to be calling me names, are you?' Jenny remonstrated.

'I should've fucking killed you when I had the chance!'

Jenny nodded. 'Yes, you probably should have. The tables have turned somewhat now, haven't they?'

'What are you going to do to me?' the killer asked of no one in particular.

'Hm… haven't decided yet. Whatever it is will be slow and painful though,' Jenny grinned at him. She looked over at the gun where Willem had placed it on the work surface by the kettle, and the killer followed her gaze, the colour draining from his face. 'I mean, kneecaps are the go-to in the movies, aren't they? Always thought that looked particularly painful,' Jenny continued.

The killer attempted a laugh and shook his head, clearly not taking Jenny's threats seriously.

'You shouldn't underestimate her,' Amy said, nodding at her friend.

'She's right, you know. Other men made the mistake of underestimating me. I'm really rather tired of it now. And when you took Bella, well, you kind of signed your own death warrant as far as I'm concerned.'

'You wouldn't… you couldn't… you wouldn't get away with it,' the killer blustered.

'Try me,' Jenny said.

The killer fell silent once more.

'She's very impressive,' Willem said to Amy.

'She is,' Amy agreed. 'But what are we going to do with him? Seriously.'

'I am serious,' Jenny declared. 'About the kneecapping anyway.'

'All that's going to do is make a right bloody mess on your kitchen floor and wake the neighbours,' Amy pointed out.

Jenny thought for a moment. 'I know, but I can shoot through a cushion or something. Or make a silencer out of a Coke bottle.'

'What?' Amy exclaimed. Willem just looked dumbfounded.

'Yeah, it's a thing. I saw a YouTube video on how to do it.'

'Jeez, I thought I googled some dodgy things,' Amy said, shaking her head.

'Nobody's going to be shooting anybody, kneecaps or otherwise,' Willem said finally, putting his hands flat on the table. 'We just want to talk to him.'

'You might only want to talk to him. I want to fucking shoot him,' Jenny said, glaring at Willem. 'My house, my rules.' With that, she got up and went to the fridge, returning with a large bottle of Coke, which she proceeded to empty down the sink.

'Er… can I have some before you tip it all away?' Amy interrupted her mid-flow.

'What? Oh yeah, of course,' Jenny said, stopping what she was doing to pour Amy a glass of Coke and offering some to Willem, who said no, before she continued to pour the rest of the fizzy brown liquid down the sink.

This was too much for Jeff. 'You're both as fucking mad as each other! Help me out here, brother,' he pleaded to Willem.

'Two things: One, I am most definitely not your brother, and two, I'm rather enjoying watching you squirm. Oh, and by the way, she's right about the silencer,' Willem nodded sagely.

While this exchange was taking place, Jenny was still at the kitchen sink, pouring a small amount of water into the bottle.

She then asked Amy to hold the bottle level on its side while she carefully taped the muzzle of the gun into the bottle's opening.

The killer watched, transfixed, as did Willem.

'Wouldn't want to be in your shoes. Brother. Looks like she means business,' Willem nodded.

Jenny spoke next. 'Could I see you in the other room for a moment, Amy?'

Amy followed her friend into the lounge, Jenny holding the now rather unbalanced gun and homemade suppressor, carefully keeping the water level below the muzzle of the gun.

'You're not really going to shoot him, are you?' Amy hissed.

'No. Well, probably not. Bit tricky with your lover boy sitting at the table.'

'Er… he is not my lover boy,' Amy protested.

'Then what, pray tell, was he doing with you at three o'clock in the morning, eh? Answer me that,' Jenny said, raising her eyebrows.

'He was just keeping an eye on me.'

'I bet he was!' Jenny winked.

'Oh shut up,' Amy said, blushing. 'Besides, he saved your bacon, didn't he? You should be thanking him, not accusing him of cramping your murderous style.'

'Whatever. Anyway, getting back to the business at hand… Have you got your mobile on you?'

Amy nodded.

'Then set it to record. Let's go and get a confession out of Jeffrey Timberlake or whatever the fuck his name is.'

Amy pulled her phone out of her pocket and found the Voice Memos app in the Extras folder on her iPhone. She hit the record button, nodded at Jenny and followed her back into the kitchen, where they took up their seats at the table once more. Jenny rested the Coke bottle on the table, pointing at Jeff. He looked like he might wet himself. He looked like he already had. Willem just looked bemused.

CHAPTER 43

Shipmates

'So, Jeff, this is what's going to happen,' Jenny began. 'We're going to ask you questions and you're going to answer them. If at any point I don't like what I hear, I will shoot you. Simple. Okay?'

'What the fuck… You…' Jeff began.

'Uh uh uh,' Jenny said, lifting the gun. It wasn't easy with the balance affected by the improvised silencer. She wished she'd had time to practise in the mirror. Spud would laugh if he could see her now.

Jeff shut up.

'That's better. Let's begin,' Jenny said. 'What's your full name?'

Jeff hesitated.

'Starting with an easy one here, Jeff. Pretty sure you must know your own name, eh?'

Jeff swallowed. 'Jeff, Jeffrey, Teller.'

'There, that wasn't so hard now, was it?' Jenny smiled at him. 'Well, Jeffrey Teller, perhaps you'd be kind enough to tell us what you've been up to in the town these past weeks.'

Jeff was silent once more, his mouth going up and down like a goldfish, but no words coming out.

'Need a little memory jog?' Jenny asked. 'Shall we start at the beach huts? I believe that was your first port of call. Come along now, Jeff, you're amongst friends here. What made you copy The Exhibitionist, the man we knew as Robert Seymour?'

'I didn't fucking copy him. I didn't copy anyone. I'm the original. Robert Seymour stole my ideas,' Jeff sneered the other man's name as if it disgusted him.

Amy and Jenny looked at one another.

'What do you mean he stole your ideas? How could he…?' It was Amy who spoke this time, a confused look on her face.

Jeff looked at the floor as he tried to decide what to tell them.

'Well?' Jenny prompted, shifting the gun a little.

Jeff appeared to have made up his mind, figuring he had nothing to lose at this point. 'I knew Robert Seymour as Bob. We worked on the boats together for a while.'

'The boats? You mean the ferries?'

'Yeah, P&O. We both worked in engineering, week on, week off. You got to know your workmates pretty well living on board for seven days at a time. Bob, that's what he went by then, and I eventually realised we liked the same books and films and stuff and we got talking one night about the kind of dark stuff we fantasised about.' He paused, casting his mind back to those long days on board ship.

Jenny jiggled the gun to encourage him to continue.

Jeff sighed, resigned to telling them everything.

'Over time, as we learned to trust each other I suppose, we talked about what it would be like to act out some of those fantasies for real. Back then I don't think either of us actually believed we'd do it,' he shrugged.

'What changed?' Amy asked.

'Dunno really. I think maybe the more we discussed actually doing it, the more we realised that was what we really wanted to do. When we left the boats we stayed friends and we'd talk about it from time to time over a few beers. Then, when they did the first Triennial exhibition in 2008, the idea began to form of tying the killings into the art installations. It was *my* idea.'

'If you were talking about it all those years ago, why the long delay?' Jenny asked.

'Bob moved abroad to work and we gradually lost touch. I s'pose I just got on with my life – didn't think about it as much without Bob to bounce ideas around with. I knew he was back in the country – came back just before Covid hit – and I thought maybe we'd pick up where we left off, but apparently Bob had other ideas. When that first body was found last year I knew it was him.'

'You must have been pretty pissed off. Felt betrayed,' Amy said.

'He totally stole your thunder, didn't he?' Jenny said, grinning and obviously delighted at the idea.

Jeff glared at her.

'You must've felt like killing him,' Jenny said.

Amy glanced across at Jenny. Was she planting the idea that Jeff killed Bob in Willem's mind and on the recording?

'Fucking right I did,' Jeff said through gritted teeth. 'Traitorous bastard. Took the coward's way out though, didn't he, killing himself. Denied me the pleasure.'

Bugger, Amy thought. *So much for that idea. Nice try though, Jenny.*

'Guess he had a conscience after all,' Jenny said.

Jeff shook his head. 'Trust me, Robert Seymour didn't have a conscience. I was actually surprised when I heard he'd topped himself. Seemed out of character.'

Amy didn't like where this was heading. 'You must've hated being called his copycat,' she suggested, trying to steer the conversation back to Jeff.

'Fucking right I did. I'm nobody's copycat. The original idea was mine. Maybe that's why he took the easy way out – knew I'd be coming for him.'

Phew, Amy thought. *That's better.*

'Well, whichever of you two sickos had the idea, it's over now. For both of you,' Jenny said.

Jeff shrugged and smirked. 'I've had a pretty good run. Completed my final exhibit. You can't take that away from me. Nobody can. A nice rest in prison doesn't sound so bad: three meals a day, plenty of rest, no bills to pay. And all the time in the world to write my story and make my name.'

The three friends stared at him. It was Amy who finally spoke. 'What final exhibit? What have you done?'

Jeff remained silent and smirking.

'Now can I kneecap him?' Jenny asked, looking round in turn at Amy and Willem.

'No!' they said in unison.

'Spoilsports,' Jenny pouted.

'What final exhibit?' Amy asked again. 'Tell us or we'll let Jenny ask you next time.'

At that, Jenny got up and filled the kettle again. Then she went back to the abduction-and-serial-killer drawer and took out a pair of pliers, which she placed on the table in front of Jeff. His eyes widened in alarm.

'You wouldn't,' he said, shaking his head.

Jenny just smiled at him and raised her eyebrows.

'This is a woman who keeps a gun in her Fruit 'n Fibre,'

Amy pointed out. 'Just saying,' she added, holding her palms out and shrugging.

Still Jeff said nothing. He watched Jenny as if he was trying to read her expression. Her grin widened. His brain scrambled to decide what to do.

Tired of waiting for an answer, Jenny got up, picked up the pliers and stepped next to Jeff, where she proceeded to place his little finger in between the metal jaws. She squeezed. The remaining colour drained out of Jeff's face. He still couldn't quite believe she would actually do it. Jenny squeezed harder.

'Okay, okay, stop, I'll tell you!' he exclaimed.

Jenny removed the pliers and sat back down. She looked a little disappointed.

'I've set up a kind of exhibition,' he offered.

'What exhibition? Where?' Amy asked.

Jeff screwed up his face. He didn't want to give them this information. It was too soon.

Jenny got up and reached for the freshly boiled kettle, turning towards Jeff. He knew this was no idle threat. 'Fuck,' he said. 'In town. Photographs of all my art installations.'

'Where in town?' Jenny pushed, holding the kettle out.

'The old BrightHouse store,' Jeff told her reluctantly.

The friends looked at each other. 'Sandgate Road,' all three chimed simultaneously.

'We need to get there,' Amy said. 'Before anyone sees it.'

'What are we going to do with him?' Willem asked.

'Give him to the police?' Amy suggested.

'Can I shoot him first?' Jenny asked. 'Just one little bullet in the knee. For Bella.'

'No!' Amy and Willem said again.

Jenny huffed. 'You two are no fun.'

Willem seemed to take charge again at this point. 'Amy, can you drive my car?'

'Yes, I think so,' Amy nodded.

'Right, this is what we'll do…'

CHAPTER 44

Bang to rights

Twenty-five minutes later and Willem was driving Jeff's van, which they'd found parked a short distance away from Jenny's house. Jeff was trussed up in the back, groaning as he bounced about like a pinball as Willem took corners at speed.

'Oops, sorry,' Willem called back to him, wrenching the wheel on another bend. The roads were empty at this time of night thankfully.

Jenny had taken great delight in slapping another strip of tape across the killer's mouth and all Willem could hear from the back were muffled moans. There was another strip of tape across Jeff's forehead and underneath it was a memory stick onto which Jenny had downloaded the recorded confession from Amy's phone. She'd written LISTEN TO ME on the gaffer tape using a black Sharpie pen and, as an afterthought, scrawled KILLER across the tape covering his mouth.

'Nice,' Amy nodded approvingly.

Then, with Jenny covering him with the gun, Willem had released Jeff's arms from the chair and bundled him out to the van, where he'd tied him up once again, hands behind his back and ankles together. Lying on the floor of the van, Jeff was helplessly rolling around, unable to stop himself.

While Willem drove the van in the direction of the police station, Amy and Jenny were headed into town in Willem's car.

Parking as close as they could to the old BrightHouse shop, they walked quickly round the corner onto Sandgate Road.

'Oh shit!' Amy said as they stood in front of the display in the front windows.

Jenny remained silent as she walked the length of the display. She stopped near the front door. When Amy caught up with her she saw silent tears streaming down her friend's pale face. It was Bella.

'Phone Willem,' Jenny said, turning her tear-streaked face to Amy.

'What? Why?' Amy looked confused.

'Phone Willem. Tell him to stop and find out exactly where he is,' Jenny said insistently.

Amy did as she was told and Willem answered on the second ring.

'Amy, what is it. Are you okay? I'm nearly at the police station,' he said.

'You have to stop,' Amy said.

'Ask him where he is and tell him to wait for us,' Jenny instructed.

Amy got the information from Willem and hung up after insisting that he wait for them, then she followed Jenny, who was already jogging back to the car.

'He's on Castle Hill Avenue,' Amy said as she got into the driver's side again.

Jenny just nodded.

'Are you going to tell me what we're doing?'

Jenny just shook her head. Amy drove. It wasn't far at all and very soon she was pulling up behind the white van Willem was driving. He got out as they pulled up.

'What's going on?' he asked.

Amy looked at him and shrugged.

'Open the back,' was all Jenny said.

Willem looked at Jenny and back at Amy, who simply shrugged again. Doing as he was asked, Willem opened one of the van's rear doors. Jeff looked up from his place on the floor. His eyes widened with fear when he saw Jenny. She reached into her pocket and drew out the gun.

'What the...?' Amy hissed. She didn't get to finish the sentence, as Jenny pointed the gun at Jeff and pulled the trigger.

Amy screamed. Willem looked stunned. Jeff tried to scream behind the tape.

Jenny then turned calmly back to the car, calling to Willem, 'You can go again now.'

'Jesus Christ, Amy! Why did she have the gun?' Willem exclaimed.

'I don't know! I didn't know she did! Oh my God!' Amy said, putting her hands to her face.

'What now?' Willem asked.

'I suppose we carry on with the plan,' Amy said. 'Nothing's really changed, has it?'

'Apart from the fact that Jenny just put a bullet in Jeff's knee!' Willem said, shaking his head in disbelief.

'Well, apart from that. Look, we need to get back to BrightHouse – he's got photographs of all his victims and the murders in the bloody windows. We need to get in and remove them before the town wakes up.'

Willem took a deep breath. 'Right, I'll park the van where we agreed and then meet you there.'

Amy nodded. 'Be careful.'

Willem parked Jeff's van just around the corner from the police station. Jeff was still groaning away in the back, his knee shattered and bloody. Willem grimaced as he climbed in the back, careful not to get any blood on his shoes or hands.

Jeff's groaning became pleading, but it all sounded the same from behind the tape.

Willem looked around the back of the van, found what he was looking for and hit Jeff hard across the temple with the Maglite torch. Jeff grunted once and then fell silent.

Climbing quickly out of the van, Willem locked it up, pocketing the keys and looking all around before walking briskly away and back towards town. He was wracking his brain for the nearest public phone box. Were there even any left in the town? He had an idea there was one in Guildhall Street and he set off in that direction, jogging as much as possible. As he ran, he wondered how on earth he'd got himself mixed up in this madness. By the time he reached the phone box he was puffing like an old steam train. 'I'm too old for this shit,' he muttered to himself as he leaned down with his hands on his knees and tried to slow his breathing. Otherwise the police would think they'd got some pervy heavy breather on the line.

His breathing slowed, Willem checked to make sure the phone was working, fully expecting it to have been vandalised. To his relief, it was working and he dialled 999, holding his breath as he waited for the ringing tone to stop and the call to be answered.

'Which service do you require?' the operator asked.

'Police,' Willem said.

When the call was connected, Willem took a deep breath: 'There's a white van parked in Augusta Gardens, Folkestone.'

Willem read out the number plate he'd written on the back of the blue nitrile glove he was wearing. 'In it you'll find the man responsible for the killings in the town. Please hurry.' He was shaking as he hung up the phone, not waiting to be asked for his name or any more information, hoping that was enough and that he'd managed to hide his slight accent.

It was a short jog down the street and around to Sandgate Road and he could see Amy and Jenny as soon as he rounded the corner.

Amy looked up as he arrived next to them.

'Okay?' she asked. 'All done?'

'Yes. Well, hopefully. What if they don't take the call seriously?' Willem said.

'I'm sure they will. They'd have to, wouldn't they?' Amy asked, looking to Jenny for confirmation.

'I don't mind going back and shooting him again,' Jenny offered, not taking her eyes off the door in front of her.

'That won't be necessary. Will it, Willem?' Amy said, looking to Willem for support.

'No, absolutely not,' Willem agreed. 'Besides, it looks as though we have a more pressing problem,' he said, grimacing as he took in the horrific gallery laid out before them.

'There's wires all along the front of the shop,' Jenny said, pointing them out to Willem, who was still reeling from the images.

Shaking his head as if to clear his vision, Willem focused on what Jenny was showing him. He bent down and used the torch on his mobile phone to take a better look.

'Looks like motion sensors,' Willem said, nodding towards the white units evenly spaced along the front windows.

Standing up, he followed the cables to the front door, raising his eyebrows at the BOOM! sign stuck there.

'What do we do?' Amy asked.

'Well, the way he's got the place rigged, if we try and open the door, or disturb the glass in any of the windows, the place will blow.'

'Maybe we should just call the police?' Amy suggested.

'I agree with Amy,' Willem said.

'No,' Jenny shook her head vigorously. 'Nobody gets to see Bella like this. Not if I can help it.' As she spoke, she lifted her hand and placed it on Bella's picture.

'But what can we do, Jen?' Amy asked gently, putting her own hand on her friend's arm. 'Just the police – they could put up screens or something.'

Jenny just shook her head.

Amy sighed and looked to Willem for help.

'Is there a rear entrance? There must be. Let me go and check it out,' he said, turning away. 'Won't be long.'

'Okay, hurry,' Amy said, looking at the time on her phone. 'It'll be light soon.'

Willem was only gone a few minutes. 'There's another BOOM! sign on the back door. I can't tell any more than that though.'

The three of them stood staring at the images, wondering what to do.

Eventually it was Willem who spoke. 'I'm going to go out on a limb here and say that he might be bluffing.'

'What? What d'you mean?' Amy asked, turning to look at him.

'Well, there might not actually be any explosives. Not real ones anyway. Think about the suicide vest he put on Jenny. This could be a fake too.'

That was enough for Jenny. 'We're going in,' she said.

'What? No!' Amy exclaimed. 'That's madness, Jenny. We can't risk it. What if he's not bluffing this time?'

Jenny took no notice. 'Come on, back door. Lead the way, Willem,' she ordered.

Seeing that Jenny was going in with or without them, Willem led them around the back of the building to the padlocked door.

'Can you break that?' Jenny asked Willem, pointing to the padlock.

'Yes,' he confirmed. 'Amy, have you got my car key?'

Amy dug his keys out of her pocket and handed them to him, telling him where the car was parked.

'Won't be long,' Willem said as he turned away and jogged back to his car. 'I really am too old for this shit,' he muttered for the second time.

When he returned about five minutes later, he was holding two spanners. 'Toolbox in the car,' he said by way of explanation.

The two friends watched as he proceeded to position the tools on the padlock before forcing them together like nutcrackers. The padlock broke as Amy and Jenny looked on in admiration.

'Something else you picked up in the army?' Amy asked.

'No, boarding school,' Willem grinned as he pocketed the spanners and the now-broken lock.

Jenny reached for the door, but Willem put his hand out and stopped her. 'No,' he said firmly, that one word conveying all the authority he could muster. 'No way, Jenny. You two need to step back. Get behind that skip,' he said, pointing to the large metal rubbish skip a short distance away.

Jenny glared at him, but allowed herself to be led away by Amy, and the two women crouched down behind the skip.

'Ooh, my knees,' Amy groaned. 'I'm too old for this shit. You might have to pull me up afterwards.'

Jenny didn't respond, just peered around the skip to where Willem was reaching for the door handle. She held her breath as he pulled open the door. Nothing. No explosion, no bang, and definitely no BOOM. Jenny was up and running towards the rear door, leaving Amy struggling to push herself back up. 'Thanks for nothing, friend,' she called out after Jenny's departing back.

Soon all three of them were in the main shop. Jenny made a beeline for the images of Bella, peeling them carefully off the window as if she might hurt Bella herself if she wasn't gentle. Either side of her, Amy and Willem were doing the same, and it didn't take long for them to remove all the photographs, placing them in a pile on the shop floor. Outside, the sun was coming up and the inside of the shop was becoming brighter.

'What now?' Amy asked.

'I s'pose we get out of here,' Jenny said.

'What about the wiring, the sensors?' Willem asked.

'Not our problem,' Jenny shrugged. 'No harm can come to anyone if we leave them, can it? There are no explosives. Let's just go, before anyone sees us.'

Willem picked up the stack of photos and they left the way they'd come in and walked in silence back to Willem's car. Amy got in the front beside Willem and Jenny climbed in the back.

'Where to?' Willem asked.

'Back to yours, Jenny? We seriously need to get our stories straight,' Amy said.

'Fine by me,' Jenny agreed, stifling a yawn.

Trooping back into Jenny's house a few minutes later, they took up their seats at the kitchen table once more.

'I'm knackered,' Jenny said.

'Me too,' Amy agreed.

'Me three,' Willem added. 'I think the adrenaline is starting to wear off. And it's been a hell of a night.'

'It certainly has,' Amy said tiredly. 'I don't think I could sleep though. Not after everything.'

'I could,' Jenny said, yawning again. 'I could sleep for a week.'

'Don't you feel anything about what happened? What we did,' Willem asked.

Jenny looked at him. 'Yeah, actually. I feel a ton of regret that I didn't shoot the fucker in his other leg too.'

Willem looked shocked.

Amy began to giggle. 'Sorry,' she said through her laughter. 'Your face, Willem! Have you met my crazy friend, Jenny? Let me introduce you.'

Willem looked across at Amy in confusion.

'Sorry,' Amy said, 'I think I'm a bit hysterical.'

'Give her a slap if you want, Willem,' Jenny advised, only half joking.

'You two are quite mad,' Willem said, pressing his fingers to his temples.

'Sorry, sorry,' Amy said again, trying to stop the laughter that insisted on escaping her lips.

'Or you could make tea, Willem. Hot and sweet for shock, right?' Jenny suggested, beginning to laugh herself.

Willem simply sat there shaking his head. 'To be quite

honest, I think I need something a darn sight stronger than tea right now.'

'Good idea,' Jenny said, getting up and fetching three tumblers and a bottle of whisky from the cupboard. She poured a generous measure into each glass and pushed one each towards Amy and Willem.

Amy took the offered glass and took a sip, grimacing at the burning liquid. Willem knocked his back in one and held out his glass for a refill.

'Steady on there, old boy, that's eighteen-year-old single malt,' Jenny said. 'Show it some respect.'

Willem glowered at her but took the glass and sipped at the amber-coloured liquid. Putting his glass down, he leaned his elbows on the table and pressed his fingers to his eyes.

'Sorry you got dragged into this, Willem,' Amy said.

'Don't apologise, Amy. He dragged himself into it, didn't you, Willem?' Jenny said.

Willem lifted his head again and looked at Jenny, bemusement showing on his face. 'You know, Jenny, I suppose I did, didn't I? Gesondheid!' he said, lifting his glass and tipping it in Jenny's direction.

Willem could feel Amy's eyes on him and he turned to see her frowning.

'Who sneezed?' she asked, looking puzzled.

'What?' Jenny and Willem said at the same time.

'You said gesundheit,' Amy said to Willem.

'Ah! You're thinking of the German version of "bless you". It means "good health" and we use a similar word to say "cheers" in Afrikaans.'

'Oh,' Amy said.

'As fascinating as this language lesson is, don't you think we ought to have a bit of a debrief and work out what we're going to say if the police come knocking?' Jenny said. 'And what are we going to do with all the photos we took from BrightHouse?'

Amy groaned. 'Can't we just drink whisky and not think about it?'

The look on Jenny's face told her that was not an option.

'I think the police should have the photos,' Willem said. 'They're evidence which could be used to help convict the killer.'

'I agree with Willem,' Amy said.

'You would,' Jenny glared at her friend.

'You know it makes sense, Jenny. I know you're trying to protect Bella, but the best thing you can do is make sure her killer gets locked up for the rest of his life.'

Jenny grumbled something under her breath, reluctant to admit the other two were right. Amy took the relative silence as acceptance.

'How do we get the photos to them? We can hardly pop them through the letter box,' Amy screwed up her face as she thought.

'I can plant them at his house. At Jeff's house,' Willem said, sounding more than a little reluctant.

'Learn breaking and entering at boarding school too?' Jenny enquired sarcastically.

Willem simply shrugged.

'Okay, that's sorted then. Now we just need an alibi,' Amy said, looking blank. 'Any ideas?'

'Can't we just say we were here? Having dinner and watching a film or something? We can see what was on and make sure we do actually watch it. Agree on what we had to eat. Keep it simple, stick to the story,' Jenny suggested.

'S'pose so,' Amy said, thinking about what Jenny had said. 'What do you think, Willem?'

'I guess it's as good as anything. Bit of an odd threesome though,' he said, pulling a face.

'Who are you calling odd, you weirdo?' Jenny answered. 'And don't be getting any ideas.'

Amy got the giggles again.

Jenny and Willem looked at her and the laughter became infectious. By the time they all fell asleep on the sofa watching their alibi movie, the police had found Jeff trussed up and unconscious in the back of his van and taken him to hospital for treatment. When he came round he was mumbling unintelligibly about 'crazy fucking women' and asking for police protection. He had a big red welt across his forehead where the tape had been removed, and even as he lay cuffed to a hospital bed, detectives were listening to the recording of his confession. It looked as though Jeffrey Teller was bang to rights.

THE END

Readers of my previous book *The Write Way to Die* often ask me what happened to the characters Rosie and Patrick in Pippa's short stories so, here for your enjoyment, is what happened next...

ROSIE AND PATRICK – WHAT HAPPENED NEXT

'That's not a Labrador, Rosie,' my husband, Patrick, said when we arrived at the dog rescue place. 'More like a flabrador,' he snorted, clearly amused by his joke.

I ignored him as I waited for the staff member to open the run where a rather overweight, middle-aged chocolate Labrador stood, tail wagging and taking most of his body with it, waiting to greet us.

'Hello, Rolo!' I said, crouching down to his level and talking to him in that voice reserved for dogs and babies. 'Hello, boy, how are you? You're coming home today.'

Rolo's tail wagged even harder and soon he was out and in my arms, licking my face and generally showing me how happy he was with that news. Soon we were an undignified bundle on the floor.

Patrick didn't join in with the celebrations, simply stood back with his arms folded and an expression of mild disgust on his face.

'I hope you don't expect me to kiss you any time soon,' he said, grimacing as Rolo continued to lick my face.

I didn't bother to reply that I couldn't even remember the last time he'd kissed me. Those thoughts had no place in this moment of pure joy.

After completing the final paperwork, we bundled Rolo into the boot of Patrick's Audi estate – he ignored my pleading that Rolo be allowed to travel on the back seat with me – and set off on the forty-minute drive home.

As we drove, I thought about our old Labrador, Nero, who we'd lost a few months earlier at the ripe old age of thirteen. He'd left such a huge hole in my life that, despite Patrick's protestations, I'd set out to find a new companion. When I saw Rolo on the dog dating site (that's what my sons called the dog rescue website) I knew he was the one for me: middle-aged, overweight and named after a chocolate – we were a match made in heaven. It was going to be so lovely to have someone in the house who listened to me and was always pleased to see me.

Every couple of minutes, I spoke to Rolo to reassure him and let him know we'd be home soon.

'For God's sake, woman, he's a dog. He's got no idea what you're going on about,' Patrick said.

'Yes, he does,' I harrumphed. 'Anyway, it's all in the tone of voice,' I added, sticking my tongue out at him for good measure.

'Nonsense. You might as well say "blah, blah, blah".'

I thought that was probably what Patrick heard nowadays, after thirty-six years of marriage, but didn't say it. What would be the point?

Rolo was as good as gold in the car and soon we were pulling up on the drive of our detached house in Laurel Close. As Patrick parked, I glanced over at the house next door where we had lovely new neighbours. The previous homeowner had had an unfortunate... er... accident and fallen in his bonfire. The new people *never* had bonfires on sunny days, which I thought was very sensible.

We got Rolo out of the car and led him through to the back garden so he could have a wee and a sniff.

'He needs to go on a diet, Rosie,' Patrick said, watching Rolo as he explored his new domain.

'Him and me both. We're going to lose weight together,' I said determinedly.

Patrick had never been overweight, nor very sympathetic to my battle of the bulge.

Patrick soon lost interest in the new addition to the family and disappeared indoors.

I sat on a bench in the garden and soon Rolo came over and settled himself contentedly at my feet. He was mine. And I was his. And together we were going to go from fat to fit. Just one tiny vowel; how hard could it be?

As I got Rolo's dinner that first night, I pondered how much easier it would be to lose weight if someone else prepared your meals. Rolo was on a prescription food recommended by the vet, who'd first eliminated any medical issues that may have caused the weight gain. He'd concluded that Rolo had simply been overfed and under-exercised. Him and me both.

One week later and I'd already lost four pounds and was feeling a little less out of breath when I climbed the stairs. The plan was working. Rolo too had started to slim down a little and this motivated me to keep going. Patrick of course noticed none of this.

After a month, my clothes were all too big and Rolo's collar needed adjusting. Patrick did notice this. The collar, not the clothes. I was still invisible.

After two months, I went and got a new haircut and colour, treated myself to a load of new clothes and make-up, and started to take a real interest in my appearance for the first time in years. I tried on the ballgown I'd worn a year earlier to put the bins out and it hung off me. My confidence and self-esteem were on the rise in proportion to the fall in weight. I remember this Rosie. I've missed her.

Rolo and I had taken to walking on the beach two or three times a week and it was on one such walk that we met Jacques. Tall, slim and ruggedly handsome in a Gallic kind of way, Jacques was charming and friendly and I began to look forward to bumping into him. He seemed genuinely interested in me and what I had to say. Before long, we had exchanged mobile numbers and accidental meetings became deliberate ones. Then we'd started going for coffee after our walks. Rolo liked Jacques too and I took that as a good sign. Dogs are such good judges of character, aren't they?

Jacques was from Normandy, but had fallen in love with England and kept houses in both countries. He was an artist – a painter – and he'd promised to show me his studio.

It was about three months after we met that Jacques finally took me to see his studio. I'd left Rolo at home and told Patrick I was going shopping. He didn't even grunt, let alone look up from the dentistry periodical he was reading.

I met Jacques at the little coffee place which had become

our regular stop. It was located at the top of the steep, cobbled street in the town's creative quarter, which was awash with galleries and studios these days. He was already waiting outside and smiled warmly as I approached. I felt a flush come to my cheeks, and was grateful not to be out of breath and puffing like an old steam train as I would have been just a few short weeks ago.

'Good morning, Rosie,' he said.

'Hello, Jacques, how are you?'

He took my arm and leaned in to kiss one pinkly flushed cheek and then the other. 'I am well, always I am well when I see you,' he smiled. 'And how are you? You look beautiful today.'

I felt the blush intensify. It was so long since anyone had paid me such a compliment. I was out of practice at receiving them and batted the words back. 'I'm excited to see your studio,' I said, changing the subject. 'You've said so little about your work.' All Jacques had told me was that he worked in oils, saying he preferred to let me see his work in the flesh.

'Then I won't keep you waiting,' he said, linking his arm through mine and leading me down the narrow street.

I had a moment of worry when he took my arm. What if someone I knew saw us? But it felt so natural and I didn't want to appear churlish. Besides, what was so wrong about two friends walking arm in arm? Because that's all we were, wasn't it?

We walked in silence until Jacques stopped about half-way down the street, outside a small gallery. In the window was a mix of work by several different artists, including some dramatic seascapes. I wondered if they were Jacques'. I'd got it into my head that he was such a painter.

We went in and Jacques nodded hello to the woman behind the desk and led me to a staircase which wound upwards at the rear of the shop. As we reached the top, he paused and told me to close my eyes.

'No peeping until I tell you,' he said, taking my hand and guiding me forwards. 'Okay, open your eyes,' he instructed a few short steps later.

'Oh!' I said, looking around me where three walls were covered in stunning female nudes.

Jacques' expression changed to one of concern. 'You don't like them?'

'Oh, no, Jacques, they're incredible. They just took me by surprise. I thought you painted seascapes,' I laughed.

'Ah! That's a relief. I thought you didn't like them.'

'I stood quietly, taking in the canvases one by one: the female form in every size, shape and colour, in poses seductive and demure. The one thing they all had in common was that they were clearly painted with passion by a man who adored the female form. I began to feel a little shy and perhaps a little inadequate. I could feel Jacques' eyes on me, trying to read me.

'I would like to paint you, Rosie,' he said finally.

'What? Why? No,' I said, shaking my head.

'Yes, Rosie, of course yes. Why would I not want to paint you?'

'Because I'm an overweight, middle-aged woman whose body – and face – have seen better days,' I dismissed.

'Nonsense. You are a beautiful, vibrant, passionate woman and it would be an honour to capture these qualities on the canvas.'

I made a sort of 'pffft' noise. Even if I believed him, the thought of taking my clothes off in front of him was unimaginable. I hadn't been naked in front of a man who wasn't my husband for nearly forty years. Although I was feeling a bit better about myself since losing weight, it was a huge leap to undress in front of someone.

Seeming to read my mind, Jacques stepped in front of me and put his hands on my shoulders. I stared at the floor.

'Look at me, Rosie,' he said, gently tipping my chin up and forcing me to meet his eyes. 'Will you please at least think about it? Seriously?'

'I... I don't...'

'Shh!' Jacques said, shaking his head and moving his finger to my lips. 'No words now. Just, please, think about it. I will ask you again in one week.'

I simply nodded, knowing that in a week's time my answer would be the same.

'Yes, you can paint me!' I heard myself saying to Jacques one week later. We were on the beach with Rolo, who was paddling in the shallows.

Jacques stopped. 'Really?'

'Yes. Really.' Until that morning, my answer had been steadfastly no, but when Patrick had failed to notice, yet again, my transformation, my bloody-minded side took over. I'd show him!

'Oh, c'est fantastique!' Jacques said, grinning and spinning me round on the pebbles.

I couldn't help laughing. I would worry about the actual taking-my-clothes-off thing another day.

Another day arrived quickly and I found myself back in Jacques' studio. Rolo was with me as he was my unwitting alibi. I'd told Patrick we were driving down the coast for a walk. I'd had a moment's worry when he looked as though he might come with us. I hoped the panic didn't show on my face. There had been a time when I would have loved him to be interested enough to come out with me.

Rolo quickly made himself at home on a blanket Jacques spread out in the corner. It was all right for him, he wasn't the one who had to get his kit off. I stood in the middle of the room feeling like an awkward teenager.

'I'm... um... I'm not sure I can do this,' I said apologetically.

'It's okay, Rosie. I would never ask you to do something you don't feel comfortable with,' Jacques said, smiling gently and taking my hands.

'Sorry,' I said. 'It's just... I haven't... I haven't... you know...' I said shyly.

'I understand. You haven't undressed in front of a man for a very long time.'

I nodded, grateful for his understanding.

'How about this,' Jacques began, 'you get changed behind the screen and put on a robe. One step at a time. See how you feel.'

'Um... okay,' I agreed.

A few minutes later and I found myself reclining on a chaise longue, wearing nothing but a silky robe I found on a chair behind the screen. I briefly wondered how many other women had worn it as I slipped it on and tied the belt tightly around my waist.

'Beautiful,' was all Jacques said. He posed my arms and

legs and tilted my chin.

I could feel my heart beating rapidly at his touch, and my breath catching in my chest.

He didn't speak, simply began to sketch using a stick of charcoal. I tried to stop my brain from overthinking the situation, and let myself relax a little. I watched Jacques as he drew, totally absorbed in what he was doing, and I tried to see myself as he did. After a while I stopped feeling so uncomfortable and my mind began to drift.

I don't know how much time passed, but suddenly Jacques was back in the present and at my side. He gently pulled the robe down my shoulders. I started to object, but then somehow I didn't mind, and I let him lower the silky garment until the tops of my breasts were revealed.

He didn't speak, simply returned to the easel and continued sketching.

I tried to analyse how I was feeling about the situation. I had thought it would feel somehow sexual, erotic, especially considering my attraction to Jacques. But it was neither of those things. It was almost like an out-of-body experience. Jacques had disappeared into the canvas and I was watching some other woman on the chaise longue. So, when Jacques paused and approached me once more, I didn't object when he untied the robe and slipped it off me.

In the following weeks, Rolo and I returned to Jacques' studio many times. The charcoal sketch began to disappear under oils. I wasn't allowed to see it until it was finished, which was a little frustrating, but I respected Jacques' wishes. The initial embarrassment I'd felt had melted away after that first sitting and I now posed unashamedly, even proudly, for him.

On the day of the big reveal, I left Rolo at home and made my way nervously to the studio on my own. As soon as I walked in I was confronted by the painting. But it wasn't of me. It was of a strong, proud, beautiful woman. She looked familiar, a bit like someone I once knew. But not me, no, not me. I stood silently, gazing at her; the strength and character in her face, those full breasts, and the curve of her hip.

'Rosie?' Jacques interrupted after a time. 'Rosie. Do you like it?'

'It's beautiful, Jacques. But it's not me. Is it? Is that really what you see when you look at me?'

'That and so much more,' he said.

'Goodness,' I said. 'It's wonderful.'

Jacques exhaled with relief. 'I'm so happy you like it.'

'I do. Thank you.'

'It was my pleasure. Rosie, I wonder... I am having an exhibition and I would like to include your painting. With your permission, of course.'

I thought of the people who might see the painting. Of people who might know me. Of Patrick. Then I thought *sod it*. 'You have my blessing,' I said.

The evening of the exhibition opening arrived. I'd persuaded Patrick to accompany me, amid much grumbling, and we were greeted at the door to the gallery by a pretty young woman bearing a tray of champagne. I smiled and took a glass, wondering if Jacques had seen her naked too before pushing the unwelcome thought away. It wouldn't do me any good to compare myself to a woman thirty years my junior. I just hoped she appreciated what she had, as God knows it

330

goes soon enough.

There were a dozen or so people wandering round the white-walled space, stopping and commenting on the nudes adorning the walls. I felt a moment of panic as I imagined them seeing my naked form, and glugged down my bubbly before looking around for another. Had I made a huge mistake in coming? Had I made an even bigger one in bringing Patrick? In fact, what the hell was I thinking?

I grabbed Patrick's arm. 'Shall we get out of here? Patrick? Let's just go, shall we?'

But Patrick pulled away and walked towards the back of the gallery, his eyes straight ahead. I followed his gaze and there, on the farthest wall, was Jacques' painting of me. Nude. Naked. Starkers.

I was panicking by this point. What had I done? Still Patrick said nothing, ignoring my protestations that we should leave. He just went and stood and looked.

I saw Jacques approaching out of the corner of my eye. Before I could stop him, he was at Patrick's side.

'Beautiful, isn't she?' he said.

At that point I would have quite liked the floor to open up and swallow me. I downed the second glass of bubbly and waited for the explosion. It never came.

Patrick simply took out his wallet. 'How much to take it down now?' he asked.

'I'm afraid that's simply not possible,' Jacques said. 'You are welcome to reserve the piece, but it will be on display for the duration of the exhibition.'

I could see Patrick had started to simmer. This was a terrible idea.

'Name your price. I want to take it now,' Patrick insisted.

I felt Jacques' eyes on me and I pleaded with my own.

'Very well,' Jacques said finally, beckoning the young woman with the tray. 'Véronique,' he said, 'would you please take payment for this piece and wrap it for the gentleman. He will be taking it now.'

If Véronique was surprised, she was professional enough not to show it, and before long Patrick and I were leaving. He still hadn't said a word to me and was silent during the drive home. I was close to tears by this point.

He still hadn't spoken when we pulled up at home. He simply got out of the car, carried the painting indoors and went into his study with it, closing the door behind him.

Rolo distracted me as best he could, pushing his wet nose into my hand and demanding my attention. He followed me into the kitchen for a biscuit. I didn't think even a chocolate biscuit was going to help me on this occasion though as I thought of Patrick brooding in his office. What had I done? I must have been temporarily insane. I'd just been so flattered by Jacques' attention and so ruddy lonely in my marriage. Why couldn't Patrick have seen what Jacques saw? Why didn't he want me? Well, he definitely wouldn't want me now, would he? You silly old fool, Rosie. No fool like an old fool, eh?

I went and stood outside Patrick's study, listening at the door. I wanted to knock. To go in. How silly that I didn't feel I could intrude. I'd been married to this man for nearly forty years, but he felt like a stranger. With a sigh, I climbed the stairs to bed.

We ate breakfast in silence the next morning. Patrick couldn't even look at me and I didn't know what to say to him. I'd snuck into his study while he was in the shower and had seen the painting turned to face the wall, as if he was ashamed of me and couldn't bear to look at it. I think that's when I knew. Maybe if he had faced it into the room, it would have been different. Maybe then I wouldn't have decided to leave him. The painting was coming with me. And so was Rolo.

Acknowledgements

Thank you for reading *Bang to Rights*. I really hoped you enjoyed it. As with *The Write Way to Die*, I had a lot of fun penning the parts of Amy and Jenny, developing their friendship and bringing some much-needed black humour to what is otherwise a pretty grisly story.

As always, there are people I need to thank: my publisher James Essinger at The Conrad Press, book designer extraordinaire Charlotte Mouncey, and eagle-eyed Emma Brown for spotting missed compound adjectives and wrangling rogue commas. A big thank you also goes to my partner, Dirk, for the brainstorming, reading and reassuring, and to my hometown of Folkestone for the inspiration. Last, but never least, thank you to Kathy for her unceasing friendship and support, and to my son Sam, my favourite child and constant source of immense love and pride.